Isla Dewar is a regular contributor to Scottish newspapers. She lives in Fife with her husband, a cartoonist.

Isla Dewar's first novel, KEEPING UP WITH MAGDA, is also available from Headline Review.

Also by Isla Dewar

Keeping Up With Magda
Giving Up On Ordinary
It Could Happen To You

Women Talking Dirty

Isla Dewar

First published in 1996
by HEADLINE BOOK PUBLISHING

First published in paperback in 1996
by HEADLINE BOOK PUBLISHING

A HEADLINE REVIEW paperback

20 19 18 17 16 15 14 13 12 11

ISBN 0 7472 5113 4

Printed in England by Clays Ltd, St Ives plc

HEADLINE BOOK PUBLISHING
A division of Hodder Headline Plc
338 Euston Road
London NW1 3BH

To Sibyl and Gordon for always
– in their own way – being there.

1

Ellen

Chapter One

There are women whose eyes lock momentarily in bars, across crowded rooms, in the street and, though they are strangers, they recognise each other. They go through that female summing up thing, the subliminal eyeflick, the quick look from shoes to haircut, and for a second their eyes meet.

I could be friends with you, they think. There goes a fellow smoker, drinker, slut, slag, domestic failure, neurotic, whatever, they think. A fellow traveller, a soul mate, they think. Sometimes they leave it at that, a moment's wondering and speculation. They do not act upon that look and make friends. But sometimes they do.

When Cora O'Brien's eyes met Ellen Quinn's across the crowded living room at one of Jack Conroy's parties, Ellen thought: Who is that vividly dressed woman? And Cora thought: I could be friends with you. And she thought: There sits one of the most insecure women I have ever seen. And she thought: Still, she's a soul mate and a fellow traveller. Cora was like that, a romantic. She went over to chat.

She had thought to say to Ellen that she was meant to enjoy it. Meaning parties, life, everything. It always amazed Cora that people forgot to take pleasure in things. 'Pleasure,' she'd say, 'it's even a nice word.' But she thought the better of it. Wasn't it always a bitch when people said things like, 'Smile, it may never happen'? Instead the first words she ever spoke to Ellen were, 'You look like you could do with some serious corrupting.' Over six years in Edinburgh had not shifted the Highland lilt. She sounded like a mist, soft, enveloping.

Ellen said, 'What makes you think that about me?' She didn't want this new woman in her life to leave her side. She wanted to listen a little longer to that voice.

3

'Oh, I don't know. I just thought it was a flash thing to say, I suppose.' Cora sat down beside her and looked longingly at her cigarette packet. Ellen offered her one. 'No. I'm a smoker at heart, I always will be, I just don't do cigarettes any more. Pity. I used to love it. I must say, though, how good it is to meet a smoker who does not disappoint. So many opt for cheap brands with ghastly packing and huge boxes of matches. I think that when you smoke you smoke for all of us who took fright and have given up. You should do it boldly. Carry an illuminated sign, "Smoking and proud". These however,' and she picked up Ellen's pack, sniffed at it deeply, 'remind me of someone. His flat smelled of these, and garlic. And sour milk.' She drifted into memories and from that momentary distance smiled to Ellen. A confiding smile it was – one day I will tell you everything. Ellen's heart was won. A small curve of the lips, a fleeting fix of eye contact was all it took.

'It's good for irritating people,' Ellen said. That, after all, was why she'd started. And why she'd chosen French cigarettes. They were so obviously smelly. She had wanted to shock her mother, who had been suitably horrified, sneering, 'Disgusting habit.' Ellen's moment of adolescent glee was, however, long past. Now she was addicted. 'If I die with blackened lungs,' she defiantly said, 'I like to think I blackened them with style.'

Cora knew when she saw Ellen sitting fiddling nervously with her cigarette packet, dressed completely in black, hair and dark glasses concealing as much of her face as possible, that she would have to be the one to introduce herself. Looking at Ellen, she knew she was looking at someone who had never once in her life made the first move.

But hell, Cora made first moves all the time. Thought nothing of it. She had beads sewn into her hair, and a black velvet band at her neck. She wore a red silk jacket and her nails were loudly lacquered plum. She raised her small self by wearing stiletto heels. Now her eyes were level with most men's chins.

She was a teacher. She taught seven-year-olds. And she knew she was a very fine teacher indeed. She loved it. Her pupils adored her. 'Come come, Billy Mackie. If you're going to grow up and marry me you'll have to learn to tie your shoelaces.' The child looked at her,

and squirmed with embarrassed pleasure. Along with his class-
mates he jostled to be head of the line every Thursday morning
when Cora took them to the swimming baths. 'Any girl who wants
to hold my hand, Laura Sutton, better be able to multiply five by
three.'

'Fifteen, Miss O'Brien.'

'Good girl.' Cora held out her hand. A little sweaty palm
squeezed it. Wide eyes looked in awe at her shiny red nails.

Cora found seven-year-olds a delight. She thought they were like
a litter of warm-tummied animals, friendly, friendly and only
friendly. At the peak of their careers as children. They had not quite
learned to snigger and rant. Innocents. It would not last. Soon
they'd be sneering and lying. 'Don't know, Miss.' 'Wasn't me, Miss.'
They'd be greedy – like the rest of us, she thought. They'd be eyeing
electrical goods and watches. Thundering through a childhood of
burgers and baseball hats, desperate to become grown-ups.
Desperate, too, to grow into the big, loud, foul language they'll have
learned from videos. As the years passed, each new batch of infants
seemed more sophisticated than the last.

'I swear,' she said to nobody in particular in the staff room,
'seven-year-olds are getting older and older. Soon they'll be like a
class of forty-year-olds.'

'And what,' her headmaster asked, 'will forty-year-olds be like?'

'Same as ever. Looking back at their childhoods and wishing
they'd had the gumption to enjoy being seven when they were
there.'

The children in her present class had a full and active range of
swear words. 'Oh fuck,' someone cried when his pot of blue paint
toppled to the floor. Cora looked up mildly and shook her head.
Pity. It used to be such a handy little stinger of an Anglo-Saxon
outcry, but overuse had rendered it bland. Now it was a Black
Forest gateau of a swear word; common as cake and completely
without meaning.

She had the gift of enthusiasm which, to their parents and grandparents' dismay, she passed on to her pupils. She was regularly
accosted in the street by aggrieved mothers and fathers who
believed their children were being given ideas above their station.

'Hey you, Miss O'Brien! I want a word. What's all this nonsense you're filling our Billy's head with? About being a New York cop? He's staying right here. He'll be a plumber like me. What's wrong with that?'

'Nothing, Mr Mackie. As long as it's what Billy wants.' She sighed hugely, clasping a batch of jotters to her chest. 'Mr Mackie, he's a child. He's seven. If you don't get to dream about becoming a New York cop when you're seven, when do you get to dream about it?'

Mr Mackie did not know. Cora's voice, words woven in a soft Highland accent, always stopped people in their tracks. She could be giving them a recipe for beef hash or reading the Kama-Sutra. Who cared? Just so long as she kept speaking.

Sitting by her side with the party humming round them, Ellen felt the same. She wanted Cora to keep speaking. Cora, however, was considering Ellen in close-up. She was younger than she appeared to be from a distance. Her nails were chewed. A worrier, Cora thought, and smiled at her, hauling her back from the little world she was plainly prone to drifting into when left to her own devices. Together they gazed across the room, watching the party. People in small gatherings, drinking and smiling, chatting and smiling, bitching and smiling and looking idly round checking that there was nobody more interesting, smiling more than they were.

'Here we are then,' Ellen said suddenly, 'trembling on the edge of the awesome world of jackets and haircuts.'

'Well,' said Cora, 'I don't think you need to tremble,' she stroked the sleeve of Ellen's jacket, 'not with this on. What do you do?'

'I write,' she said glumly. She hated telling people what she did. 'Write!' they'd exclaim with interest. 'Oh, what?' Then she'd have to admit that she was no Kafka, Virginia Woolf wouldn't have to roll over and Iris Murdoch had nothing to worry about, Ellen had nothing fabulous to say. She wrote comic strips.

'Oh,' said Cora. 'Who are you? What do you write?'

'I'm Ellen Quinn. I do some of Jack's strips. Two of Jack's strips.'

People nearby switched from surreptitious eavesdropping to blatant eavesdropping.

'Which ones?' Cora wanted to know. Jack Conroy had output. It seemed he never stopped working. Nobody quite knew how many strips he drew. There was from his drawing board (at which he sat, perched like a little gnome on his high draughtsman's chair) a constant outpouring of action-packed, slam, bam, kapowee exquisitely drawn stories of tumbling-haired, pouty-breasted, warm-lipped women and steel-jawed men saving the world.

'I do *Gangster Women* and *Engels of the Forest*.'

'Ah,' said Cora. She had no idea what Ellen was talking about. She had never in her life read a comic strip, and had no intention of ever doing so. But the eavesdroppers nodded amongst themselves. They'd heard of Ellen Quinn. *Gangster Women* and *Engels* weren't bad. In fact they were almost good. In the awesome world of jackets and haircuts almost good was as good as anything got.

'Do you work at Starless, then?'

'Yes. With Stanley. Do you know him?'

'We nod. Actually I know where you are because it's round the corner from where I live.'

'Really?' Ellen was pleased. 'You live in Giles Street?' This was a fine coincidence.

'With my two boys,' said Cora. 'You must drop by for coffee sometime.'

'I will,' said Ellen. Then, changing the subject because she absolutely hated talking about her work: 'Jack Conroy has a corn on his bum,'

'I know,' Cora replied smugly.

'Aha,' they said in unison and exchanged mutually knowing smirks. Ellen worked round the corner from Cora's home. They had both had intimate access to the Conroy bottom. This could be a basis for friendship. A couple of things in common. They could be chums.

It was not until this evening at this party that Ellen had considered fucking Jack Conroy as anything other than a sophisticated and rather raunchy thing to do. It was the look of loathing Jack's wife, Black Fingernails – Maureen, actually, but known as Black Fingernails because, well, she painted her fingernails black – flashed at her as she came into the room that changed her mind. She knows, Ellen thought. And flushed shame.

One day she had taken some work to him. She stood in his studio, awed by its fascinating messiness. There were jerseys, tapes and

CDs spread on the floor and the sofa. It was as if someone had opened the roof of the house and poured in a fifteen-year collection of newspapers, magazines and books. They were everywhere. There were shelves, sagging at the centre, cluttered with a vast selection of reference books, old jars filled with pens and glossy plants. His drawing board was covered by bits of paper: measurements, letters, scripts, memos, reminders, and jottings from Jack to Jack. There were rows of inks along the top, a jar of murky inky water, ceramic palettes and the floor was a thick mass of rubbings. Jack drew his strips in pencil first, inked over the approved rough, then feverishly rubbed over the finished job, removing all extraneous pencil lines. He then pulled the sleeve of his battered, stained sweat shirt down over his hand and swept all the minuscule bits of rubber from his board to the floor. He'd been doing this for years but Black Fingernails and her vacuum cleaner were never allowed into his studio. His work then, was perfect. His surroundings approached post-holocaust devastation.

'Let's have a chat,' he'd invited Ellen over the phone. But they hadn't chatted, had they? Jack Conroy's bed smelled of Musk. Jack Conroy's bed smelled of Jack Conroy's wife. Maybe that's what turned Ellen off. Maybe it was Jack Conroy's wife's silk underwear draped over the chair beside the bed. Maybe it was his breath on her face, the unashamed maleness of him. He was sure of himself, knew what he wanted. When he took her wrists and held them firm on the pillow above her head, she panicked, squirmed and kicked. 'Let go. Let go.' Then, maybe, it was that when she ran her fingers down his back, over his bum, she felt, small and hard, the corn.

'How was it for you?' she stupidly asked when they were done.

'I didn't think anybody actually asked that,' Jack said. 'You don't want an answer, do you?'

'Yes,' said Ellen.

'How was it for me? Truth or bullshit?' He was sitting on the edge of the bed casting hopefully around for his boxers which he had kicked off. Naked from the back, Ellen decided, Jack Conroy was more exciting than naked from the front. He was hairy. This man was not born, she thought. He was knitted by his grandmother on a cold day.

'Bullshit,' she said.

'There,' said Jack. 'That's how it was for me. I don't want the truth either. Good way that of telling how you're doing. When things are fine you can fearlessly face the truth. When they're not you want a little comforting bullshit.'

'I asked for bullshit,' Ellen insisted.

'Oh, the earth moved,' Jack said flatly.

Now Cora hooted a great guffaw from her tiny body that cut through the brittle and glittering socialising that was going on all around them. 'What an arse he is! A corn on the left buttock! That's what happens when you spend too long sitting at a damned drawing board doing those comic strips. He never stops, I swear. It's just little.' She indicated the size with her fingers. 'The corn I mean, ha ha.' She had fabulous nails. Ellen considered them with envy. Hers were shamefully chewed. She worried too much. When she'd nothing to worry about, she worried about worrying. It was as bad a habit as smoking.

Cora smiled at her. 'I'm Cora O'Brien. And what's that you're drinking?' she asked.

Holding up her glass Ellen said, 'White wine.'

'White wine? What sort of uptight middle-class drink is that?' Cora asked, noticing as she did that behind her dark glasses Ellen Quinn had been crying. She took the glass from Ellen's hand and, before she could protest, opened an abandoned handbag and emptied the wine into it. 'You want some vodka.'

'No I don't.' Ellen waved her hands, dismissing this suggestion. 'I can't drink spirits any more. They make me ill.'

'Nonsense.' Cora would have none of this. 'You have to learn to drink. You must master the vices. You know that if a thing is worth doing it's worth doing well. If, however, a thing is not worth doing then it's worth doing fabulously, amazingly, with grace and style and panache.'

She fetched a bottle and poured them both a huge drink.

Ellen stared at hers. 'I can't drink this. I get drunk. I get headaches. I feel wretched. I hate not being in control.'

'Ah,' said Cora. 'It isn't getting drunk you fear, then. It's getting sober again that scares the shit out of you.' She raised her glass. 'To being out of control,' she said. 'Best feeling in the world.'

Ellen drank but she did not agree. 'To being in control,' she said. She knew, however, that it was not the best feeling in the world.

Chapter Two

Ellen's mother, Janine, always worried about her. Ellen was distant and secretive, like her father. There was no real knowing what went on in her head.

'Douglas was the same,' Janine said. 'He had a wayward mind. You'd be trying to talk to him about the phone bill or if the lawn needed mowing and he'd be nodding his head and agreeing but he'd be looking up at the light thinking about goodness knows what. You could never pin him down.'

Janine had a straightforward mind. She liked to think she was a straightforward sort of a person living a straightforward life. Mondays you washed. Tuesdays you ironed. Wednesdays you did the bedrooms, cleaned out the bath and polished the sideboard. Thursdays you baked and Fridays were for all the things you couldn't fit in to the rest of the week. Janine liked routine. She felt it kept her right. She had routines within her routines. Ironing: cool iron first, then hot iron. Clothes then towels, sheets, etc. She liked ironing, the rhythm of it, the comforting creak of the board. If it was Tuesday she would be ironing. If she was ironing it would be Tuesday. You knew where you were with routines.

She shook her head, thinking about Ellen and her father. She did not know how they got by. Them with their dizzy minds, dreaming and messy. She did not understand either of them. Sometimes she thought when she saw one of them gazing silently at the wall or out of the window that she would like to smack them out of their dreamings, reminding them that she was here and she was the one who did their ironing and cooked the food they ate. Then again sometimes she thought it best not knowing the nonsense that went on in those drifting minds. It would, she concluded, drive her daft.

It always surprised Ellen when she returned to the leafy,

suffocatingly polite Edinburgh suburb where she was brought up that as a child she had seen these streets of quiet boredom as a seething hotbed of low life, intrigue and tribal rituals.

She was convinced Mrs Paulo three doors up was a film star. And if she wasn't a film star she definitely had dazzling connections and lived the film star life. This because once Ellen had seen her standing at the window speaking on the phone. Not only did her phone have a cord long enough to stretch to the window, but it was white. A white phone – only film stars had such a thing. Ellen kept a beady young eye out, keen to spot Audrey Hepburn or Rock Hudson should they come by. She was sure they would one day. Of course they'd call first – on the white telephone.

Mr Martin, four doors down on the other side, was a spy and Mrs Robb next door to him was a witch. But better than all of that, Ellen knew beyond a shadow of a doubt that a whole Sioux tribe lived on the golf course at the end of the road. For an entire summer Ellen rode out nights to the great plains on that scrubby municipal golf course and led the Sioux nation. Nobody knew about this except, of course, in time, when she became Ellen's closest friend, Cora.

'God, Ellen,' she said when she was told, 'you must have been born stupid. I just had stupidity thrust upon me. Well, I more rushed towards it, the way you do. Marriage, men, life, children . . . and such.'

'You have never been married,' Ellen said.

'OK. Men. Life. Children. That's stupid enough. I don't go the whole hog.' Cora would not be put down or corrected.

Ellen told her everything. But then she would. She was one of those people, a puppy at heart, who had not mastered the simple art of thinking before she spoke. Dressed in black, looking shyly out at the world from behind a thick fringe, she was not as distant and dark as she seemed. Give her a crumb, give her a smile, give her a sliver of affection, a kindly word, and she was yours, she was anybody's. She was easily won. This is me, she would say. And, pouring out a pile of emotional rubble, this is my life. Look at it, what a mess. Look at this bit, I really screwed up there. She was as enthusiastic about her failures as her successes. It never really crossed her mind how judgemental people would be with the information she freely dished out. That was why she was loved, if only she'd known it. Cora's outrageousness, her vividness, on the other hand, was a façade. She only told Ellen almost everything. Some of her shame, some of her rage and most of her regrets were secret. She believed in holding a little of herself back.

That summer, the summer of the Sioux, as Ellen thought of it whenever she brought it to mind, she climbed from her bedroom window almost every evening when her mother and sister were sleeping. She wore her pyjamas under her dark blue, elastic-waisted corduroy trousers and hand-knitted polo-neck jersey, her playing clothes. On her gleaming black horse, Thunder, she trotted under sodium lights down the middle of Wakefield Avenue, reins jingling, saddle creaking. Thunder was, of course, part of that play. He was only real to her. Beloved imaginary horse, for that small part of her life he was the only thing she could cling to. The only thing she allowed to be real to her. Her father had just died. As she went she sang songs of the day, favourite tunes from the radio. She listened to her own whisperings, 'Hey Jude, too-ti-too-ti-too.'

It was one of the silliest things she ever did. But when you're eight and the Sioux are waiting on the eighteenth green, danger is the great iron horse steaming over your hunting grounds, the long knives, the rolling wagon trains of white men who do not know the ways of the buffalo. It is a mountain lion, a renegade Pawnee, nothing that would faze someone mighty and wise, who does not realise she is only eight summers tall, and who has the ear of Sitting Bull himself.

'I was happy then,' she'd say wistfully to herself in those mindless moments when, idle-brained, she'd be washing the supper dishes, or just vacantly staring out of the window. Then she'd draw herself up sharply. 'No I was not.' Of course she wasn't. When a child takes to wandering a golf course at night with a whole tribe of imaginary companions something is wrong, very wrong indeed.

Thinking back it seemed like another time, when she'd been another person – the human being she was before Cora was in her life, before Daniel, Emily Boyle and Chippy Norton. Chippy, of course, was only a figment of her imagination. But of all the characters she created he was her favourite, and he was also the most successful. So in his fat, dreamy and fictional way, he was the most important of all. It was he who paid the rent, bought all the clothes, footed the grocery and fuel bills and kept Ellen in French cigarettes and Russian booze.

It started in March. Daniel Quinn was a long time into her future, she was Ellen Davidson then. She remembered the night her father died well. Every moment, every look – her mother's furrowed concern, her sister's goody-goody smirk as she finished every scrap of her liver and wiped the plate clean so that now she could have her almond slice; every sound – the muted babble of the television her sister, Rosalind, had left beaming into the empty living room up the hall, the clatter of pots in the kitchen; every scent – burned liver, that fresh air smell of just-ironed clothes – was with her always. It was a snapshot, mindbite memory she could take out and relive whenever she was low and needed to go even lower.

It was Tuesday. Tuesday in the little two-bedroom bungalow in Wakefield Avenue was liver and a bath. Ellen hated liver and always ate slowly, carefully cutting the dread meat into tiny bits and shifting them about her plate, waiting for her mother to leave the table. Then, with her disapproving sister watching, she would with one swift practised move empty the liver into the plastic bag she always kept handy on Tuesdays. She'd scrunch it into a little roll and shove it up her jersey. It lay warm against her tummy. Later she would bury it in the garden. Even now the sight of liver lying flaccid, bleeding slightly on the butcher's slab, could cause her to retch.

Her father came home late that day. Still wearing his tweed car coat he slumped on the armchair by the fire that was his armchair and nobody else's, complaining that his head hurt.

Her mother laid his liver on the table and looked at him, with furrow-browed concern. 'You won't be wanting your supper, then?'

He shook his head.

'Go wash the dishes, Ellen,' her mother ordered. Ellen protested. She'd cleared the liver from her plate, eaten the regulation piece of bread and was planning to have an almond slice. 'Wash the dishes,' her mother ordered in that final flat voice mummies had when no arguing would be tolerated.

Ellen went into the kitchen, filled the sink with hot water and washing-up liquid, and started to play submarines with the plates and a cup. The cup, pink with a thin gold rim, was the enemy lurking in the deep, waiting for the innocent plate to pass overhead. It would strike. Boom, whoosh. Torpedoes on the port side. The liver in the bag was getting cold as she pressed against the sink keeping it in place. She would have to get rid of it.

'For heaven's sake, Ellen, can't you do anything properly?' Her mother came into the kitchen and, shoving her from the sink, took over. 'Go have a bath.'

'But it's early. What about my programme? I want to see my programmes on television.'

'Have a bath.'

Her father groaned. She watched him as she passed on her way to the bathroom. His face was grimly grey under a filmy sweat. He had just been sick. His head lolled back, mouth slightly open. He held his hand on his chest, his breathing sounded pained, rattled in his chest. He looked at her and called her, ' . . . Um.' He always called her that. There were so many little girls running around his house – his daughters, his daughters' friends, neighbours' children – he lost track of them. He knew of course that Ellen was his. But he was weary. His job took all of him. So he couldn't always single out her name from the mass of little girl names that flooded into his mind whenever he saw her.

' . . . Um . . .' he said. That was the last time she saw him.

She filled the bath, dutifully took off her clothes and folded them according to her mother's strict guidelines. Janine Davidson's great achievement in life was the acquisition of a bungalow. One hundred and ninety-two Wakefield Avenue was a bungalow in a mystifying maze of post-war bungalows and from the time she and Douglas moved in, Janine had spent all her time and energy living up to the sanctified respectability she imagined was the stuff of bungalowees. She was too rigid with the fear of getting found out – found out that she was from poor working-class stock, from tenement housing, and shouldn't really be living in this hallowed, badly heated, insufferably clean little house – to relax and enjoy her life, her family.

There was, then, according to Ellen's mother, a right way and a wrong way to do everything. In the Davidson household everything was done the right way, even folding of the clothes prior to getting into the bath.

Ellen hid the liver under the perfect pile. Now she wouldn't be able to bury it in the garden. She'd hide it in her schoolbag and drop it in a litter bin on the way to school. Her tummy gurgled. She was hungry. She thought longingly of her almond slice still on the table, waiting for her to come to claim it. Still, baths were good. She resumed her game of submarines. The sponge was the enemy waiting in the rocks – her left knee – for the face cloth carrying a load of bananas and sugar cane to sail by.

'Hello, Dr Phillips? Mrs Davidson here, a hundred and ninety-two Wakefield Avenue . . .' Ellen heard her mother's voice. It was her posh voice, the one she used for the doctor and the insurance man who came by on Thursdays.

Ellen liked her address. It rhymed. One hundred and ninety-two Wakefield Avenue. A wide street, well lit. A row of houses amidst rows and rows and streets and streets of houses all the same. Wakefield Avenue was posh though; it led onto the golf course.

'It's my husband, Douglas. He's not well. He's having trouble breathing and . . . yes . . . in his chest. Thank you. The house is on the right-hand side of the road, just past the bus stop . . .'

Dr Phillips would come in his Jaguar. Ellen held her breath, something was happening. If you held your breath when things happened people forgot you were there and you could watch the grown-ups being grown-up. She was Ellen Davidson, she was eight years old, she had straight browny-black hair, brown eyes and a small face. Her favourite person in all the world was Burt Lancaster. Her favourite things were a luminous yo-yo that shone in the dark and a bumper book of the countryside. But the thing she wanted most was a horse. If she only had one she'd be happy, and she'd never ever ask for anything else ever again. Every year she wrote to Santa asking for a shiny black stallion, but she never got one. Every Christmas morning she would run through to the living room and peer into the garden. 'Please let it be there. Please.' She dreamed it would be standing on the lawn, just behind the lilac tree, black and magnificent, pawing the ground, snorting and waiting for her to come to him. She would call him Thunder.

'Ellen, we can't possibly have a horse,' her mother repeatedly told her. 'Where would we keep it?'

'In the garden. In the shed when it rains. It could fit in beside the lawnmower. I'd look after it. Brush it. Ride it. I'd ride it on the golf course.'

Every Christmas she and her mother went through this dialogue. Every Christmas Ellen hoped wildly and every Christmas her mother sighed. She would disappoint her daughter yet again. Games compendiums, new frocks, a dolls' house, a little pocket radio – nothing, absolutely nothing would ever be as good as that black horse, glistening and tossing its mane out past the lilac tree.

The doctor arrived. Ellen heard him booming down the hall. Why did doctors have such big voices? She held her breath. She could hold it for a count of two hundred and forty-seven, though the last sixty or so had to be rattled through, top speed. This would be handy should she ever have to hide underwater from renegade Pawnees.

'An ambulance, please.' The doctor was on the phone, using their phone. Would he have to put the money in the little box like Mrs McKenzie across the road when she phoned her mother in Inverness every Sunday afternoon? ' . . . a hundred and ninety-two Wakefield Avenue. Heart attack . . .'

Ellen looked at her fingers. They'd gone all white and wrinkly. The water was cold, but she was scared to get out. She didn't want to appear at the bathroom door in the middle of all the fuss. They wouldn't want her there. Best stay put. She stopped her intricate little sponge and face cloth games and sat absolutely still, listening. She could hear herself breathing here in the bathroom, hollow, throaty against the damp. Further off, house noises: the television, the pipes clanking. Somewhere in the distance a dog barked, Mrs Barr next door came out, put some rubbish in the bin, slammed the lid down and went back into her kitchen. Ellen was getting goose pimples. It was cold in here.

'I wish I had a horse,' she said. 'I wish, I wish, I wish . . .'

The ambulance arrived. The doorbell rang. Her mother went out.

17

Ellen heard the fuss, the rush of footsteps thumping down the hall. Ten steps it was from the front door to the living room. It never changed. She counted every day.

'Davidson? Ambulance. Where is he . . . ?'

'Down the hall . . . down the hall . . .'

They left the front door open and the chill rushed in under the bathroom door. Ellen shivered. She imagined the ambulance outside in the dark, light whirling, flashing blue across the night into neighbours' living rooms. They'd come to their windows to watch surreptitiously. 'Something going on at a hundred and ninety-two.'

She heard the stretcher being carried back out the door, down the path. The ambulance men would be big. Her mother said she'd go with them. 'I'll get my coat and bag.' She sounded strange. 'Rosalind, look after Ellen. See she goes to bed. And go to bed yourself at ten o'clock. I don't know when I'll be back.'

'Where is Ellen?'

'Oh goodness, in the bath. She's been in the bath all this time.' Bang bang bang on the bathroom door. 'Are you all right, Ellen?'

'Yes,' small, squeaky voice.

'I'm going in the ambulance with Dad. You go to bed. Do what Rosalind says.' Her sister would bully her. She'd have to be careful with the liver.

Shivering Ellen climbed from her bath, dried herself. She went to bed without saying her prayers.

Every night Janine Davidson insisted her daughters pray before sleeping. It was what respectable people did. Every night, then, she reinforced in Ellen the conviction she was going to die before morning.

> Each night as I lie down to sleep
> I pray the Lord my soul to keep.
> If I should die before I wake
> Take me to heaven for Jesus' sake.

Alone in her bedroom, muted noises of living-room life sounding through the wall, Ellen would lie waiting for death to come for her.

Death was a man in a hat with a thin moustache, glittering cruel eyes, pointy two-tone shoes and a little black, gleamy gun that he would use to shoot her. Or, he might strangle her with his strong, black-gloved hands. And death was a lady in a white dress that rustled in the hall just beyond the bedroom door. She had a thin and taunting face, white like her frock. In her hand she held a silver stiletto that she would plunge into Ellen's heart shrieking, 'Die. Die. Die, child. Die.' Ellen spent the hours between bedtime and morning in a state of terror. She slept with the blankets over her head so that when death came it would take her unawares. She would not hear the approaching tiptoe of pointy two-toned shoes or the abominable rustle of the silken white frock.

Her mother got home after midnight. She stood leaning against the door, stark, ashen. Her face had been painfully stripped of its old expressions and stamped deeply with a new look of shock, horror and grief.

'He's dead,' she said, leaning forward, clutching herself. 'Your father is dead.' She started to cry, deep, deep sobs. She couldn't breathe. Her shoulders shook and she gulped air with a huge sniffing, yelping sound, like an animal. In their pyjamas, still warm from sleeping, Ellen and Rosalind watched. Ellen froze. She didn't know mothers did that. She didn't know mothers hurt, cried. Hesitantly, she stepped forward to put her arm round her. But her mother, face streaked with sorrow and sudden surprising loathing, looked at her.

'Not you,' she spat, shaking her head. 'Not you. I don't want you.'

It was dark in the hall, cold. Rosalind stepped forward and pulled their mother to her. 'Sssh,' she said. And, 'It's all right.' Cradling her. Rocking her. Patting her. The unnerving yelping stopped, calmed into weeping. The two locked in that embrace walked down the hall, disappeared into the living room.

Ellen stayed alone in the dark, her private chaos fixed on her face, small, shiny with the need to please, creased with anxiety. She felt her flesh crawl. Self-loathing moved through her, over her. She wasn't loved, her mummy didn't want her. Should she stay here for ever in the dark and cold or go into the living room? She didn't know what to do. An icy draught swept under the front door. She shifted slightly from chilled foot to chilled foot. She looked hopelessly down at her arms and at her unwanted body. Then went back to bed. Her life hinged on this moment. It shamed her, and she couldn't bring herself to tell anybody about it.

Later, much much later, when all the crying and mumbling and chinking of teacups was over and her mother and sister were sleeping, Ellen rose. She took the crumpled bag of liver from amongst her clothes and crept out of the window to bury it in the garden. What with her father dying and her mother not wanting her and everything, she thought she'd better get rid of it quickly. If her mother found it now it'd be too much. Goodness knows what she'd do. It was a perfect night – a thousand stars in the sky and the lawn frosty under her feet. Ellen stood in her pyjamas and blue furry slippers and looked about in wonderment. She hadn't known that as she curled in terror under the blankets all this was out here, waiting for her. It was not scary here.

She fetched a trowel from the garden shed and dug a small hole on the far side of the lilac tree that was not visible from the living-room window. She entombed her guilty parcel in it and smoothed it over, patting the loose earth down. There, now nobody would ever know. She turned round and that's when Thunder came to her.

Had anyone been watching they would have seen a little girl in blue polka-dot pyjamas standing on tiptoe in furry slippers in a small, frighteningly tidy garden. They would have seen her stretch out her arms in ecstatic greeting into the chill empty air, patting and stroking nothing, nothing at all. They would have had to have seen the world through Ellen's eyes, been part of her little world, to know that she was embracing the love of her life, a muscled and magnificent black stallion that gently stamped the perfectly mown, immaculately edged lawn.

Prancing across the garden, gleaming and gorgeous, mane tossing, he came to her. Snorting gently he nuzzled her and she put her arms round his neck and kissed him. His mouth was velvet, shoving gently into her hand. She loved him and he loved her, only her and nobody else – ever. Nobody knew. Nobody in the whole world knew the friend she had.

Chapter Three

Sometimes Ellen ran through her life, the edited lowlights, a series of ifs. If she had not been such a harum-scarum child, running about the golf course at night on a pretend horse, she might have been more alert during school hours. If she'd been more alert during school hours she might have developed the habit of paying attention to what her teachers were saying. If she'd paid attention to her teachers she might have passed more exams and left school with a few more qualifications than she did. If she'd had more qualifications she would have been able to get a better job than the one she got in the stationery and book department of a large store. If she had not got that job she would not have started reading the comics they sold and she would not have met her friends and soul sisters Karen, Sharon, Alice and Katy. If she had not met them, she would not have thought up *Gangster Women*, her first comic strip creation – 'Hit the streets, Gangster Women, we have sisters to avenge' – and sent it to Stanley Macpherson, sole proprietor of Starless Enterprises, entrepreneur and dreamer, and she would not have been given a job writing science fiction scripts. If she had not been given a job, she and Stanley would not have been lunching in the Oyster Bar, and she would not have noticed Daniel Quinn leaning on the bar, staring at her. If she had not gone through the small flirtatious routine of noticing him noticing her, then pretending not to notice him noticing her, he would not have come across to chat and she would not have gone out with him that night, gone to bed with him that night, married him six weeks later and lived through years of absurdities, guilt, swearing, good sex, bad sex and long convoluted arguments that he always won. She would not have been the constant butt of his energy and fury or witness to his frenetic search. Search for what? Neither of them knew.

Sometimes Ellen thought that all she was searching for in life was another moment to match those of sheer joy she'd known that summer, the summer of the Sioux.

She first slipped out for another meeting on the lawn with Thunder on the night of her father's funeral. She brought him a piece of shortbread and a salmon sandwich, which she ate herself. Next night she went again to find him. Then a couple of nights later she slipped out again. By that time she was becoming addicted to her late-night sorties. Every night she lay in bed resisting the temptation of the night outside her window, the stars, the soft spring grass, the fabulous horse. Every night she gave in to it, till at last she was lost in her fantasy.

When Thunder became real to her, she thought that the little lawn was not big enough for him. After all, he lived a secret patient life waiting by the side of the house for her to come home from school. He needed a larger expanse of grass, somewhere to gallop. It seemed natural to trot out of the garden gate, down the street to the golf course. Once there she took the horse at a canter, then a gallop down the fairways and across the putting greens. She moved further and further into her dreams. Once when she was riding she turned round and there they were, the Sioux. Feathered and proud on painted ponies, they were gathered behind her. She was not alone. She had a whole tribe of warriors with her, looking after her. She was quite safe now. After that they were always there. Ellen painted her own body with her mother's lipstick and eye shadow, red and blue whorls and daubs that spelled out the story of her life: her father, the mighty chief's, glorious death; her tepee with her mother; her sister; the smack she'd got from her teacher because she was always falling asleep in class. With the night life she had it was hardly surprising she dropped off in the classroom. But she could not resist the night. Bareback and semi-naked she rode, arms spread into the air, yelling and whooping. She was a little girl, tamed and house-trained in the daytime, feral at night. A wildness came reeling from the depth of her and as she galloped across the summer grass it turned to exultation. When she was grown-up and returning to the scene of her imaginings, Ellen would stare out over the golf course and long to know such uninhibited freedom again.

* * *

After her father died Ellen's family became dowdy. Or rather dowdier. They drifted into a quietly harmonious gloom. It was undemanding and it suited them. Though they ate supper at the same time they would have, had they been waiting for him to come home from work, mostly they carried on as if Douglas Davidson had not existed in the first place. They never spoke about him. Only sometimes, at four or five in the morning when Ellen was arriving home after her adventures with the Sioux, she heard, drifting sorrowfully from her mother's bedroom, the muffled sound of sobbing. But in time even that stopped.

Her mother found solace in a dreary culinary routine: Monday stew, Tuesday liver, Wednesday mince, Thursday mince again and Friday fish – though they weren't Catholic. Saturday they heated a pie and Sunday was roast beef. The house became bleak, comfortless. They came together over Janine's grim meals. The woman had the knack of taking good nutritious food and turning it into cardboard. 'Set the table, Ellen,' she would call.

Ellen would obediently leave the television. Put on the tablecloth. Then forks and knives at each place, salt and pepper in the middle and sugar and milk at the head of table, where the man sits, though the man didn't sit there any more. Nobody was going to take his place. They ate and they rarely spoke except to say things like, 'The fish is good.' 'Better than last week.' 'Tasty.'

Then, and now, Ellen couldn't understand such conversations. Why talk about boring fish when there were so many fabulous things in the world to discuss? She couldn't, of course, tell her mother and sister about the movement of the buffalo on the golf course, or the heron frozen still on one leg silently waiting for eels that swam the great water beside the bunker at the tenth hole, or the wild ponies, or the war dances or the furious gallops on Thunder over the prairie. But there were other things.

Clutching her fork, she leaned over the table, little eyes gleaming deep in her small, pale face. She had the mark of an unfed and sleepless child. Her mother, however, was too absorbed in her mourning to notice. There was so much Ellen wanted to say, so many stories from the little life she led after school finished and before supper was served she was desperate to share, she did not notice her jersey trailing in her ketchup.

'Jumper,' her mother said, waving an exasperated hand at the little indiscretion. Ellen stared down at the gaudy stain and lifting her jersey to her mouth sucked it clean. Her mother sighed in despair. That child would be the death of her.

Ellen shrank into herself, hiding from the disapproval and hiding, too, who she really was, her thoughts. Now they would never know the things she knew. Mr Martin was a spy – she was sure of it. She'd seen him one day last summer in dark glasses and a white hat. And Mrs Robb across the road was a witch. How could she tell her mother these things? Her mother did not want her. Best keep quiet. Best not make a pest of herself.

Ellen had discovered she could crawl into Mrs Robb's back garden through a hole in the hedge. She spent hours huddled behind the gooseberry bushes watching the old lady bustling about her kitchen. She imagined she was cleverly hidden. But, of course, Mrs Robb knew she was there. Poor child, she thought, I hate to think of the nonsense that's going on in her head. She knew Ellen. She had seen Ellens before. She was a small, underfed suburban waif who rode everywhere on a glorious pretend horse. Nobody cuddled her, nobody tucked her up at night. And nobody had ever told her she mattered.

Looking back on it, and she wasted a deal of time looking back, recriminating, regretting, Ellen realised that crouching low in Mrs Robb's garden and riding out at night was when she started inventing lives for other people and for herself. That must have been the beginning of me – this me that I am now, she thought. But then she was prone to sudden bouts of indulgent self-examination.

The three lived separate lives. Janine Davidson disappeared into her head, coping with her grief and guilt, mourning the man she married, chastising herself for not knowing him better, not trying to understand or communicate with him more. Ellen rode out on her beloved Thunder, and Rosalind, seven years older than her sister, discovered sex. She was, then, the only sane one in the house. Friday and Saturday nights she would come home, her neck covered with lovebites.

'What a mess, Ellen. I told him not to do that. Don't tell Mum.' The only sisterly thing she ever did was show Ellen how to reduce the glaring redness by rubbing the lovebites gently with Janine's Nivea cream, then covering them with pan stick makeup. Ellen sat on the bath watching. This was fascinating. What she longed to know, but didn't dare ask, was, how did they get there? And why?

What she did know was that it was part of the huge secret that her mother knew and her sister knew and all the smart and popular people in the playground knew and she didn't. Oh, what a tortured soul Ellen was then. And oh, what a tortured soul she was still.

Chapter Four

Every day after school Ellen rode to where Mrs Robb's garden backed on to the golf course. Leaving Thunder tethered to the flagpole on the second hole, she squeezed through the gap in the hedge to do some spying. She was keen to spot some actual witchery, spells in the making. Maybe there was a cauldron in the kitchen where toads were stewing nicely with nettles, slugs, cat's spit and school dinners. Blech. Sometimes she craned up hoping to catch a glimpse of a pointy hat or a broom, though she knew for a fact not all witches had such things. Perhaps this was the sort of witch who stuck needles into little dolls whilst chanting in a scary drone. Maybe she could make things move just by glaring at them.

To her surprise Mrs Robb grew fond of the little solemn face peeking from behind the gooseberry bush. Ellen was a skinny child peering at the world from under a thick dark fringe. Her hands and feet were large. She was going to be tall and needed feeding. Mrs Robb could see that. Though she warned herself that no good, no good at all, would come from interfering, she decided a few scones and some chocolate cake of an afternoon would not go amiss.

She lured the girl into her garden as she lured bluetits and sparrows, with titbits. Ellen found small brightly wrapped parcels hanging from the gooseberry bush, like baubles on a Christmas tree, waiting for her when she took up her daily vigil. At first they confirmed her suspicions. Aha, she thought, a trick, some sort of witchy ploy. I'm not falling for that. Next day there was another parcel. And the next, and the next. In time they became irresistible. She opened one and found three sweets glistening in transparent purple wrappings. She wouldn't eat, though. They might make her float above the ground gushing fountains of sick. Oh yes, she was a match for any witch, any time. But there the sweets were, lying in her hand, chocolate-covered and overwhelmingly tempting. She unwrapped one and slowly put it into her mouth, then lay back on the ground watching the world turn purple through the paper.

Each day, then, she went to the garden, and each day a new surprise, brightly wrapped and tied with gold ribbon, was waiting for her. She crouched low, sucking home-made toffee or chocolate fudge, patiently waiting for witchy doings, breathing in the brown smell of earth, listening to the sounds of the suburbs; a dog barking, blackbirds in neighbouring gardens, Mrs Rush two doors down taking in her washing, Mr Johnson noisily revving his car engine, distant children playing. Ellen knew everything that everybody did. On chilly spring afternoons she watched her breath splay out into the late frosty air as she whispered her favourite word. The one her sister said when she dropped her lipstick down the lavatory. Over and over she said it. 'Bugger.' It was a fabulous word. 'Buggery-buggerybuggerybug.'

She listened to the sounds of the golf course. Two golfers in checked trousers and tweedy caps strode by trundling their trolleys, discussing their game. Far across the fairways she heard a wagon train roll, the whistle and shout of drivers encouraging tired horses. It's a might late for 'em to be movin', she thought. They ought to be getting bedded down. Get some fires lit. Let the wimmen folk rustle up some beans an' coffee.

A group of boys going home, dragging sticks, passed nearby. She could hear their strange conversation. Boys were tricky. You never could understand what they were talking about. They seemed to provide their own soundtrack when they spoke. 'Then the black car spun over and over, eeeee, boom, spadoom . . .'

A lone brave rode slowly by, a deer slung over his horse. They'll be mighty glad to see that back at camp, Ellen thought.

The world was budding, too cold still for blossoms. Ellen looked at the buds on the gooseberry bush, and on the silver birch tree by the fence. Little greening knobs waiting to happen. Did it hurt? Did plants breathe and cry like the women she'd seen in cowboy films on Sunday afternoons on the telly? 'There ain't time to git her to the doctor. The baby's acomin' now. Fetch some whisky an' boil up water, and jes' keep it comin'. We'll be aneedin' plenty of it. Give her somethin' to bite on.' There'd be a close up of the mother-to-be's face, twisted in agony. She'd be gripping the brass bed, knuckles white, sweat dripping from her face. Her hair would be matted. Then the action would switch to the father, walking anxiously to and fro whilst his wife screamed from the birthin' bed. Screamed and screamed and screamed. Ellen wasn't going to do that. Oh no. She was never going to have a baby, never ever. It was nippy. It hurt. It hurt worse than getting the strap at school or falling down on your knee. She did not like, even, the idea of growing up. Becoming a woman frightened her. Did it mean she'd be like her mother? Would she have to wear a girdle? And curlers in bed? No. No. No.

After a week of shiny little gifts, Mrs Robb knocked on the window. Ellen froze. She was not expecting this. Obviously the witch knew she was out here spying, but she didn't think she would ever actually speak to her. Also, she was beginning to suspect Mrs Robb of being disappointingly ordinary. But you never knew with grown-ups, especially witchy ones. The witch held up a plate of chocolate cake and beckoned her in. Ellen knew she shouldn't go. Her mother often told her to beware of strangers. But a look round the witch's kitchen, a chance finally to see if there was a cauldron or a black cat or anything witchy at all, was too good to miss. Besides, the chocolate cake looked like real chocolate cake, large and fluffy with proper icing on top and gooey stuff in the middle. It was the sort of thing children in storybooks ate and was also, therefore, too good to miss.

It was a strange kitchen, not at all like the one at home. Gleaming copper pots hung from a beam above a white Aga. Ellen's mother cooked on a three-ring Belling using two big pots, one little pot, a chip pan and a frying pan for everything. Here the walls were lined with shelves, cluttered with rows of blue and white plates, jugs and bowls. Cups hung in perfect order from neatly spaced hooks. But there was no sign of anything evil. Ellen peered round. There were no dubious brewings, no toads, no foul-smelling weeds, no tiny bottles of rancid liquid. She'd hoped there might be a huge book of spells, ancient, leather-bound, stained with years of dire spillages; rat's blood, horn of unicorn, eye of crow sort of thing. But no, the house smelled of lavender polish and baking. Ellen felt let down. This woman led a warm and comfortable life. How dare she?

'Is this a potion?' Ellen asked at last.

'A potion?' Mrs Robb looked mildly surprised. 'It's tea. Tea and chocolate cake.'

Milky tea lapping in a wide-brimmed blue and white cup, a glistening slab of cake – such treats, such riches, such difficult crockery. It would need two small hands to steady such a vessel from saucer to lips. Should she, though, drink the witch's brew? Eat the witch's fare? What might it do to her? Turn her into a hat stand or a creepy-crawly? Then what would happen? Would anybody miss her? She would go bustling home tiny, so tiny it would take a week to cross the road, and nobody would know she was there.

'Where's that child?' her mother would snap. 'She hasn't been home for four weeks. Well, we'll just have to sell her bed and forget all about her.'

'But I'm here. This is me in the larder,' Ellen would say smally, voice whisper-shrill vanishing unheard into the air around her, tears in her eyes. But nobody would know it was her. They'd stamp on her or chase her out into the cold waving brooms and pokers.

'So,' said the witch sitting opposite her, 'why do you spend so much time in my gooseberry bushes?' Her voice was deep and old, cracked with use. Like her cups, Ellen thought.

'I'm watching,' she said.

'Watching what?'

'You know. Everything that has to be watched. Birds, starlings.'

'Ah. I see.'

'Don't you get scared?' Ellen asked suddenly. 'On your own?'

Mrs Robb shook her head. 'I like my own company.'

'Don't you have children? A husband?'

Mrs Robb shook her head again. Her children were long gone, they rarely came to see her, and her husband died over ten years ago.

'I get scared when I'm alone in the dark,' Ellen confessed. 'At night there's people coming to kill me.'

'Nonsense.'

'No. Not nonsense. You don't know. I'm alone, aloner than anything.' Out riding with the Sioux she wasn't alone. She was lonesome. There was a difference. 'There's a lady in white and a man in a hat. Sometimes they fight about who is going to do it. "Let me," says the lady,' Ellen shrilled her voice, ' "No, me," says the man,' a deep voice for the man, chin down. ' "You did it last night. It's my turn." '

'Goodness,' said Mrs Robb, reaching over to pat the child's hand. 'You need a brave.'

'A brave?'

'Yes, lots of people have them. A guardian angel who looks after you. Imagine him standing at the end of your bed, arms folded whilst you fall asleep, and promising to stay watching over you all night.'

That night Chief Golfing Moon stood at the end of her bed. Ellen did not fight to stay awake watching out for manic murderers or waiting till it was time to ride. She slept deeply from eight thirty at night to seven in the morning. Maybe it was the brave keeping her safe. Or maybe it was Amy Robb's magic potion – food.

All summer Ellen rode on Thunder. 'Ellen, for goodness' sake will you stop galumphing about on a pretend horse,' her mother chastised. 'Soon you'll be nine. You're an embarrassment.'

Ellen shamefully looked at her feet, scuffed tennis shoes. Soon as she left the house she heaved herself on to Thunder, yanked the reins and headed off.

Summer evenings she was allowed out after supper. She trotted up Wakefield Avenue along Wakefield Road to North Broadway. She loved that name, Broadway. This could be America. Maybe one day she'd see Ben E. King with his steel guitar that he could play so he'd be a star on Broadway. But it wasn't just the name attracted her. There was the chip shop. Ellen spent evenings Gene Kellying round the lamppost outside it, utterly happy. The air was magic, the scent of chips in the making mingling with the roaring jangle of early sixties favourites on the juke box: 'Da Doo Ron Ron', 'Leader of the Pack', 'Then He Kissed Me'. Ellen swung and sang along. 'Met him on a Monday . . . too-ti-too . . .' But her constant waif-like presence annoyed Enrico Ross, the owner.

'Go away. You can't hang about here. You're putting off my customers.'

Ellen hung her head.

'Piss off. I'll tell your dad.' Enrico waved her away.

'Don't have a dad.'

'OK. I'll tell your mum.'

'Don't have a mum. They're dead. In a car crash. My leg got hurt.' She began to limp. 'I háve to go into hospital to get it fixed.' She was tempted to tell him that she was going to have it sawn off, but realised that would stop her coming. He would notice the leg was not missing. And, she would miss that fabulous vinegary waft and thick blast of Detroit music. 'They're putting a pin in it.'

Enrico felt terrible. How could he tell such a tragic infant to piss off? He believed her. Pale, thin child looking up at him. She had too much hair and was growing out of her clothes.

A tear slid down Ellen's cheek. She believed herself. She could imagine the crash vividly. The car was overturned, a pool of petrol spread across the road. Her father lay crushed behind the wheel and her mother, who had been thrown clear, was lying splayed out, arms wide, legs apart, clutching her best black handbag. She was wearing her green coat with the velvet collar buttoned to the neck. Her mouth was wide open. She had a faint look of surprise on her face.

'Hey,' said Enrico, 'have some chips. On the house, OK? Good for the leg.'

Ellen took them. They were hot in her hand. She was a poor orphan child, and was almost too choked with grief to eat them. Grief and giggles. She thought something hugely funny about the vision of her mother spread-eagled on the tarmac, astonished and, well, dead. Heartened at the chip coup she decided to go see her new best pal, Mrs Robb.

They had formed, Ellen and Mrs Robb, an instant and deep understanding, isolated child, lonely old lady. They fell easily into a little pally world of private jokes and small secrets. 'Come,' Mrs Robb would say, 'put on my other apron and we'll bake flapjacks.' Or, 'Let's put crumbs out for the birds.' Then she and Ellen would sit by the window watching the squabbles on the bird table and making up stories about ebullient sparrows and cheeky bluetits. Mrs Robb knew of Ellen's desperate struggle with long division and her constant failure to leap over the horse at gym.

'No mind,' she'd comfortingly pat Ellen's shoulder. 'Albert Einstein couldn't leap a horse as far as I know. And I'm absolutely certain neither could James Dean, Maria Callas, Leonardo da Vinci or Dostoevsky or—'

'Who?'

'Never mind. Just know that leaping a horse is no sign of future achievement. In fact, I'd go so far as to say those who can leap a horse at nine may well be peaking. This could be as far as they go. Downhill from now on for them, I'm afraid.' Ellen had no idea what she was talking about, but knew it was heartening. She wasn't the failure she thought she was.

Tonight the garden was silent. The house was still, deserted. This is a new sort of quiet, Ellen thought, creepy. She licked her salty lips and wiped the grease from her hands on the seat of her pants before setting off across the lawn. She crouched. You never knew. This sort of silence needed careful investigation. She peeped into the kitchen window. Mrs Robb sat in the chair by the Aga. Ellen knocked heartily on the pane and waved. Mrs Robb did not move. Must be sleeping, Ellen decided and rapped more heartily. Still nothing. Ellen pressed her face to the glass. Mrs Robb stared ahead. She did not see her. She did not, Ellen realised, see anything. Her arm dangled by her side. She seemed strange, all lop-sided. Dead, Ellen thought, tremblings starting in her stomach, tears glazing her eyes. Damned folks are always dying.

She knew enough to get help, but didn't dare fetch her mother. 'What are you doing sneaking about other people's gardens?' she would say. She ran next door and rang Mr Martin, the spy's, doorbell. Together they peered into Mrs Robb's kitchen.

'I'll have to call the police,' the spy said. Then he shocked her deeply. He turned and snapped, 'You bugger off.' There was that word – bugger, bugger. Fancy a grown-up actually saying it. As she turned towards her bolt hole in the hedge Mr Martin, suddenly, as if he had been waiting to get hold of her, said, 'I see you. I see you running about this golf course at night. What do you think happens to little girls who do things like that? Silly little cunt.'

It was the worst word she'd ever heard. It curdled into the

evening and hung between them, still ringing with the coarseness and malice in his voice. Ellen fled. But that word – it penetrated her innocence. She instinctively knew she could not ask her mother what it meant.

She watched the departure of Mrs Robb from her front room window. The police came and broke down the door. Shortly after, an ambulance sirened down the avenue. She wondered if it was the same one that took her daddy away. There was fuss and people in uniform being important. And then they brought out her friend on a stretcher, cosily tucked, Ellen thought, in a bright red blanket. She could see that the old lady's face was not covered. 'Not dead, then,' she comforted herself. That, however, was the last time she ever saw her.

A few days later, she overheard her mother discussing the business with a neighbour. 'A stroke,' they said, shaking their heads. 'She'd been sitting there all day till Mr Martin found her. Poor old soul.' Ellen didn't like that. Mrs Robb, she knew, wasn't, never would be, a poor old soul. In time, though, Mrs Robb's family turned up and emptied the house of all its treasures – the blue and white cups, everything. In time new people moved in. Ellen didn't like them. Whoever they were, she didn't like them.

She was a Jesus-stricken child, Ellen. There were Bible readings in class first thing on weekday mornings, and on Sundays she was sent out, buttoned and polished, in her best clothes to Sunday school. Hardly a day passed, then, that she was not warned that the Lord was watching her, knew all her thoughts and deeds. There was no doubt then about who'd been spying when she'd lied to the chip shop man and giggled at the thought of her mother lying hugely splayed out on the road. The big Who, that was who. And now He'd smote down Mrs Robb as a punishment. That was what He did. He was always smiting folk. He worked in mysterious ways and she felt awful about it, just awful. It was quite obvious. She'd done a terrible thing. She'd sinned, a right piece of sinning and Mrs Robb had copped the blame. Poor old bugger. At night she lay in bed wondering about Mrs Robb and wondering if Mrs Robb, wherever she was, lay in bed wondering about her.

Then there was the Sioux. She hadn't been out to see them for weeks now. She was torn in two about all her imaginary friends. She knew, of course, that they were not there. But at the same time she thought they might be missing her.

It was round about then she started to stammer. It had been bad at first, a fierce impediment which put a panicked, gasping gulf between what was in Ellen's mind and what was on her lips. Red of face and shaking with frustration and embarrassment, she would stumble and stop at hard letters and sounds. 'P-P-Pass the salt, pl-pl-pl . . .' That, and her skin, which began to flake and scruff from her face and hands, made her the object of a deal of horrible, hurtful whispering in the school playground. Her mother took her to the doctor.

'Has she been under any stress lately?' he asked.

'No,' Janine told him. 'Well, her father died. But that was months ago and to tell the truth she showed no signs of upset when it happened. And now she's started wetting the bed, too.'

'Delayed shock,' the doctor nodded. 'You never can tell with children. You just don't know how they turn things about in their little minds.' They spoke about Ellen as if she wasn't there. As if she wasn't real. Ellen watched them exchange views about her, little head moving back and forth, as if she was at a tennis match.

'Don't worry,' the doctor said. 'It'll pass. Vitamin C and time. Great healers, you know. She'll grow out of it.'

That was the sort of doctor he was. The age of him, the times he'd lived through, he believed in Vitamin C, time and massive doses of antibiotics. He was convinced she would grow out of the stammer. She didn't. The spluttering calmed after a year. But in moments of distress that unconquerable gulf between what she wanted to say and how it staggered and lurched from her lips came reeling back.

In time fortunes in the depleted Davidson household improved. There was, after all, nothing else for it. Money ran out and Janine was forced to get a job. She was taken on at the local supermarket where she started out stacking shelves, worked up to the checkout till and ended up as under manageress. She wore a green and white striped overall and she made friends. Ellen saw her laughing and telling jokes and could hardly believe her eyes. Her mother was a person after all. And the cuisine cheered up. There were super-market treats – fishfingers, hamburgers, beans and packets of chocolate biscuits. The supper time conversation moved beyond the tastiness of fish to her mother's anecdotes about work.

Going out to work suited Janine. To her it was just another routine. And she did like her routines. She was good at them. Now it was wake, get up, put on underwear, wash available uncovered bits, finish dressing, make toast and coffee, get children up, fed and out the door. She matter-of-factly did this every morning. At night she came home, took off her overall, snapped on the radio in the kitchen, stuck something under the grill, opened a tin of beans. She clung to the rhythm of her ways. It stopped her thinking. It was thinking got to you, she decided. If you could keep your thoughts at bay you'd get through.

Sometimes, though, she could not help herself. She'd watch couples at the supermarket making their way up and down the aisles, choosing what they were going to have for supper or bickering over breakfast cereals and she'd wonder: Had Douglas lived, would we have been like that? As years passed she replaced the quiet, bookish, somewhat grumpy husband she'd had with the jolly, outgoing, even-tempered one she secretly fancied. She imagined the things she might have done with this fantasy husband. They would have watched favourite sitcoms on the telly. They would have gone for drives on Sunday afternoons. They would have had a cup of tea together on the back doorstep Saturday mornings as they made up the week's shopping list. They would both have been fond of a nice bit of salmon (tinned, of course, they couldn't be doing with real) for a treat. Anniversaries and birthdays he would bring her a cup of tea in bed. All in all she was happy with her daydreams. One thing she was sure of, it was a lot easier to mould a dead husband into your perfect man than it was a live one.

In time Ellen started to leave her childhood behind. She still banged into doors and apologised to them. When her mother was about she dropped cups and mumbled. But time was distancing her from that moment when her mother, grieved and scorned, had said to her, 'Not you. Not you.' The horror, the loneliness of it faded and Ellen rarely thought about it. The rift between her and her mother became part of her life. It was simply how things were. They didn't talk about it.

Sometimes, sitting on the bus going to school, and later going to work, she would gaze out over the golf course. There was that special little valley where golfers played blind over a high ridge from the sixteenth to the seventeenth hole. She used to ride along the small canyon and look up at that ridge. There the Sioux stood in a long magnificent line, silhouetted against the sky, waiting for her, watching over her. Looking back at it from her almost-adult standpoint, it was hard to come to terms with how vividly real they had been to her. She could only shake her head at how silly she'd been. It was time to get on with the business of growing up.

Chapter Five

When she was eighteen Ellen left school and started work in the stationery department of a city store. She loved it. She could play with the pens, practise writing her name over and over in different coloured inks. She could watch the folk who came and went into the store, what they bought, what they wore, listen to what they said to each other. She could pore over the comics on the newspaper and magazine counter. Lunch times she went to the staff canteen and sat drinking foul tea from a thick white mug, eating ham sandwiches and listening to the shop girl gossip. It was wonderful. Girls getting together and talking dirty. The fabulous world of sex was new, or newish to them. They took to it with relish. They discussed men's cocks; size, shape, the difficulties of sex in the back of a car, difficulties with gear sticks and ashtrays, and how to get really drunk really quickly and really cheaply. They laughed bawdily, ate low-cal sandwiches because they were always watching their weight, followed by huge puddings, apple pie and custard, chocolate cake, crisps and bars of Dairy Milk, because wasn't weight-watching a bore? They spoke about men as sex objects, accessories, necessary nuisances, messy pets and objects of ardent and utter adoration. They took their love lives more seriously than anything else. Their conversation was incandescent. They chirruped in unison like sparrows roosting in an evening hedge, nudging up to each other. Ellen sipped her tea, ate KitKats, eavesdropped and was happy. But she did not, could not, join in. All her life joining in was a problem.

Occasionally one raw voice would break free of the giggling chorus and tell a tale of derring-do and sexual extravagance. 'I was in Jimmy's car an' he wasn't gonney take my pal Norma home. He was going to leave her at the end of the street. It's dark, I says, she could get attacked. An' he says, who'd attack her? Well, I'm not havin' that. I got his balls. He's thinkin' he's in for a treat. But I says, you'd better take her to her door, look what I've got . . .' There were guffaws of approval for that. Ellen was impressed.

'Hey, Ellen,' Alice from Hosiery asked once. 'Ever been clubbing? Louie the King's?'

Ellen shook her head.

'Oh, come on Friday night,' Alice said enticingly. 'It's great. Good laugh.'

Ellen shrugged. 'Maybe.' She was surprised to be invited. She didn't think they liked her. But then, she didn't think anybody liked her.

'The girls in the shop have asked me to go out with them on Friday night,' she told her mother.

'I hope they're not going to that dreadful disco in Leith. What is it? Louie's or something.' Janine stiffened with sanctimonious censure.

'Louie the King's,' said Ellen. That disapproval, however, was what Ellen needed to hear. She went.

Friday night and they'd just got paid and, arms linked, shrieking youth and cheek and freedom, five abreast they went looking for sex and booze and rock'n'roll. But mostly sex. The girls were barely recognisable out of their shop outfits. Hair spiked, lips painted brown or black, skimpily covered thighs flashing, they strutted to the pub, found a table and set about smoking, talking filth and drinking themselves into oblivion.

'Five Bacardi and Cokes, please.' They rummaged in their purses and were histrionically democratic about who paid for what. 'No, Ellen. You bought the crisps. I'll get the peanuts. And another round. Ha, ha, ha.'

The night was beginning to reel. They made lewd comments to men, innocent bystanders who simply had the misfortune to be standing in the wrong place at the wrong time, mildly sipping a pint of lager. 'Ever had a blow job, mister? Well, you're still not gettin' one. Ha, ha, ha.' Ellen didn't know where to look.

Now and then, suddenly it seemed, they'd used up all their conversation, so they filled the vacant spaces in their minds, singing

snatches of favourite songs. Shoulders moving in rhythm, fags
drifting smoke, they had such sweet voices. Nobody thought it rude
that someone would suddenly turn vacuous and start singing, mid-
sentence. 'No woman, no cry. Oh I love that.'

At eleven they went clubbing. 'We switch to cider now,' Ellen's
companions and bebop cohorts ordered. 'Spirits cost too much
here.' The night stopped reeling, started to colour and rage. Ellen
was scarcely capable of standing up. She lurched into the club,
handbag flapping, hair askew, eyes glazed, face flushed, mascara
streaming. Lights roared. Music more than roared. It was a hard
presence. When she moved she moved through and into the sound
that filled the whole building. For days afterwards her ears were
hot. She was hot-eared from the disco. Love is the Drug, blast, blast,
blast. The noise blew her thoughts away. She could not speak,
communicated by mouthing wildly and pointing. 'Another drink?'
waving at the bar.

Her friends put their bags, shapeless from the weight of junk
within, on the floor and shifted from foot to foot round them. If they
were dancing together nobody could tell. They shut their eyes, sang
along and moved, waving their heads and haircuts in rhythm.
Lights flickering jarred and splattered the movers and shakers on
the floor like light through splintered glass, and everyone was
dancing in action replay. If a boy was foolish enough to ask one of
them to dance, he was mouthed, 'Fuck off.'

Ellen went to the loo and, opening the door, entered a Fellini film:
a wall of noise and the air was impenetrable – smoke, hairspray,
perfume and swearing. There were girls on the floor fighting,
rolling over and over, scratching, biting, kicking and screaming,
'You shite. You fucking shite. If you go near my Pauly again I'll kill
you. I'll kill you.' Over and over they rolled, pale little arms flailing,
fists flying. Nobody paid them any attention. Bloodied and bruised
they staggered to their feet and glared. Nobody won.

Girls stood in thick ranks making pouting lipstick faces in the
mirror and squished gallons of Charlie scent on to every available
bit of their bodies under the arms, behind the ears, down the
cleavage, wrists and up their skirts, 'You never know I might get
lucky. Ha, ha, ha.' Howls of laughter. The veil of hair lacquer

squishing from spray cans was thick. Girls were gluing not only their hair but the air surrounding it, cigarette smoke was caught and stuck in blue waft fug. All the cubicle doors of the lavatories were open. Girls sat, knickers round their ankles, roaring drunken angst to friends leaning on the wall, legs crossed, waiting their turn. 'I love him, Sandra. I really, really love him.'

Ellen thought she was going to die. She knew she would never get to pee. She wanted to lie down. Bacardi, cider, vodka, lager and she thought perhaps some brandy were coursing vilely through her veins. She slumped to the floor, sat, legs splayed before her, gazing at the carpet which, close up, was not as plush as it appeared from the upright position. It was dark blue nylon and pock-marked with cigarette burns.

'Are you all right, darlin'?' one of the wrestlers asked. Ellen didn't even have the strength to nod. 'Here,' the wrestler grabbed her by the hair. She really was going to die. This was it. 'Put your head between your knees. Best place for it, ha, ha, ha. Stop anyone else's getting up there. No. Only joking, darlin'. Deep breaths. Fresh air'll help.' Fresh air? What fresh air?

And at three in the morning they hit the streets again. Arms linked again. Singing. 'Here we go. Here we go. Here we go. Here we COME. Here we COME. Ha. Ha. Ha.'

Alice and Katy needed a pee, disappeared top speed up an alley, and reappeared squealing in triumph. 'Alice's pee won,' they shouted. 'We had a bet about whose would run down to the litter bin first and Alice's won.' They all bawled and laughed and bent double with mischief. Vulgarity? Wasn't it lovely?

'I love you, Alice,' Katy wept. 'No, I mean it. You're my pal. And no man could replace that. I mean, you need men, but you need women to be your pals. Women are best.' They all agreed and cried. And Alice was sick.

'Great night,' she said. 'Brilliant. Best night ever. Are you coming next week, Ellen?'

She shook her head. 'No,' she whispered weakly. She felt brittle and frail. The very sound of her own voice was too much to bear.

On Monday, tamed and pale, they'd appear at work again. Next

Friday they'd be out here again, screaming and drinking. Always after that, when she was sitting at home watching television, or working late in the office, and the shrieks of women out on the town came careening through the night to her, Ellen thought it would be them lifting their skirts, running down the street, yelling. She thought them wild and wonderful. They made her feel she was not very good at life. She rolled wearily home and fell asleep unwashed, half dressed, battered and beleaguered, under the knowing black-and-white eye of Humphrey Bogart on the poster above her bed.

It did not take her long to reinvent her new friends and what she imagined to be their savage sisterly love. She had seen the name Starless Enterprises on some of the comic strips in the local Sunday newspaper. It was the brainchild of Stanley Macpherson. He was the regular subject of interviews. He appeared colourful, and his characters made an interesting splash on dull pages.

Dear Mr Macpherson, *Ellen wrote a month later.*
I have written a comic strip story about four gangster women who live in an old tower block and who vow sisterly love and seek to save their fellow women from the injustices of living in a man's world. I've called it Gangster Women, and I am sending it to you to look at . . .

Then she dried. What did people say in this sort of letter? She abandoned her plan and left the letter lying in her bedroom drawer. Two weeks later she added, 'Hope you like it.' Then, before she could change her mind she swiftly posted it and expected to hear nothing. She always expected the worst.

'You can't work in a shop for ever,' her mother worried. 'You have to decide what you are going to do with your life.'

'OK,' said Ellen. 'I will. Soon.' She walked out of the room, banged into the doorpost and apologised to it. 'Sorry.'

Her mother rolled her eyes. That girl, what was she to do with that girl?

Two weeks after she posted her letter, Ellen got a reply.

* * *

Dear Ellen,
   Loved your scripts. Come and see me, four o'clock next
Monday afternoon.
Look forward to it.
Yours, Stanley.
PS: Give us a bell if this doesn't suit.

Chapter Six

Stanley Macpherson was scruffy. Ellen hadn't imagined that. She had him in a suit answering phones, making decisions, being ruthless. His office was a heap. There were heaps and heaps, and heaps bundled into more heaps. Heaps of papers on his desk. Heaps of files on the shelves behind him. More heaps on the window sill along with an ivy plant, dried and clinging to life. His phone rang constantly. He wore a sweat shirt with a hole in the sleeve. The crotch of his jeans was about to collapse under the constant strain of containing his thighs. The threads that held it together were worn and tired. He drummed his fingers as he spoke, and when he moved he moved quickly, in short enthusiastic bursts.

Ellen delighted him. She was exactly what he'd been looking for since he started up. There was something about her uncertainty and indecision that pleased him. She was immature, inhibited and wildly imaginative. Here was a writer he could mould and shape. Furthermore, here was a writer he was sure would stay put. His last two had moved on, one to work for New York comics from London, the other to San Francisco.

He rubbed his stubby beard and felt only slightly guilty about his motives as he offered her a job. He would in time, he knew, take her home to his family. He would feed her, introduce her to food and wine she plainly knew nothing about. He'd show her a new world of books, music and films. He could see it already. He'd done it time and time before with other writers, artists and, well, just people he took a shine to. He was shrewd and he was kindly. He, however, thought he was jaded and a soft touch. He was never particularly kind to himself.

'You can't take a job like that.' Ellen's mother clasped her hands in dismay. 'What will become of you? There's no future, no security.'

It was just what Ellen needed to hear. Her judgements and decisions were always measured by her mother's disapproval. The greater the disapproval, the more likely Ellen would do whatever was disapproved of. She took the job.

On her first day Stanley took her to 'meet the gang'. She stood uncertainly in the doorway, gazing round.

'This is Ellen,' Stanley said. 'And,' gesturing the room with a sweep of his arm, 'Ellen, this is the gang.'

They were all men. Ellen was shocked. She hadn't expected this. Nor, apparently had they. They shifted in their seats and tried to look welcoming They were all young. There was a script editor, and a central-casting designer/art editor with wire glasses and pony tail. He spent hours poring over typefaces, constructing words – different typeface for every letter. It looked odd, Ellen thought, likeably odd. There was another writer, Don, and Billy who did things. He sold advertising space, unloaded bundles of comics from the van when they arrived from the printer, answered the phone, fetched sandwiches, nipped to the bookies to place bets and probably worked harder than anyone else. And, whilst all the others would, eventually, move on, Billy would in time combine his job as fixer and fetcher with that of script editor. He'd stay put, then – along with Ellen.

They all stared at her suspiciously. A woman writer was a creature rarely glimpsed in the world of comic strips. This wasn't right. Women were, well, women, weren't they?

Ellen nodded hello and sat at her desk. Her hair was drawn over her face, she smelled of patchouli. Apart from that first hello she hadn't a clue what to say. For two weeks she sat quietly, scarcely moving. If she needed a pee she waited till she could wait no longer, she felt so awkward and embarrassed just walking across the room. Her shoes squeaked, or so she thought. She felt the faint rustle of her thighs to be thunderous. People stopped work and looked at her, she imagined. Her shyness came wheeling from deep within her. She sat considering her fingers, did not want to look up, and when she spoke, she mumbled.

She arrived dutifully at nine, left at five. Her lunch lasted precisely one hour. It took a while for her to realise she was the only one closely observing office hours. Though she relaxed enough to let her lunch hour roll on past two o'clock to three, or half-past, she never relinquished that hour between nine and ten when she had the office to herself. That was when she did her best thinking.

In time her quiet presence was accepted in the office. She learned to join in the banter, discussed television programmes, favourite songs on the radio, and the best way to dunk a biscuit. She won ten pounds betting that Stanley's jeans would last till the end of the month, if not for ever. 'It's physics,' she said. 'Stressed thread and thighs. The thighs are not going to get any bigger so the threads will not be stressed any further.' Everyone was impressed. They took her in. She might be a woman but she did not speak of womanly things. She did not spend hours putting on makeup or fiddling with her hair. In fact, Ellen hated her face. She thought it absurdly eager and shiny, as it had been on the night her mother said, 'Not you.' She looked at it as little as possible and was fairly adept at putting on foundation and lipstick without a mirror. They forgave her the patchouli. She was, they agreed, as near to a bloke as a woman could get. She'd do.

Stanley gave her the desk next to the window, nearest the door. He figured that if she was smitten by a sudden bout of femaleness – which could be, he knew from experience, messy – or if the maleness of the office got too much for her, there were escapes. She could either run out of the door and away. Or she could leave them all behind staring out the window. Mostly she chose the window. She looked out at people in the street below. Other people's lives always fascinated her. Often Stanley would pass the office door and catch her sitting watching the world, and he'd smile. The fruit of her starings would soon be written down, incorporated in her strips.

Though fat and scruffy, Stanley Macpherson was no fool. His life plan was to be a millionaire by the time he was forty. He had the ideas and energy. But his heart's gentle reputation kept his bank balance low. He left the writing of story strips to others and concentrated on what he could do best – the quick three-framers. He had a knack for them. They were simple, he explained. 'You start at the end with the joke and work forwards to the beginning.'

He'd been doing this reverse thing for years and years. 'Man and boy,' he smiled. But he was beginning to think he was doing this in reverse, too. He was sure he'd been a man when he started. Now, though, working back, he was beginning to doubt his maturity.

His wife, Brigit, visited him at work regularly trailing children. It never seemed to Ellen that it was the same children she brought along.

'How many children do you have, Stanley?'

'Five. Brigit had two before she met me, then we've had two, but the new baby, Jackson, isn't mine.'

'Goodness. Don't you mind?'

'What has minding got to do with things?' he said. Sadly. 'I believe in monogamy but the woman I'm monogamous with doesn't.'

He had, however, an impressive way with a business plan. His idea was to specialise in small, joky strips for advertising companies and local newspapers. It was only after he met Jack Conroy that he moved into science fiction. These he sold to Sunday supplements and freebie papers, then syndicated on. Jack Conroy drew his stories, usually double layer, eight-frame serials for an agreed sum, took standard syndication fees, and got slowly richer and richer. Stanley ran the office, met people, shook hands, paid bills, handed out money, supported children he hadn't fathered, kept his wife in clothes and a Volvo and struggled.

He'd started out writing all the strips but in time got too busy running his business to do what he started his business to do. He knew most of the writers he interviewed were ambitious and he had spent some time looking for someone who, like him, would stay put. Someone who would sit behind a desk for years and years and one day would look up and notice time had passed. Ellen was a find to him. He knew she was the one the instant he read her bawdy script and the shy little letter that went with it. He suspected, however, that in time he'd end up looking after Ellen and sorting out her life, just as he looked after and sorted out just about everyone he employed, married, befriended or, it seemed, happened to sit next to in the pub. He was a soft touch's soft touch.

He was right about Ellen. She had not meant to stay working at Starless Enterprises for long. She had intended to raise enough cash to see her through university. But she got comfortable behind her desk. She liked the monochrome view from the window and the people she shared the room with. She slipped into a laconic relationship, slow lunches and small talk, with Stanley. And she got paid to daydream. She had landed on her feet. Though *Gangster Women* palled on her – their strutting and posturing bored her – she continued to write them. She was convinced that one day she would come up with a character she could give her heart to. Someone humane and kindly and yet real. She knew it was there, somewhere, waiting for her and one day she would come to it.

Stanley liked Ellen. Her lunch time company was refreshing. She still hadn't mastered small talk so her conversation was a mass of speculation and daydreams. Also she did all the speaking, leaving him free to eat and dream. 'What would you do with five hundred pounds to spend on yourself, Stanley?' 'What's the most boring evening you ever had, Stanley?' 'Have you always been faithful to Brigit, Stanley?' 'Have you ever wondered about God, Stanley?'

'Christ, Ellen. I don't know. There have been so many boring evenings they all seem to blend into one these days. Brigit – no. No, I haven't. Don't ask about that. Anyway, I'm not as bad as she is. And no, I have not and will not ever wonder about God. Why do you ask that?'

'I was reading an article that said God is a woman. It's an old idea, but I'd forgotten about it.' Ellen had been working for Stanley for four years. 'Only now I don't think He can be a woman.' She yanked at her T-shirt, peered glumly down at her body in there. 'Look at me. No woman would do that to another. God's a bloke or a cat.' Across the room at the bar a man was looking at her. His stare made her uncomfortable. She did not like men staring at her. She felt her chin was too big and her forehead shone luminously if she did not keep it covered. Bryan Ferry was searing on the juke box, 'Over you . . .' A saxophone crooned.

'A cat?' Stanley sighed and eyed her sandwich left abandoned on her plate as she keenly conversed, a pursuit she found more absorbing than eating. He, however, was more of an eater than

49

talker. His wife had recently been warning him that if he did not do something about his weight she'd leave him. He was in a quiet torment. Brigit or the sandwich? The sandwich won. It was nearer. 'Do you want that?' he asked. She shook her head, a gesture he took as meaning he could have it. 'Why a cat?' A shower of crumbs flew from his mouth as he spoke and landed in the middle rumple of his sweat shirt. The sole was coming off his training shoe.

'I knew this old lady, Mrs Robb. She had a cat. She fed it chopped liver and bits of fish. It lay in a basket by her Aga. I never saw anyone or anything so adored. Cats are made to be adored. Yes, a giant celestial cat in a huge gleamy basket.' She was pretending not to notice the man who was very openly and obviously noticing her. 'Don't you ever feel, Stanley, that your life is being messed about for no real reason? It's the celestial paw playing with you, the evil way cats do, batting you around, then leaving you alone only to turn and pounce again. That's cats for you. That's God for you.' The man was walking across the room. He wore a black suit with a white T-shirt and grubby baseball boots.

'Presumably the great cat in the sky only gave us thumbs that we can operate tin openers,' he said.

He was like that. He joined in the conversations of complete strangers if they interested him. In the years to come he would often leave Ellen alone in bars twiddling a glass whilst he went to sit with people he did not know to marshal their arguments or participate in discussions he found too amusing, too puerile, silly or fascinating to miss. Sometimes he made new friends. Sometimes he got a smack in the mouth.

'Absolutely,' agreed Ellen.

Daniel picked up her drink and drained her glass. 'If I wait for you to finish lunch time will be over and you'll be gone. And I won't be able to buy you another.'

'I'll have a pint, too,' said Stanley. Then whilst Daniel was at the bar he told Ellen she'd better watch herself with that one. But Ellen was charmed. She was ripe for a spot of adoration.

That night, after the first meeting in the pub, Daniel was standing in the street waiting for Ellen to finish work. He was leaning on the barrier at the edge of the pavement, smiling at her, looking fabulous. He took her for a drink, bought her a pint of Guinness and a cheese sandwich. And he took her back to his flat – to bed.

Years later, remembering, feeling vaguely cheap, she complained to Cora, 'A Guinness and a cheese sandwich and I'm anybody's. It didn't take much. I was easily won.'

'*Was*,' said Cora. '*Was*? I just love your use of the past tense.'

It rained. When they got to Daniel's flat they were both soaked. He brought her a towel.

'I'm all right,' she only feebly protested.

'You're wet,' he said.

'I've been wet before. It doesn't hurt.'

'You're shivering,' he pointed out.

'I'm a woman of the world. I've shivered before.' She thought that such a clever answer. She was twenty-two. She thought she was cool. But she did not know as much as she thought she knew..

She worried that first night with Daniel that she would not be good enough for him. She hated her body and did not want him to see her without her clothes. She was under the impression that everyone in the world was better at sex than she was. She slipped uneasily out of her T-shirt and bra and looked glumly down at her tits. 'Do you think one's bigger than the other?'

'Perhaps,' he agreed. He was older than she was. He could not count how often he'd had this conversation before. 'Which one do you think is larger?'

'The left.'

'Is that your favourite tit?' He thought he could tell a great deal about a woman by how she answered that question. But then it was hard, sometimes, to understand women. They were all far more intimate with their own bodies than any man was. A woman would always have a favourite bit of her body. If she went through life believing she had a fabulous arse she was usually outgoing, vibrant, confidant. But an awful lot of the women he'd been with just liked their wrists. He supposed this was the bit they saw most, or maybe it really was their best bit. As they got older many women seemed to think one side of their face wrinklier than the other. Then again a woman might break her nail and cry out in dismay, 'Oh, it was my best nail, too.' They had things like that, women – one eye baggier than the other, and favourite nails.

'No. I like the small one best,' Ellen said.

'Ah.'

She was frightened of having big tits. She stood holding them, considering them. He knew who she was when he first approached her. That comic strip woman, Ellen something-or-other. She was sort of famous, locally famous, though she plainly did not know it. He sensed money. If she did not have any now, she would in the future. Seeing her chatting to Stanley, he recognised a glistening chance and hated himself for his opportunism. But he couldn't help himself. She was not without experience, he could tell, but lacked the self-confidence to relax and enjoy the pleasure her body could bring her. He was the man to put that right. He ran his hand slowly over the favourite tit and surveyed the other with critical care. 'Perhaps this one is the nicer. Let me consider it from another angle.' He moved round to the back of her, and, kissing her neck, reached round, continued his research. He told her to take off her jeans. But please leave on her knickers. He'd like to take them off himself.

Afterwards she lay listening to the building. People who were soon to become her friends were moving about, getting on with their lives. Had they heard her? Ronald and George upstairs had finished supper and were washing up together. She could hear them walking back and forth across their kitchen. Mrs Boyle downstairs opened her door and called for her cat, 'Fergus!' Her deep and fruity tones echoed down the corridor. The cat came running, yowling. Ellen loved this. She could lie in bed eavesdropping on the people around her. There was something comforting about the nearness of neighbours. She did not feel alone.

In the bungalow of her childhood where she was for ever alone, neighbours kept themselves private. When Ellen wanted to spy on them she had to climb on their garden fence and stare through the window. In her glory days this had been a favourite game, but she no longer indulged. Well, a person gets too old to gallop about on a pretend horse. Thunder, then, was no longer around for swift getaways when people furiously burst from the sacred isolation of their living rooms waving fists and bawling, 'Bugger off! Nosy little brat!'

Daniel fetched them some bourbon and said he hoped she wasn't going to do anything boring like get up and go home. Ellen phoned her mother and lied. She said she was staying with a girlfriend. She found lying to her mother a very easy thing to do. As she spoke Daniel ran his hand up the insides of her thighs. They drank and when the bottle was empty Daniel went down to the pub for another. She paid.

'What do you do?' she asked when he got back.

'Stuff,' he said.

'Stuff?'

'I'm working on my PhD.' He hadn't looked at it in years. Doubted he'd ever finish it. 'I do a few bar shifts. Three evenings, a couple of afternoons.' Since he spent so much drinking, it seemed reasonable to make some cash doing the odd stint on the other side of the bar. 'I pick up a bit on the horses.' He gambled. Mostly he gambled.

In the kitchen the phone rang and rang. Daniel paid it no heed. Neither did Ellen. She was in love. She loved Daniel's flat; the lumpen corduroy-covered sofa in the living room, the postcards and bills stuck behind the clock and candlesticks on the mantelpiece, the multi-patterned rugs, the clusters of unwashed cups and glasses everywhere, the small collection of jackets and coats hanging behind the door. The pictures throughout the flat were all framed and all of women, women by men – Man Ray, Degas, Aubrey Beardsley, George Grosz and in the hall there was a part of a Robert Crumb strip cut out and blown up. She loved the strange musky, joss sticky smell and the ragged chenille curtains. An entire wall in the living room was taken up by his record collection. The only thing that was cherished was his stereo system. There was nothing about Daniel's flat that Ellen didn't love. There was nothing about Daniel that she didn't love. His body was soft. When he took off his shirt, she saw he had a mole under his left nipple. He was skinny like a boy. His ribs showed.

He turned to her, took her glass and laid it on the floor by the bed. Then he kissed her. They both tasted of Jack Daniel's. His mouth was soft on hers, his tongue moved, and probed into her. His hands slid over her, over her back. She loved that. She felt him between her legs and desperately wanted him, pushed herself up towards him.

'No,' he said. 'No. Go on top. Sit on me. Let me look at you.'

'I can't.' She hung her head. She was embarrassed. She didn't like anybody to look at her.

'Leave the light on and let me see you,' he whispered and he pleaded and she could not resist him no matter how awkward she felt. She sat on him, feeling high up and vulnerable. But then the pleasure of it took hold of her. He moved up into her and let her curl her legs round him. He kissed her neck and the lobes of her ears, stroked her hair. 'You are beautiful,' he told her. She was, too. For the first time in her life in that flat with summer rain splattering the window and starlings from the park roosting and chorusing and complaining outside, in the quiet nine o'clock gloom she thought she was beautiful. In the morning she'd re-join the world, bang into doors and apologise to them, say sorry to strangers when they stood on her foot. Move along streets, eyes down, shoulders slumped.

The phone rang again. And again. Behind the door, swept against the wall, there was a huge collection of unopened letters and bills. Ellen was dealing with a rogue. All the signs were there, but she did not recognise them. She was twenty-two. She was ardently working on her cool. And she *really* did not know as much as she thought she knew.

Chapter Seven

Her mother hated Daniel. 'What do you see in a man like that? Can't you tell he's the worst sort of man? Too good-looking for you. What does he do anyway?'

'Stuff,' said Ellen.

'What sort of stuff?'

'He's working on his PhD.'

'Pah. Nonsense.'

'He works in a bar.' Her mother thought it beneath her to say anything about that. Ellen didn't mention the horses.

Daniel wasn't enthused about Ellen's mother. It was plain to him, however, that the more she loathed him, the more Ellen would adore him. He felt he'd be letting himself down if he did not exploit the situation. When Ellen and her mother were standing face to face chatting he would get as close to Ellen as possible and slip his hand up her skirt, down her knickers, round her bum. He would stare Janine in the eye and do secret intimate things to her daughter. 'She is mine,' his look of derision would say. 'She is mine and you can do nothing about it. I am groping her arse as you speak to her about the macaroni and cheese you ate last night.'

Once, after supper, when he and Ellen were washing up together, he suggested she bend over the small Formica-topped kitchen table so that he could take her from behind whilst her mother was in the other room watching *Sale of the Century*. And, though she refused, Ellen was surprised at how much the suggestion turned her on.

'Well, if you won't do that, marry me,' Daniel said. 'You'll be Mrs Quinn. The fabulous Mrs Quinn.'

It was as overwhelmingly tempting as the purple-wrapped sweets in Mrs Robb's garden. Daniel scarcely looked at her. He was drying some forks, slowly laying them out in a neat row. He wanted

Ellen to be the fabulous Mrs Quinn. He felt he deserved a fabulous Mrs Quinn in his life. He could take her, mould her. Show her all the things she knew nothing about – art, films, books, food, sex – life, dammit, life. He could shape her into the wife he longed for. He, of course, had no intention of becoming the fabulous Mr Quinn. He wanted a wife, but no way was he going to become a husband.

'It will be wonderful,' he persuaded. 'Just as long as we don't start acting like husband and wife. That's the sure-fire way to kill a marriage.' She hadn't a clue what he was talking about but she agreed with him willingly. She finished washing the dishes, wiped the sink, folded the dishcloth and placed it neatly between the taps, and went through to her mother.

'Daniel has just asked me to marry him,' she said.

'He what!' Her mother was appalled. 'Marry him? Marry a man like that? You can't. I forbid you . . .'

That did it. She married him.

Chapter Eight

Ellen and Daniel got married, and, too broke to afford a honeymoon, they drifted into their own world of comfort and passion. A sort of second childhood, only with sex. They cocooned themselves in Daniel's flat for a fortnight, dining in, and in bed, on carry-out fish and chips, Chinese or pizza. They made alcoholic concoctions with vodka, rum, Kahlúa and Coke, and sat on the lumpen sofa scarcely dressed, drinking, eating Chocolate Olivers and prawn cocktail crisps. They bought champagne, shook the bottle jubilantly and ran round and round the sofa spraying each other. They got sticky. They whooped and laughed and danced, a slow semi-naked shuffle, draped over each other listening to Roxy Music. They fucked themselves to a standstill. Towards the end of their fortnight of junk food and love a spot of actual fresh air seemed tempting, and sane. Hand in hand they set out across the park. Shaky-legged and pale they made it to the nearest bench. They sat a while staring bleakly ahead before heading home.

Watching from the upstairs window, Ronald said to George, 'Oh look, our young lovers have shagged themselves witless. They can hardly walk.'

George said to Ronald, 'Oh, jealous.'

Next day the two tried to make it over the park again, and still couldn't. It became a joke: if they ever could make it over the park together their love would be finished. They sat on the bench.

Daniel kissed her. 'My tongue's having a better time than I am,' he said, slipping his hands up her T-shirt.

She loved that, loved his hands on her. In years to come when the big fights started he would turn his back on her, leaving her helpless. She never could deal with rejection, 'Not you. Not you.' 'Touch me, you shite,' she'd scream at him. 'T-T-T-Touch me.'

57

She loved to be touched. The people she held dearest were touchy, feely people. George upstairs, who would grip her hand in the pub and say, 'Now, Ellen, you must tell me what you've been up to. Lots of naughty things, I hope. And if it isn't naughty don't bore me with it.' Mrs Boyle downstairs, who would link a frail arm in hers and say, 'Come, Ellen. We'll go on a mushroom quest to the Italian deli on Elm Row. Mushrooms and wine. You'll pay.' Cora, who would tidy her hair, fix her collar and say, 'Ellen, you can't possibly go out like that. Let me sort you out.' And Daniel, of course Daniel, who more than fucked her, he cuddled her. It was the cuddling that more than anything kept her married to him. Sex was, of course, a fabulous bonus. But she loved having him next to her in bed, arms round her, clinging to her. She loved to hear him breathe.

In times to come friends would show Ellen pictures of their honeymoons. She would look at pictures of people as they had been years before, thinner, smilier, looking enthusiastic and slightly foolish in luminescent beach outfits and straw hats.

'What did you do for your honeymoon, Ellen?' they would ask.

'We went to bed for a fortnight,' she'd say. There would be silence. Was it disapproval? Or maybe envy? Ellen never could tell.

After two weeks of hectic bliss she went back to work, a relief really. She needed the rest.

The initial burst of married life over, Daniel thought his life would continue as before. He did not think of himself as a husband. He had a fixed notion of husbands. They were dull people who faced south-west.

'Husbands,' he explained to Ellen, 'are people who stand outside shops, wearing tweed caps, vacantly facing south-west, whistling vague tunes through their teeth whilst their wives shop. That's not for me.'

He was adamant about that. At the time, Ellen had no wish to have a man in her life wearing a tweed cap, whistling vaguely, whilst facing south-west. Daniel in her bed was more than enough. She brought in food, and, in a martyrish sort of way, thought she was making her relationship work when she did not, in any way, impose her taste on his flat.

'Don't be bringing pink things in here,' he ordered. Actually until he mentioned it she hadn't thought to bring home something pink. After that she was constantly tempted. When she discovered that Daniel slept regularly with Friendly Mary, who owned the fruit shop at the end of the road, she painted the bedroom the colour of tinned salmon. 'Have that, you bastard.' That she loathed the effect as much as he did made no difference. This was not a piece of design. This was an act of vengeance. She was only just beginning to consider their flat as much her home as it was his. She'd been paying the rent since she moved in.

On her first afternoon alone she spent a gruelling couple of hours going through the pile of mail that she'd seen lying mouldering behind the front door that first night with him. She settled on the sofa with a cup of coffee, thinking this a glorious opportunity to discover more about her new husband. She wanted to know everything about him. There was so much he did not tell her. She imagined there were mysterious businessy things, deals and intrigue, that she would not understand. She was thinking Humphrey Bogart in *Casablanca*, a man with a past and a gritty integrity. This was not naïveté, it was stupidity. She opened eviction notices, dire threats from the electric company, police warrants about his parking fines – she was not even aware he had a car – and warnings that the bailiffs had obtained a warrant to enter the premises and would be doing so unless payment was received within seven days. There was a letter from Daniel's mother – he'd told Ellen she was dead – pleading with him to get in touch. Where are you? Why don't you call? There were hysterical outcries from credit card companies and a letter from Daniel's bank manager demanding he hand in his cheque book and card.

Ellen had no idea that the simple act of opening mail could have such a foul effect on the digestive system. She sat in the lavatory, rocking back and forth clutching her stomach. Her beloved was not a man of gritty integrity after all. Any moment now the door might be battered down and heavy men in porkpie hats would remove all their furniture. Oh God.

She put the sordid mess into a box and next day poured it dramatically on to Stanley's desk. 'What do I do, Stanley?'

He always knew what to do. 'Run away,' he suggested. 'Leave

the bastard. I did warn you. That first day – remember?'

Then with a heaving intake of breath he pulled the financial ruin towards him. He sat her beside him at his desk. Together they slowly sorted out the mess. At the end of a churning day Ellen had taken charge of her husband's finances. She handed over most of her savings to clear the back rent. She agreed monthly sums to pay his credit card debts. She settled with the electric company, and had the phone connected again. She didn't know what to do about his mother. Though she no longer had anything to fear, the chill of the threats and the panic they set up within her remained. The dread sounds in her life were no longer the awful rush and swish of silken dress or the slow menacing fall of pointy shoe on chilled lino. They were the simple sounds of morning mail tumbling through the letter box or the sharp insistent tapping of someone knocking at the door.

None of this really changed her feelings for him. She would lie in bed watching him move about the bedroom vaguely humming some favourite song of the moment, and she would think how beautiful he was with his boy's body and his perfect haircut and she would wonder what such a person saw in her. In the end it didn't matter what he did, what debts he brought home for her to sort out. All he had to do was kiss her; all he had to do was touch her; indeed, all he had to do was walk, smiling, across the room to her and she was his.

The notion of just was lodged in the depth of her psyche. She was just . . . She was just a plain sort of a person with short dark hair and big hands who never thought someone like Daniel would ever look her way. She was just a person who wrote silly comic strips. When Stanley told her she was beginning to have a following she thought: It's just me. They must all be wrong. Or they must have terrible taste. If she told Stanley her plans for a new script he'd say, 'Sounds good.' She'd think: Sounds good. Only sounds good. But *is* it good? It's just a comic strip.

Chapter Nine

She did, of course, challenge Daniel about his heap of hate mail and debts. But he was unrepentant. In fact, he couldn't understand why she was so upset by it. She let her resentment grow and fester within her for a week before she said anything. She was not used to confrontation. In her bungalow days, confrontation had not been on the agenda. It did not fit into her mother's emotional routine, which was a round of smiles, frowns and disapproving hostile silences directed at anybody who stepped out of line.

Daniel wasn't one for confrontations either. He didn't really reckon any of life's biggies – birth, marriage or death. Birth – well, he'd done that obviously, but what was it to him? He could remember nothing about it. Death – well, he didn't mind really. As long as it took him by surprise. And marriage was just something he'd done. He liked Ellen, he fancied having her around on a regular basis, but he'd no intention of letting this marriage thing interfere with his gambling, his hanging out with his mates, working at the bar – his life, in fact.

'You have a mother,' Ellen accused.

'Yes, don't we all?' He raised his eyebrows. Why should that surprise her?

'But she's alive. You didn't even invite her to our wedding.'

'So? You have a problem with that?'

'Yes I do. I should imagine she would too.'

'Nah.' He shook his head. He was adamant she would not have a problem about missing his wedding. 'She doesn't like me. I'm not her sort. I didn't grow into the person she planned. I think she'd rather forget about me.'

Ellen stared at him. She found it hard to take in what he was saying. 'Your own mother. You never ever go to see her.'

He shrugged again. 'She doesn't ever come to see me.' There was always something reasonable about Daniel's arguments – no matter how atrocious he was being.

'I go see my mother once a week.' Ellen was fairly saintly about this. Priggish, almost.

'But that's another of your lies,' Daniel told her. 'You don't want to go. You just kid yourself you're being a dutiful daughter. Don't even bother to open your mouth to tell me you enjoy it or she enjoys it. I won't believe you.'

Ellen shut her mouth and left it at that. A few days later, however, she phoned Daniel's mother and introduced herself.

'Um,' she said when she heard the voice at the other end. 'Um . . . Mrs Quinn? Um . . . I'm Ellen. Daniel's wife.'

'Who? Who's this?'

'I'm Ellen Quinn. Um . . . I married your son the other week.'

There was a long silence. Breathing. Then, 'Well, well. There's a turn up for the book.' Ellen could almost hear her battling against making scathing comments. Eventually she simply said, 'Well, there you go. You never can tell with Daniel. You can never accuse him of being predictable, I'll say that for him.'

'Um,' Ellen said again. 'Um . . . would it be all right if I came to see you?'

Ellen could tell that it wouldn't. But Daniel's mother was too polite to say so.

'Yes,' she said stiffly. 'Why not? I'm sure we've lots to talk about.'

'Tomorrow?' asked Ellen.

'Tomorrow,' the older Mrs Quinn agreed. And did Ellen hear her say – let's get it over with?

She was tall, straight back, hair that had once been blonde but was now just pale, palely grey. It was obvious where Daniel got his looks. She was still beautiful, though she wore her beauty badly. It irritated her. People stared, or they were absurdly polite to her.

She showed Ellen into the living room. This is where Daniel sat as a child, Ellen thought, looking round. It was infinitely more comfortable than the living room she'd sat in as a child. Through the window she could see the garden. All the love Daniel's mother had left in her was lavished on that quarter-acre or so. It was lush and vibrantly blooming. The little patch that came with the bungalow Ellen grew up in had been tamed and clipped, mowed and tidied into bland submission. A polite row of lupins grew along by the far hedge and some pansies lined the flowerbeds by the lawn. The only thing that flourished was the lilac tree and now Ellen's mother was talking of having it chopped down. The brutishly vigorous way it bloomed every year offended her. 'Chop it down,' she muttered. 'That'll show it.'

'I'll make us tea,' Mrs Quinn offered. She brought them a pot of Earl Grey and a plate of exquisite home-made almond biscuits. Ellen ate an abstemious one and refused a second though she longed to take more. She didn't want her new mother-in-law to think her greedy.

'Perhaps you'd like to see Daniel's room?' Mrs Quinn asked.

Ellen nodded. 'I'd love to.'

It was up a small staircase. Ellen could imagine Daniel as Christopher Robin coming down these stairs wrapped in a blue dressing gown, dragging a favourite teddy, bump bump bump, behind him. The room made Ellen draw her breath. It was perfect. A shelf of stuffed toys – a white cat, a hen, several teddy bears, a scruffy dog. There was a wooden yacht for sailing on the park pond, several model vintage cars, shelves and shelves of books – all the classics. Ellen writhed in envy, remembering the sparse and linoed bedroom where she lay waiting for the man in pointy shoes or the lady in the white dress to come to kill her. Look, he had *Winnie-the-Pooh* and *The Wind in the Willows*. She'd been past twenty when she discovered them.

'He had an idyllic childhood,' she gasped.

'I like to think so,' his mother said. 'It goes to show, don't give your child everything. It simply isn't enough for them. Shall we go downstairs? We'll have more tea and see if we can find something to talk about other than Daniel.'

They didn't succeed. By the time she left Ellen had seen his school reports, the cards he made for his mother for Valentine's Day, the holiday seaside snaps of him in blue swimming trunks sitting on a beach donkey, the breeze ruffling his hair. His dream childhood was packed neatly into three shoe boxes and a few photograph albums.

'Where's his father?' Ellen wanted to know.

'He left,' Mrs Quinn said with withering finality. Ellen didn't dare push for more.

When she got home she told Daniel of her visit. 'She wants me to go see her again. Next week if I can manage.'

'Does she?' He didn't seem to mind at all. 'I bet she liked you. You're much more her sort than me.'

'What do you mean by that? She's your mother, you could go see her sometime.'

'Oh, she wouldn't want that. She doesn't really want to see me. Not now that I'm no longer the perfect son. Actually, I'm not her sort.'

'Not her sort! Not her sort!' Ellen was exasperated with him. 'How can you say that?'

'Look, Ellen, just because someone gave birth to me, it doesn't mean to say I'm the kind of person she'd like to have round for tea.'

On Thursdays Ellen went to the pub where Daniel worked to watch him hold court. He moved up and down the bar serving opinions and drinks. 'A tequila and a half of lager. You didn't buy that album, did you? There's only one decent track, third one in side two. The opening riff's pure early Hendrix.' Then down the bar, different punters, different booze, different opinions: 'Two pints and two Bells. No, I didn't bother with Misty Morning. Not on that turf. He's had a bad season.' Back down the bar: 'A Glenfiddich and a Guinness. Thing about David Lynch is his weirdness, that's why you go to see him.' Daniel knew about things she didn't. He knew about proper things.

Once she overheard some boys discussing him.

'Bastard,' said one.

'Fuck never paid us,' said another.

They sat in a pathetic row on bar stools. They were all much younger than she was. And they were paler than she, thinner, raggier, grubbier and hungrier. They were a band, Five Believers. Daniel had hired them to play in the bar. Though the owner had left cash for them, Daniel had pocketed it.

Ellen was shocked. 'These poor boys.'

They had holes in their jeans, long bony hands dangling from denimed sleeves, spots on their faces. They had that well-honed weirdness of youths who were sure they had something to say if only they knew what it was; multi-coloured hair, pierced noses, shaved and tattooed heads. They spoke Scottish, but they dreamed in American. But then, Ellen thought, didn't everyone everywhere do that at some time or another in their lives.

When she and Daniel got home she berated him. 'How could you? How could you treat these boys like that? They're children, Daniel. Children.'

Daniel scratched his head laconically. He was unrepentant.

Shocked at how little he seemed to care, Ellen continued her tirade. 'That's a terrible thing to do. You didn't just steal their money. You stole their dreams. You took their dreams and turned them into some sleazy gain for yourself. These boys want to be musicians.'

'They're not musicians,' Daniel said. 'They're not even dreamers.' He crossed the room pulled out a Charlie Parker album. 'This is a musician, and a dreamer.' He threw down a tattered copy of *Electric Ladyland*. 'And here's another. What are these boys? Greedy. They want to be stars. They want to be in the pop charts. They want little girls to call their names and unzip their flies. They want sex and booze and big cars. They want adoration.' He turned to Ellen, face gleaming and saintly. 'I have done them a favour. I have shown them what it's about. The disappointments, the graft. That's what evolution's about. Adapting to the facts. Getting real with the truth.'

'Is it?' Ellen was sure there was something wrong here, but Daniel at full stretch could convince her grass was blue and dogs didn't bark.

'They should thank me,' he decided. He threw his arms about, ran his fingers through his hair, paced the room. He even started to have faith in his own rant. 'Greedy. Greedy. They're all greedy. They want. Everybody wants. They want now. They don't want to work. Perfecting a craft? Forget it. They are filled with the hysteria of having. They look round at jackets and haircuts and mobile phones and hi-fis . . . and . . . Jesus Christ, I don't know what else. And they think, I want some of them . . . some of them . . .'

'Apples?' suggested Ellen weakly.

'Apples! Apples!' Daniel screamed. 'Fuck apples. We all got apples. Tasteless. A ruined fruit. No, they want kumquats and papayas, passion fruit and mangoes. Juicy exotic things.'

Upstairs Ronald said to George, 'Daniel's on the rant again.'

Downstairs Mrs Boyle raised her eyes to the ceiling and turned to the cat and tutted, 'Such bollocks, Fergus, don't you think? Well no, I suppose you've quite forgotten what bollocks are.'

But Ellen was impressed. Hysteria of having. Kumquats and papayas. Oh yes, she was impressed. Considering Daniel's hero and his hero's writing on his bookshelf, *The Origin of the Family, Private Property and the State*, she sat in the office next day and wrote *Engels of the Forest*. She had not, of course, actually read anything Engels had ever written. And had, in fact, no intention of ever doing so. Well, she was just . . . just an ordinary writer. It was, she thought, well beyond her understanding. So she imagined what it was about.

In her version, Engels came from his hermit retreat in the Amazonian Forest to save the world. A chicly shabby soul in a white baggy suit and black T-shirt, he stood high on the parapet of the multi-storey car park where he slept on a small rush mat that he unrolled nightly. This was his only shelter. 'I do not seek comfort,' he cried. 'Comfort weakens me.' He spread his arms in despair and, Jesus style, wept for the world. 'We are consumed by the hysteria of having,' he sobbed. 'What has become of us?' He was a martial arts champion. He lived on junk food, unwrapping a chocolate bar: 'Oh God, sugar, chemicals, additives. I must have them. Junk food. Street nutrition.' The first story, 'Engels and the Five Believers', was an instant cult.

Stanley read it and said to Billy, 'Do you know, I believe this is Daniel. This is how the silly bugger sees him.'

But Billy said, 'No. I mean I know she's a bit ingenuous but she's not *that* bad.' Then pausing a moment, thinking about this: 'Is she?'

One Sunday morning Mrs Boyle waylaid Ellen when she and Daniel were returning from the newsagent's, arms laden with newspapers. 'I have been lying in wait for you,' she said. She had a deep and fruity voice. She hung on to words as if she loved them, and wanted them to last a long time on her tongue. 'It's time we got to know each other. I'm Emily Boyle, your neighbour downstairs. You must come for a chat. Sometime soon.'

'Yes,' Ellen smiled. 'I'd love that.'

'You must tell me all about yourself,' said Mrs Boyle. 'I want to know it all – how you met Daniel, everything.'

'We met in the pub.'

'That's right,' said Daniel curtly. He did not like Mrs Boyle. He sensed she had the measure of him.

'You spied her across a crowded room,' crooned Mrs Boyle. 'And you had to make her yours.'

'Something like that,' said Daniel. Ellen carried on up the stairs. She was eager to study her horoscope for the week ahead.

'You came, you saw, you conquered.' Mrs Boyle eyed Daniel – a challenge.

'Something like that,' Daniel repeated, making sure Ellen was out of hearing range. 'Wrong order,' grinning now. 'I saw. I conquered. I came.'

'Ah,' said Mrs Boyle. Wasn't it always the same? These young people thought they could shoo her with shock back into her flat. As if the very hint of sex would set her scuttling to the safety of her own fireside. As if she, in her time, hadn't had her share of shagging. 'Oh Daniel,' she said, 'you came. I know you came. Ronald and George upstairs know you came. I do believe the people who live on the other side of the park know you came.' Daniel said nothing. Ellen appeared looking over the banisters at the hostilities below. She did not realise what was happening.

'Come for coffee this afternoon,' Mrs Boyle called up to her. 'Come chat to me, my dear.'

'You're not actually going?' Daniel demanded when they got inside the flat.

Ellen considered this. 'Are you telling me what to do?'

'No,' said Daniel. 'Just I didn't think it was your scene to spend afternoons with old ladies.'

'As a matter of fact . . .' Ellen said, 'as a matter of fact it is.'

Mrs Boyle was delighted to see her. 'Come in. Come in.' Ushering her down the hall to her living room, a sunny south-facing place: a dark green velvet sofa covered with cushions, long green curtains, blue walls, white ceiling, bookshelves, pictures, a tiled fireplace with actual fire flickering and, centre stage, a Steinway grand piano.

'You play?' asked Ellen.

'Of course I do. Less and less these days. But I play. You don't really want coffee?' Mrs Boyle asked. 'It's such a bore boiling a kettle, checking for clean cups, finding milk. We'll have sherry.'

'Sherry?'

'Absolutely,' pouring as she bossed. 'I do not allow myself gin before teatime. It's my rule. So I have sherry.'

Ellen knew she was dealing with an older, superior digestive system.

'So,' Mrs Boyle sat on the sofa looked at Ellen and said, 'tell me about yourself.'

Ellen shrugged. 'I write. I'm married to Daniel. I live upstairs. That's it, really.'

'What do you write?'

'Stuff. Comic strips.' She looked glumly out the window. She was always slightly ashamed of what she did.

'I know you,' Mrs Boyle pointed triumphantly. 'You do that *Gangster Women* thing. I read that.' Then, qualifying her little admission of bad taste, 'Normally I wouldn't, but I quite like that. It's rude. I like rude. Are you famous?'

'Good heavens no. I haven't got the face for fame. It's not thoughtful enough. Deep. You need to look deep, even if you're not. Don't you think?'

'No,' Mrs Boyle spoke slowly, 'I don't think so.' Young people said such young things. 'How old are you? Though that's only a technicality really. Well, with women anyway.'

'Twenty-three.' Ellen felt suddenly shamed by youth. She was only just twenty-three.

'That would make you seventeen, then.'

'Twenty-three.'

Mrs Boyle grinned, old teeth. 'I have this idea that woman reach seventeen and stop. They still thrill at men and long for love. They stay seventeen till they get to thirty-five then they panic about becoming fifty one day. So they have a tense few weeks facing the future, giving up cigarettes, coffee and wine. Then they get fed up and go back to seventeen again. It's more fun. Of course, in between they are all sorts of ages. Depends on the time of the day. Me now, I'm seventy-three. First thing in the morning I'm well past ninety. At noon I'm fifty without the panic. Just capable with warmed up semi-functioning joints. At night I'm me again. But there's a spot in the depth of me that's for ever seventeen. Eager to please and wondering about it all.'

Ellen smiled and looked down. 'At seventeen I was too busy rebelling against my mother to thrill at anything. Besides, women have careers. They take themselves seriously. I don't think they bounce about from one age to another these days.'

'Oh,' said Mrs Boyle. 'Perhaps. But I think most of us feel seventeen inside all our lives. In my heart there is still the spark of what I once was. And sometimes when I look in the mirror the face I see surprises me. The creature I used to be haunts me.' Then, changing the subject: 'I think you need bringing out. Perhaps one day I could teach you how to behave badly.'

'I don't think I need to be taught that.'

'Oh you do. I can see you do.'

'I do not need to be taught to behave badly,' Ellen said. This conversation was not what she wanted. She wanted to chat like she chatted to Mrs Robb. Then with the sherry, in the warmth of the fire, she relaxed and confided. 'Actually I always wanted someone to talk to who was handy with the free advice and Kleenex tissues. That sort of thing.'

'Oh,' said Mrs Boyle. 'That sounds like a surrogate mother. I'd avoid that at all costs. One mother is hard enough. Far better to behave badly. I mean, you might choose someone for your surrogate mother and find yourself rebelling against and speaking back to some poor person who simply imagined she was your friend.'

'This conversation is a bit sudden,' said Ellen. 'We've only just met.'

'I'm seventy-three,' Mrs Boyle reminded her. 'I may well pop off at any time. I have no time for sodding small talk.'

Chapter Ten

There was, Daniel decided, something wonderfully unashamed about Friendly Mary's bedroom. Everything was pink. Pink wallpaper, pink curtains, pink sheets, pink duvet, fluffy pink rugs on pink carpet. Christ, he couldn't live here. But the odd afternoon lolling in bed, dreaming, was wonderful. Across the room, on the pink dresser, lay a formidable collection of pots, jars, tubes, tubs, mascaras, lipsticks, blushers, eye shadows, mousses, lotions, creams and gels. Mary spent a deal of time on her complexion. Which was also pinkish.

There was, too, something unashamed about sex with Friendly Mary. It was sex and only sex. Sex with gusto and lust, but nothing more. There was as little conversation as possible. Mary just wanted to get on with it, then sleep for half an hour. Actually Daniel suspected his attentions were only part of Mary's intense complexion care, but obliging her had its compensations. There was time to himself afterwards to lie back wallowing in all that wonderfully horrible pink and consider his life.

His most vivid memory of his childhood was of himself, six years old, standing on a high wall that he had climbed up but couldn't climb down again. His father stood below. He was wearing his holiday sports jacket, tweed check. The collar of his shirt was open. There was a small triangle of tan at his neck. His arms were spread open. 'C'mon, jump. I'll catch you.' Daniel jumped. His father dropped the welcoming arms and stepped back. Daniel landed on the tarmac at his daddy's feet, a small crumpled body. There was screaming, such a terrible noise that it took Daniel a moment to realise the howling was coming from him. It was more than the pain, though the pain was awful, it was the hurt and confusion. Why?

His father loomed over him. 'Let that be a lesson in life. Never trust anybody.'

His mother came running, 'Oh my God, Bill,' she screamed at his father, beating him with clenched fists. 'What have you done?'

'I've taught the lad about life. A short sharp lesson. He'll thank me—'

'You've broken his leg, you idiot.'

It was true. The crumpled crying child was bawling in agony. The pain was huge and engulfing, and through it he saw his mother and father argue. She hit him, over and over she hit him. 'You fool. You fool.' He turned. Shoulders hunched, hands plunged deep into his pockets he walked off. Neither of them paid any attention to Daniel and his awful pain.

He was in hospital for weeks, lying in striped pyjamas, plastered leg covered in autographs and silly rhymes. His mother visited, bringing toys and books and fussing round his bed. Nurses cuddled him, stroked his hair, ran their fingers round his chin and smiled lovely smiles whenever they caught him looking at them. 'Oh,' they would softly say, wrapping him to them, 'he's such a gorgeous boy. I think I'll take him home with me.'

He changed from a boisterous, ebullient infant, the hero of the football park and playground leader, to a bookish boy, mummy's darling. He became a nice lad. 'Ah Mrs Quinn,' neighbours and friends would say, ruffling his hair. 'You must be so proud of your son. What a nice lad he is.' Feeling safe and approved of, Daniel would grin sheepishly.

All his life he'd done as he was told. In fact, his mother had him so fine-tuned she didn't have to say anything. A look, a sigh, a firming of the lips was enough, and if he really did not come up to snuff, if he failed an exam or was home late from school, his mother would stiffen. Stiffen and turn her back. Sometimes she would not talk to him for days.

This loss of affection made his stomach ache and he trembled within. Thinking about it now, he decided it made him soft. He was a man now, but he did not know what kind of man. Macho bored him – he did not want to run about a football field and he had no interest in fixing cars. If he had to define the sort of macho he sought, it would be more than a man's man. It would be a thinking man's man. Robert De Niro in *Taxi Driver* or *Goodfellas* would do. Daniel thought yes, he could be my hero and pal.

Daniel had been a nice lad through his school days and on through university and a double first in psychology. And then . . . and then . . . he did not know how it started, or when. He found himself walking faster, jaw constantly clenched. Once he went to a dinner party at his professor's house and, finding the conversation shrill, pretentious and utterly unbearable, he grabbed a bottle of Rioja and emptied it on to the table. 'I can't stand this. I can't stand this.' Horrified at himself, he stood listening to the gloop gloop of escaping wine, watching it soak into the perfect Irish linen tablecloth. Then he left.

Not long afterwards he'd written a passionately rude letter to the head of his department. When he'd finished it he rushed out to post it. He hung about the mail box waiting for it to get lifted. As soon as he saw the postman collect the pile of letters and put them in his sack, Daniel decided he was doing a very foolish thing. He should not send that letter. He should get it back. He ran shouting, waving his arms after the post van till his legs shook. He stood heaving and sweating in the middle of the road, hoarsely repeating, 'I've changed my mind. I've changed my mind.' Remembering now, he covered his eyes and whispered, 'Christ. What got into me?'

Whatever it was, it now got into him regularly. He behaved badly whenever the opportunity presented itself. But since he nutted his father, his rages had calmed. Seeing the man standing before him crying and bleeding and saying, 'Well, that was a pretty laddish thing to do,' had made him feel both horribly satisfied and horribly guilty.

Not long after he had written his famous foul letter to his professor, he'd been drinking and thinking about his childhood. He missed the laddish child he'd been before he broke his leg. Remembering how he'd trustingly leaped into his father's outstretched arms, and the shock when he hit the tarmac filled him with wild loathing for the man. 'Shite,' he said through clenched teeth. 'Bastard. Shite. Shite.' He'd been in the Café Royal at the time, drinking too much malt. Whisky always brought out the worst in him.

He shoved on his raincoat and set out east across the city for his father's flat in London Road. It was raining. He did not fasten his coat. It flapped and flew out behind him as he strode, eyes fixed, staring insanely ahead, hair flattened against his head. 'Bastard. Bastard,' he said. People moved aside to let him past. Passengers on the city's maroon buses watched him, faces pressed against the window. He could have jumped on one as it trundled past him. But sitting still on a bus would do nothing for his rage. No, a bit of fierce striding was called for.

His father was alone when he arrived. He was usually alone. He didn't make friends easily. His marriage had fallen apart not long after he'd stepped aside and let his son fall. 'I break things,' he said when he was drunk. 'I break everything.'

He was surprised to find Daniel on his doorstep. His son was soaked and obviously enraged.

'Daniel,' he said pleasantly. 'What brings you here this time of night?'

'You bastard. You bastard, why didn't you catch me?'

'I didn't mean to hurt you,' his father said.

'Well, you did. Look at me.' Daniel stepped back, let his father view his lean body. 'I used to be one of the lads. Look what's happened to me. I'm soft. A wimp. Bastard.' He nutted his father. Heard his nose crunch under his head. 'Oh God. What have I done?' he cried. 'Oh sorry. Sorry.'

But his father waved away his apologies. That was when he'd said, 'That was a pretty laddish thing to do.' Blood streaming down his face. He'd been consumed with guilt about his son for years. Now he was released. Well, almost. And now, though Daniel rarely saw his mother, his father was a regular at the bar where he worked. The two got along together.

Now Daniel was being disgraceful again. Three weeks married and screwing around already. Not that he found women easy. They scared the shit out of him, and they confused him. No, women found him easy. Brought up by his mother, denied access to his father he did not talk man talk. He was not threatening. He understood about favourite fingernails and beloved lipsticks. It did not demean him to walk down the street carrying a bunch of flowers, and he thought nothing of going into the chemist's to buy Tampax. Women found it easy to tell him what they wanted, 'No. No. Touch me there. And there.' He did not think it a problem to give them exactly what they wanted.

When he wasn't gambling or dealing in the pub Daniel wandered the streets. He loved street life. The insistent thud of rock'n'roll blaring from shops, lead in the air, the chunter of buses, gleamy windows draped with stuff to buy with money he didn't have, the boozy waft from pubs, the hot blast of junk food flooding from restaurants. He breathed it in. He couldn't get enough. He moved with a young man's recklessness keenly through crowds. People always stared. His sudden handsomeness shook them. Looming through the throng at Woolworth's pick'n'mix he stood out. Women nudged each other asking, 'Isn't that...' 'Wasn't he in...?' 'Didn't he ...?' 'Who is that...?' Daniel ignored them. He hated the attention. Some people seemed to be on the point of adoration. He detested them for it. Once, two teenage girls, pale and thin in this week's style, swooned when he went by. Then burst into giggles at their silliness.

Daniel thought them sweet and reached out to stroke the cheek of the nearest one saying, 'I forgive you. I forgive you.'

The girls were outraged. 'What an arse,' they whispered.

Daniel heard and turned to them grinning, 'So I am. But I'm so good at it.' He was gentle with women, he was sweet to them. Then he could not help being hateful.

He sighed, sniffed deeply at Mary's perfumed sheets. In half an hour he'd be back out there. What he enjoyed most about sleeping with Mary was her rudimentary approach to the act. She liked the missionary position. She didn't feel herself or pant urgent instructions, habits he'd noticed in younger women. And she never, absolutely never, indulged in any sort of post-coital conversation. She fucked with abandon. She came. She rolled over and slept soundly for half an hour.

She lay beside him now, breathing deeply, a slight snore. He had ten minutes left to consider her back before she woke. A fine back.

It should be fat but heaving sacks of potatoes, crates of apples and oranges kept the flesh firm. Fascinated, he ran his fingers through her frizzed and bleached hair. Friendly Mary was deliciously tarty. Ellen rarely bothered with the frilly fripperies of being female. But he loved them; the smell of makeup, perfume and hair-spray. Ellen's female fripperies were the dark and messy sort that turned him off: old tights strewn across the bedroom floor, abandoned knickers, tangled hair embedded in brushes, empty Tampax packs on the bathroom shelf.

The clock beside him flicked over another minute. Daniel chastised himself for his day so far. He had risen early that he might take Ellen a cup of coffee in bed, a small considerate act to relieve his conscience. The night before he had taken money from her handbag. He regularly took money, so regularly he had rules about it. He never took big notes, something she'd miss. He took sums made up of coins and small notes. He reckoned she never knew how much she had anyway. He always swore to himself that the money was for food. And always in the racing pages he found an irresistible horse which always let him down.

Recently Daniel had developed a new approach to his gambling. Once he had studied form. Had in fact taken life as a gambler as seriously, as scientifically, as he had his life as an academic. Now, however, he trusted to luck. But he was meticulous about it. He kept a lucky book. In it he noted winnings and losings and set against them the exact pattern of the day.

Today he'd written: '7.45 rose. Ellen coffee. Wore white sweat shirt, red boxers, tennis shoes. No socks. Breakfast me: coffee, black, two cigarettes. Didn't shave. Played old Springsteen. Watched breakfast telly, got pissed off.'

He detailed every moment right down to putting money on Small Wonder. At the end of the week he'd study it all and try to discover some link. Did he perhaps own a shirt that was luckier than the rest, or was there a pair of loser's underpants in his drawer? Was there a winning breakfast? If he could unravel a common denominator constant through his losings he could eliminate it from his life and build up a winning routine from that.

Mary woke, rolled over and groaned. 'Make us a cup of tea, love,' she said.

She was a bad waker. It was on Daniel's mind that when he, if he, returned to academic life he might write a book, a paper at least, on how women of different body types and from different socio-economic backgrounds behaved after sex. He considered himself an expert. Some women were depressive, some joyous, some silly and some just liked throaty low talk, a kind of verbal replay on the action that had just taken place.

Ellen had quite a line in post-orgasmic prattle. She always spoke about sex. Sex speculative: wonder what divas are like in bed. Wonder what they sound like when they come. Sexual lament: do you know, we've never done it in a car. Sexual inquisition: have you ever done it in a car? Who with? Was she better than me? Sex on a heightened intellectual plane, almost: Isn't sex clever? If I was God I'd never come up with sex. I'd have people exchanging eggs orally, some sort of disgusting party game type thing.

She was so withdrawn, but when she opened she really opened. He smiled, remembering Ellen.

Last night he had found her sitting on the sofa yanking at her hair, crying. 'Look at my hair,' she wept. 'It's been cropped. I look like Martha Klebb in that James Bond film.'

'You do not.'

'I do. I do. I'm never going out again. Everyone will laugh at me.'

'Why did you let him cut it like that? Why didn't you tell him what you wanted?'

'I don't speak hairdresser,' Ellen wailed.

Daniel had a rush of rage. How dare some absurd hairdresser person treat his Ellen like this? He longed to protect her. He had a flash of himself as a New York Italian, De Niro, in a perfect suit, holding the hairdresser by the collar and instructing him with chilling good manners, 'When the lady wants her hair cut you cut it the way she says. Know what I'm sayin' here?'

'Will you fetch us a cup of tea?' Irritated, Mary reached over and punched Daniel's thigh.

'Sorry. I was thinking.'

'Too much of that'll give you hairs on the palm of your hand.'

He walked naked through to the kitchen, a yellow room. Whilst he waited for the kettle to boil he rummaged through the cupboards for food. A meal for Ellen was expected of him this evening, and he'd lost all his money on Small Wonder. Was it the red boxers?

He always left his jacket behind the front door so that he could fill his pockets as he made the tea. Two packets of soup into the top inside pocket, a handful of chocolate biscuits and a tin of sardines into the right-hand side pocket, a wedge of cheese into the left. Everything had to be flat. But, that should do it. A teabag into each of Mary's sex'n'chocolate mugs and still time to read his horoscope in her newspaper. 'Aries: a problem that has been plaguing you will soon be solved. A windfall will relieve stress on a close relationship.' Cheered he took the tea back to the bedroom.

'You've been ages. What have you been doing?'

'I was reading my horoscope.'

'What did it say for me, Pisces?' Mary wanted to know.

'It said,' Daniel told her solemnly, 'that you should watch your friends closely. One of them is taking more from the relationship than you realise.'

Chapter Eleven

On the Saturday after their first meeting Emily Boyle invited Ellen to go shopping. 'We shall go on a mushroom quest to the Italian deli, and I shall teach you how to behave badly.' She linked arms.

Ellen did not quite know how to say that she did not want to learn how to behave badly. 'Why would you want to do that?' she asked.

'Because I can. I have been waiting all my life to get away with being naughty. Who is going to throw out a little old lady? I love behaving badly. It's my hobby.'

Ellen didn't have a hobby, didn't really understand hobby culture. However, when she went to work in the stationery department she'd been asked to fill in a job application form. Name, address, age and hobbies. The first three were routine. But hobbies? 'Tennis,' she wrote (a lie). 'Squash' (another lie). 'Learning new languages' (complete and utter bullshit). 'Reading, writing and appalling my mother' (the truth). As soon as she had it down on paper she regretted it, but as it was in ink, she could not rub it out. Still, she got the job. She wondered if management thought that was what shop girls did, or if they even bothered to read the form. But it was official, then, and noted down for posterity in some filing cabinet somewhere. She was Ellen and her hobby was appalling her mother. Perhaps it would be slightly less adolescent to take up behaving badly.

They went first to buy some fish. Emily fiddled with the trout that lay gaping vacantly in the window.

'Please don't handle the fish,' the assistant called.

'But I will handle it. I am going to buy it. I'm allowed to fiddle with it.'

'No you're not. Please leave it alone.'

'I will not leave this trout alone. I intend to be very intimate with this trout.'

Other shoppers turned to stare. Goodness, what was she going to be doing with the fish?

'I am going to eat this fish. You don't get more intimate than that. Well, not at my age you don't. I want to look at it. I want to see if its eyes are bright, its scales shiny. I want to know if it has been a happy little trout before it came into my life.'

They glared at each other, the fishman and Emily. The fishman took a sharp intake of breath and heatedly said, 'There are other folk interested in my trout. And they'll not be interested in something you've had your hands all over.'

Emily snorted, tossed the trout back on to its tray and rounded on the fishman. 'Have you the vaguest idea who you are talking to? Have you the vaguest idea who I am and what these hands have accomplished? Fiddling with your trout is beneath them. Beneath them.'

She waved her hands in front of him. Ten fine fingers flapping before a man who plainly did not know superior merchandise when he saw it.

Ellen looked round. Did anybody know they were together? Was there some way she could slip into the street and wait round the corner? She hated scenes.

'I am Emily Boyle,' Emily Boyle crowed.

Emily Boyle? The fishman was baffled. He turned for support to the queue. 'Emily Boyle?' he mouthed and received a unanimous shrug. They hadn't heard of her either. But she said her name with such withering authority they all felt they must be wrong, must be missing something not to have heard of her.

'I am a concert pianist. And these hands that you so deride have played a duet with Rachmaninov.' There was a hush. Emily played an air piano, little, strong fingers dashing over an imaginary keyboard, head moving to the music in her head. 'Rachmaninov, I tell you. And he did not find my hands to be anything other than magnificent.'

Defiantly then, she picked up one trout then another and decided in the end to have some plaice. As they left Ellen overheard the fishman say that if effing Rachmaninov came in he wouldn't let him fiddle with his trout either.

'Did you really know Rachmaninov?' Ellen asked.

'Indeed I did.'

'And did you really play a duet with him?'

'I did.'

Ellen was impressed.

Emily linked arms again and proposed they continue the mushroom quest. 'I suspect,' she said, 'that you have never eaten a proper mushroom in your life.'

Ellen suggested they go to Friendly Mary's fruit shop, but Emily Boyle refused. 'That woman is too friendly by far. No, we shall go to the deli on Elm Row and we shall listen to *opera* as we choose. How dull life would be if all there was to buying a mushroom was just buying a mushroom. So, mushrooms and Puccini it shall be, and a bottle of Barolo. You'll pay.'

It had been a good day for Daniel. He had, he was sure, finally cracked the lucky routine. Up at eight, coffee to Ellen, white boxers, putty-coloured chinos, black sweat shirt, baseball boots, no socks. Breakfast, two cups black coffee, two cigarettes and the Atlantic Soul Classics – Otis Redding, Wilson Pickett, Aretha Franklin. He did a small jive as he drank his coffee and read the racing section. Urban Domino, he thought. It'd been a black and white sort of a morning so far. He walked down the left side of the street, stuck his head round the door of the fruit shop to see if there was anything required of him. Mary dismissed him with a small decisive flick of her hand.

At noon he grazed in the supermarket. A croissant from the pick'n'mix bread section, eaten with a couple of slices of salami from the deli as he slowly wandered the aisles eavesdropping on shoppers and reading the labels on ketchup bottles. He opened some ginger biscuits took out three and replaced the packet behind the others on the shelf. He'd return to it tomorrow and eat some more. Then he wiped his mouth, brushed off any telltale crumbs, and bought a can of Coke as he passed through the checkout. All this he noted carefully in his lucky book before he went to place his first bet of the day.

He put the five pounds he'd taken from Ellen last night on his chosen horse. It won. He put his winnings on Monochrome City. It won. Now he put all his winnings on Two Tone Alley. It won. Daniel had a simple gambling system. He simply put all the money he had on his fancied horse to win. He didn't really gamble to make money, he gambled for thrills. This simple all-or-nothing method made his blood rush, heart pound, palms sweat. He loved it. Now, scarcely able to breathe he scanned his paper for another likely horse. Metropolitan Black And White was running in the four thirty. It was too good to miss. He put everything he had on it.

He couldn't stay in the place. Couldn't watch the race. Couldn't even bear to hear it. He sat on the pavement outside the bookie's drinking his Coke. He knew how he looked. His hair stuck on end from the excited way he ran sweaty fingers through it. He was wild-eyed and mumbling to himself, 'I'm right. I'm right. You bastards, I'm right. It'll do it. It'll win. Win. Win, you fucker, win.' People passing walked wide of him. His face was streaked with sweat. His Coke can caved in under his wild grip, Coke flowing over his fingers on to the pavement. He hardly noticed. He didn't care. Didn't care about anything. The lucky gods were with him. There were angels at his side. The good planets were shooting through his sign. Everything was going for him today. He couldn't lose.

When he got home, he emptied his pockets on to the sofa. He had a thousand pounds. 'A grand,' he said. 'I did it. Me.' Actually he'd turned his fiver into one thousand and fifty-seven pounds and forty-six pence. But he'd rounded it down to a neat sum and spent the difference on wine and steaks and records.

Unable to contain his excitement he paced the room, fists clenched saying, 'Yes. Yes. Yes,' over and over. He'd cracked the lucky routine. He knew how absurd this was. And he knew too that he'd have to go with this new flow. Thing was, when he started on this lucky routine he'd nothing. Now he had all this money. Plainly he had to start every lucky day with nothing, or at least five pounds pinched from his wife's purse. He couldn't have money. He couldn't let Ellen know he had money. She would want to do sensible things with it. Pay bills, save up for something nonsensically sensible, like a holiday or a new car. Oh no, he was having none of that. 'Hide it,' he urgently told himself. 'Hide it from me, and hide it from her.' He unzipped one of the cushions on the sofa, stuffed in the notes, plumped it furiously and replaced it. 'Now,' he said, 'pretend it hasn't happened. Don't talk about it. Don't acknowledge the luck and it won't leave you.' This was lunatic. He was logical, sane with an above average IQ. He didn't believe any of this, not really. But what could he do? He was hooked. 'Put on some music,' he urged himself.

He keened across the room, ripping a new record from its sleeve, put it on the turntable and skipped frantically through it, moving the needle from track to track, searching for the sound he needed. A rock'n'roll fix. He needed that. Gambling was not his only craving. Sometimes he'd leave home and not make it to the end of the road before he was filled with some kind of howling angst, a teenage thing, a great hole in his psyche that could only be cured by hearing – and hearing at full blast – certain bits of certain tracks. It started with Jimi Hendrix, those first few bars of 'Burning of the Midnight Lamp' and moved on in time to Neil Young's 'Like A Hurricane'. On it went through the years – now he was dozing on brain-numbing smashes of James Brown – live. He flirted with Little Feat. Had a through-the-earphones affair with Talking Heads, 'Letting the days go by. Watching the river . . .' Then it was 'Rock the Casbah', 'London Calling' or 'Transmetropolitan', 'Yes aye yeah,' he'd sing along. When he'd finished deifying The Clash and The Pogues he went in search of new heroes. The ache, then, ran constant through his life. U2, Public Enemy – the more music he bought, the more he was addicted. He'd stand beside his precious stereo still in his thin raincoat, eyes shut, 'Ah, yes. That hit the spot.' He'd have enough to get him through the next few hours. Then he'd come reeling back, needing more, telling himself the while that it was time he grew out of this.

Today's acquisition was discarded. He shoved it back in the sleeve and would probably never play it again. 'I'm too old for this,' he said to Ellen when she came back. 'Somewhere out there, on some album is the ultimate track. I'll find it, play it and be cured of rock'n'roll for the rest of my life.'

'Did you know Mrs Boyle downstairs knew Rachmaninov?' she said.

'Oh that. She didn't tell you that old story, did she? She tells everybody that.' He groaned indifference. 'You didn't believe her, did you?'

'Of course I did. She played a duet with him.' It was Ellen's turn to play the air piano, demonstrating.

'Oh, bollocks,' Daniel sneered. 'Rachmaninov's dead. All these old classical boys are dead.'

'Rachmaninov died in 1943,' Ellen said. 'He was born in 1873.'

'Did he?' Daniel was surprised. He vaguely imagined that everybody who wrote symphonies lived in an age of frilly shirts and powdered wigs and that they all knew each other. Rachmaninov, Mozart and Beethoven, he thought, probably lived next door to one another. They'd be chums. 'He was born exactly one hundred years before Lou Reed recorded "Walk on the Wild Side",' he said. 'We've come a long way, babe.'

Ellen was angry at being so dismissed. 'I believe Emily Boyle did meet Rachmaninov. She did, too, play a duet with him,' she said hotly. 'I was impressed.'

'I am a siren. I am a woman,' she had written in her notebook. 'I am timeless, sister. I have played violin with Paganini. I have sung with Caruso. Danced with Vaslav Nijinsky. I have been carved in Carrara marble by Michelangelo Buonarroti. I have spanked Freud's bum, taught Einstein sums, discussed scansion with Keats, dined with Escoffier and droned along with Leonard Cohen. But it is my time now. Time to strip the centuries from my face and I am Boudicca, Queen of the Iceni, warrior. I am Jeanne d'Arc, sanctified seventeen-year-old, scourge of the English at Orléans. And I am Patti Smith, godmother punk, chemical dreamer and abuser. Hit the streets, gangster women, we have sisters to avenge.'

'Good script,' Stanley would say. 'Loved the old woman.'

'We shopped for mushrooms and pestered the fishmonger,' Ellen told Daniel.

'Sounds fun,' he sneered, running his fingers through his hair.

The collar of his shirt opened as he did, so Ellen saw the mark on his neck.'What is that?' she said.

'What is what?'

'That mark on your neck.'

'I've got a rash. Dunno. Maybe it's this shirt.'

'Shirt my arse. That's a lovebite, you bastard. I know a lovebite when I see one. At your age. How gross, Daniel.' Ellen was eight again, sitting on the edge of the bath again, getting lessons in lovebite camouflage from her sister. She stayed eight for a few moments, before the full implications of the mark on her husband's neck sank in. 'You've been with someone else.'

Daniel did not look at her. 'Fancy some sardines?' he asked.

'You've been with another woman,' Ellen told him. 'Who is it?'

'You wouldn't know her. God, Ellen, there's no need to make such a fuss. It's only sex.'

'What do you mean, it's only sex? Only sex. What else is there? You shite. You shite. I've been shopping and you've been fucking another woman.' She glared at him. 'I had a lovely time. I bought mushrooms,' she cried. 'I bought mushrooms and you were doing that.'

'No I wasn't,' he said. 'I was . . .' No, he couldn't tell her he was winning. He tapped his neck. 'That was yesterday.'

'Yesterday,' she howled. 'I was working and you were . . .' she pointed accusingly at the guilty patch, ' . . . you were doing that.'

She wanted to hit him, wanted to hurl herself at him and punch him and punch him till he hurt and she didn't. But she couldn't. She had never in her life hit anybody. She had hardly ever lost her temper. So, unable to deal with confrontations, she turned her face to the wall and slowly banged her head over and over. 'Bastard. Bastard. Bastard,' she moaned. 'I hate you. I hate you.'

She picked up her best black leather jacket and left. 'I'm going out. Cook your own effing mushrooms.'

Hands deep in her pockets, she wandered back streets, sniffing and choking. Tears spread mascara down her cheeks. 'Bastard, bastard,' she blubbed to herself. She was cold, but that was good. Cold was good. It served Daniel right that she was so cold. Maybe she'd get a chill that would spread to her lungs and develop into pneumonia. She'd palely lie on a chaise longue, glittery-eyed, dying a tragic, operatic sort of death. That would show Daniel. Then he'd be sorry.

Eventually a small gang of boys, cottoning on to how defenceless and low she felt, started following her, calling to her, 'Hey, darlin'. C'mon over here. Hey, wait.' She heard their steps quicken. She moved faster and eventually broke into a half-walk, half-run with them hard on her heels, hollering into the night. 'Bitch. We're going to fuck you.'

Heart pounding, she stumbled and started running. She did not turn to look at how far behind they were. She just headed for Leith Walk, hailed a taxi, climbed in and gave Jack Conroy's address.

It was his birthday. 'I'm having a party, young Ellen. Come and bring that dreadful man of yours.' She had imagined herself sipping wine, Daniel by her side in his white linen suit. He was gorgeous in that suit. He'd worn it to their wedding. Everyone agreed, though nobody actually said it to her face, the groom was prettier than the bride. She stopped at Oddbins and bought a bottle of chardonnay to take with her.

Black Fingernails opened the door. She was not pleased to see her, Ellen could tell. When she slept with Jack she thought she was oh so cool, oh so sophisticated. Just a swift roll in the hay, a bit of an afternoon frolic with a married man. She was a woman of the world. She did that sort of thing. Now she knew. She was a cuckold too. It hurt. Sinners had fun. Those sinned against felt stupid, inadequate and naïvely trusting. That feeling of standing in the dark and cold, unwanted and her face shiny with the need to please. 'Sorry,' she whispered as she was let in. Not that Black Fingernails understood. Well, Ellen was always apologising and saying sorry.

So Ellen found a corner, sipped her drink and fiddled with her cigarette pack. Across the room a vivid woman flirted and laughed and watched her. At last she came to her. At last she sat down beside her. 'You look like you could do with some serious corrupting,' she said.

2

Cora

Chapter Twelve

When she was ten Cora O'Brien ran away from home. She packed her school bag with a few of life's essentials and took off, top speed, along Tobermory's main street, past the lavatories and past the distillery and up the brae. She hadn't an exact plan as to how she was going to get to the terminal at Craignure and on to the Caledonian MacBrayne ferry that would take her off Mull to Oban and the mainland. She figured she'd deal with that when she got to the top of the hill which was steep, extremely steep. The faster she tried to go up it, the steeper it got. Running made her heart pound. She gasped for breath, but kept going.

That was the first time her father saw her run. He was driving down the hill into the village when he saw her. The speed of her shook him. He stopped the car, got out and called to her. 'Cora! Cora O'Brien, just where are you going battering up the brae like that?'

'I'm running away,' Cora wheezed.

'Oh good for you,' her father said mildly. 'I'm all for that. Could you not have taken one or two of your brothers with you? Only it gets a bit crowded in the house with you all around.'

Cora was part of a sprawling family. Her oldest sister was twenty and her youngest brother six. She was in between, along with two older brothers and a younger sister. Bill and Irene had six children. Sometimes Cora thought her life too crowded by far, hence the bid for freedom.

Cora shook her head. 'I'm not doing that. If I hadn't all those bloody brothers and sisters I wouldn't need to run away.'

'Too right. I quite agree,' her father nodded eagerly. Like his daughter he had the gift of enthusiasm. He leaned towards her, smiling. And she loved his face, such a comfortable face, her dad's.

You could curl up in one of its little curves, that gentle rounded place where cheek reached down to chin, where the smiling happened – you could curl up there and sleep for ever, Cora thought.

'Let me come with you. Let's run away together. Have you brought enough for two?' Her dad unzipped her school sports bag, peered in. 'Oh yes,' he nodded approvingly. 'You've got everything a person could need.' And so she had. She'd packed a copy of the *Beano*, two Mars Bars, a spare pair of socks, a torch and two extra pairs of knickers. What else could a person possibly need in life?

'No,' Cora shook her head. 'You can't come. It isn't running away if you come.'

'Sure enough,' her father agreed. 'Well,' he extended his hand, 'goodbye then. It's been lovely knowing you. And I'll miss you.'

Cora shook the proffered hand. 'You won't do anything silly like cry, will you?'

'Oh, Cora, when you're gone I think I will. I'll cry.'

She couldn't bear the thought of her precious dad weeping. Just imagining it brought tears to her own eyes. 'Don't cry. Please don't cry, Dad.' Tears flowed now. Great fat, wet drops of sadness for her father's sadness ran down her little freckled face, gathered at the point of her chin and actually splashed to the pavement.

'Tell you what,' said her father. 'Stay home and I won't cry.'

So she did. She stayed till she was seventeen. But it was ten years and two children before she went back. Meantime she drifted into and out of her father's enthusiasms.

In the summer of the great escape, Bill O'Brien, having seen the speed that she was taking her leave of Tobermory, decided that Cora had the makings of an athlete. Actually, not just an athlete, but a famous athlete, a fast and dazzling athlete. He was famous, fast and dazzling with the hyperbole.

He bought her a tracksuit and a pair of running shoes. He devised an athlete's diet that consisted mainly of bananas and steak. He took her every evening out to the fields behind the house to train. When it was raining they did squats together in the back bedroom to strengthen her thighs. Had he known the mischief she'd later get up to with her strengthened thighs and the pleasure they'd bring, he would not have bothered. At the time he simply thought he was covering all the angles. His training advice was short and sweet. 'Blister and hurtle, Cora,' he'd say. 'Blister from the starting blocks and hurtle for the tape. Don't look round. Don't think about anybody else, just go for it. Blister and hurtle.'

Cora's running career was short and, well, spectacular. That summer she blistered and hurtled her way to becoming star of the school sports. She won two cups, a medal, and a box of Dairy Milk. Cups and medals bored her, but the chocolates were worth the effort. Heartened by their success her father entered her for the 100 metres at the Oban Games. Most of the village was on the ferry going across to the mainland. A party afloat. For Bill O'Brien it was forty beer-filled minutes. He was more nervous than his daughter.

The track was part of the main arena, cordoned off by ropes. When they were not in the beer tent, people sat on bales of hay, watching. They took their drinks into the sunshine to lubricate this watching. Cora attracted some interest. There was her tracksuit, bright red and covered with butterfly badges she had sewn on. But it was her height that caused most nudges and grins and knowing nods. As soon as the entrants for the first heat were lined up it was plain there was a good six inches' difference between Cora and her nearest rival. That six inches was all leg.

'A fiver on the wee one,' someone said. Cora flinched.

'Never mind them,' her father whispered. 'Go for it. Blister and hurtle.' He reeked of alcohol. Cora shrugged. All this bored her. She had no real desire to run faster than anyone else. Just running was enough. As the starter lined up the competitors, she handed her dad the orange lolly she was eating at the time and received some rapturous applause from the crowd for that. She took her place, heard the gun, shot from the blocks and flew for the tape. And won. It was easy. Very, very easy. She won the next heat. And by the time she hit the quarter finals she had a small following.

'Come away, the wee one.'

At the semis the now ritual handing over of the lolly was received with whistles and roars of approval. Her father took it with pride, gave it a lick for luck, and held it aloft to the crowd. Cora stepped back from the fiery blast of his breath.

'You know what to do, darlin'. Just do it. Know what I mean?' he reeled, pointing waveringly at the tape. Cora adored him. Sober he was wonderful, drunk he was more wonderful. Drunk he always cried. She looked at that special little bit of his face where she would curl up and lie if only she were tiny enough and she promised to win. Bill O'Brien was high. He was a man on the make. Why, he had a knack for this. Cora could, he drunkenly believed, go all the way – whatever that meant. And he would go all the way with her – wherever that was.

As the afternoon moved on, the waft and fumes of booze filled the air above the park. The very air was alcoholic, and the mood was jubilant. People sang. There was a new heroine to sing for, 'Come away, the wee one.' They were Scots, and they would all their lives root for the wee one. It was part of what they were, automatic underdogs. Those who were not naturally small had delusions of smallness. Tall people could not enjoy with grace and style their height, they longed to be down there blistering and hurtling with the wee ones. They wept for Cora and her courage, and bought her Cokes and ice creams and chocolate, all of which she ate with relish. A small euphoria was cooking, people were betting on the wee one. Money was changing hands, drinks were being got. And was everybody happy? You bet your life they were.

Come time for the final Cora was, naturally enough, awash with confectionery and fizzy drinks. Though she was a bit worried about how tired she felt, Cora did not think her alarming consumption of Coca-Cola, raspberry-ripple ice cream and Mars Bars would, in any way, slow her up. They lined up.

Her father was incoherent with joy, hope and whisky. 'Do it, Cora. Do it, my lovely. You can do it.'

Strategies, sadly, meant nothing to them. They both thought a strategy was something a general did to manoeuvre an army. It had more to do with winning wars than races. Cora did not know about holding a little back, or saving her best till last. She heard the starter's pistol and felt the rush and bustle of others passing her, the desperate urgency. It was the urgency of those who knew to blister and hurtle only when it mattered, only when the real winning was at stake. She came last, then. But last to a wild roar and thunderous applause. She bowed and opened her arms to the crowd as she crossed the line. 'Come away, the wee one.' That cheer was for her and she imagined people would hear it miles away. It would sound clear across the water to Tobermory, a yell like that. She lost. But only gloriously.

'You humiliated her,' Irene O'Brien scolded her husband on the ferry home. 'How will she ever live this down?'

Bill hung his head. The fool he was. But Cora slipped her hand into his and told him not to worry, she'd had a lovely day. 'The loveliest of my life,' she said. She had learned to play a crowd. She'd had more goodies than she thought she could ever eat. And she knew that there was joy in moving. She could listen to her body as she went, her heart and her breathing. All her life, then, in joy or sorrow, she ran. But winning meant nothing.

When her children were old enough to leave unattended she would run through the Edinburgh mornings by the Water of Leith, watching starlings, listening to the rhythm of her feet and the sounds of her breathing, thinking about her father. It was the only time she managed to mull over the things she found in her head. The only time she had herself to herself.

Chapter Thirteen

When Cora arrived in Edinburgh she was seventeen. She was dressed for safety. Her hair was pinned back and she had one of those faces that looked like an infant's drawing, two bright eyes, small nose and a tumble of auburn hair. All that was on her face was a child's candour. It was innocent, waiting for life to happen to it. Waiting for a few expressions to add to its repertoire.

She had a place at Edinburgh University. She was going to be a chemist. Chemistry came easily to her, she had a natural understanding of the mixing of solids, liquids and gases. Ever since her teacher at Tobermory High had explained about the nature of matter – anything that occupies space and has mass.

'Matter can go through physical changes – ice melts, solid to liquid; water boils, liquid to gas,' her teacher said. 'These changes are easily reversed. Chemical changes, now, chemical changes are tricky. They are hard to reverse.' Cora thought it easy. Chemistry was a delight, its precision a comfort, its colours a delight, its changing forms, reversible and irreversible, a constant fascination. It had a kind of poetry for her. That, and she fancied she cut a dash in her white lab coat.

She went home for Christmas. She was changing. The life she was living was on her face. Irene saw it right away. A firmness about her daughter's jaw, a resolve. All Bill saw was the shorn hair, the pierced ears, the extravagant eye makeup. He saw the short skirt and huge boots. Neither of them saw the moth tattooed on her bum. Neither of them would ever know about that.

'Don't you ever tell your grandmother about my tattoo,' Cora warned her boys when they were still little enough to be allowed lingering looks at her backside.

'Why not?'

95

'You know,' she nodded to them. 'There are some things you just don't tell your mother.'

'But you're our mother.'

'Well, don't tell me, then.'

'Don't tell you what?' Children were so persistent.

'Don't tell me whatever it is you don't want me to know when the time comes for you to have things you don't want to tell your mother.' They stared at her, baffled.

'How're the studies going?' her father asked.

'Oh fine,' she lied.

'Well, that's all that matters, isn't it?' he smiled. Irene looked at him witheringly. Men were such fools. What on earth was going on in that dim head of his? Didn't he see? Didn't he see anything? God, she could see it. She turned the glare on to Cora. Cora winced.

'The girl's got in with a bad crowd,' Irene told Bill in bed that night.

'Oh, she'll be fine,' Bill said. 'Cora's got a good head on her.'

Irene tutted and turned over. He just didn't see it. And Cora was his darling. How could she tell him? Cora wasn't a girl any more, was she? Cora was a woman now. And furthermore it was plain to Irene that Cora was turning into the wrong sort of woman. The naughty sort.

The next morning Cora went round to see her grandmother. Irene phoned an advance warning.

'The child's had a mental aberration,' she said. 'If that's what university does for you, you can keep it. Strikes me education only makes you daft.'

'Well, I wouldn't go as far as that.' Gran O'Brien always felt Irene was too dismissive of everything and everybody. 'It's a child she is.' She was from Orkney, had met Bill's father in Inverness over sixty years ago and had lived here in Tobermory since she married. As a child she'd been beaten in class for speaking Gaelic, the tongue she spoke at home. It had left its mark. Now she spoke English, thought in English, but dreamed as a Gael. And her everyday linguistic constructions were the ones she'd learned almost eighty years ago from her own mother: 'A child she is.'

But when Cora arrived in her kitchen her grandmother saw a

child she wasn't. 'Have you walked here through the streets dressed like that?'

'Yes.' Cora was proud. 'We all dress like this. Well, all my set anyway.'

'Is that the style?'

'Yes.'

'It'll be a reading you're after.'

Cora nodded. 'Yes.'

'Well, put on the kettle.'

Cora's grandmother read tea leaves. As far back as Cora could remember her grandmother had been peering into people's tea cups, telling them their lives. As a little girl she'd played with her favourite doll under the huge table in her grandmother's immaculate kitchen listening to the readings.

'I cannot tell the future,' her grandmother said. 'It's the present I'm making sense of. Help you see the broader view.' They'd drain their cups, keen to know what was happening to them. Many an afternoon was spent standing by the window holding a cup up to the light, making mystic sense of the shapes in the gathered leavings, dredged at the bottom. Cups would be passed to young Cora that she would stare in and say what she saw. 'Stars,' she'd say. 'A tree.'

'She has the child's eye,' her grandmother would explain. 'She sees what she sees. We see what we wish we saw. Ah now, look. Right enough. A tree. Great branches reaching out. It's good fortune you'll be having.' Then again, when the news wasn't good, the bad tidings were delivered gently. 'Oh my, now. Things are getting away from you. You're not at all happy at the moment.'

It always seemed to Cora that people would know what was happening to them without her grandmother peering into a cup. But they liked it. It was a comfort. Her grandmother offered people understanding, sympathy and hope, always hope. She never charged. She saw trips across water (considering they lived on an island this was hardly surprising), lucky dark strangers. She saw more than people knew – black crows and dogs, deep depressions.

'You have to ask the person to drain the cup. And it's good tea you use. Proper tea, big leaves. And it isn't just the cup you read,' Cora's grandmother told her. 'It's the people behind the cup you look at. It's their moods you're interpreting. Then again, you're letting them know what other people think of them, and what they think of themselves.' She sighed. 'Women,' she said. 'They're always looking for something more. A deeper meaning. "This can't be it," they say. How can I tell them it is?'

She understood this desperation well. Like the drinkers from the cups she read, she imagined she had dedicated a good part of her life to the elimination of dirt and was, like them, seriously doubting the validity of such devotion. She imagined she was a domestic despot declaring war not only on dust and muck but on the bringers of filth into the house – but she was wrong. Her house was old-fashioned clean. Kept pristine, not with aerosols, but with polish and elbow grease. It gleamed darkly, smelled of polish, and soup simmering and home baking. Visitors lingered, savouring its old-fashioned warmth and safety. Still Cora's grandmother regularly chastised herself for bustling through life duster in hand. She was a wiper and a guardian of household surfaces.

'It'll all be here long after I'm gone,' she said, indicating the sideboard with a sad flap of her hand. Then, realising the finality of that remark, 'Long after I'm dust. Everything . . .' This time she indicated the world beyond her dresser with a dramatic sweep of both arms. Everything, the furniture, the house, the street, the village, all the towns out there she'd never visited. Streets and streets of houses with wiped sinks, gleamy draining boards, shiny baths, perfect skirting boards and all the dust. All that dust that she and a million other women vigorously worked to eradicate would return to settle on picture frames, television screens, whatever, for ever. 'I'll be the dust. It'll be me getting wiped off mantelpieces, shaken out the window only to come back and settle again.' Shocked by this vision she slumped on to her perfectly plumped sofa. The truth? God, you could die from it. 'Maybe that's why women search for something mystic – a meaning. There must be more to life than just getting on with it. Men now, men think getting on with things is the meaning of their life. That's what they do, they get on with it. What do you think, Cora?'

'Yes,' she answered, though she hadn't a clue what her grandmother was on about. Well, she wouldn't, she was four at the time.

But she always remembered those words. It helped her later to understand the indestructibility of matter and the uselessness of a life as a guardian of household surfaces.

It was inevitable that Cora should pick up her grandmother's gift. Now she was earning quite a reputation as a mystic back in Edinburgh. Her friends considered themselves sophisticated and cultured. They wore their rebel clothes, listened to outrageous music but couldn't resist a bit of no-nonsense, down-to-earth mysticism when it was on offer.

When Cora left, clumping down her grandmother's tiny front path in her boots, Jenny O'Brien phoned Irene.

'Well, I did a reading. She's just finding a new way. A road for herself to follow.'

'I suppose it's natural at her age,' Irene said. 'Was there anything else?'

'No,' Jenny lied. She could hear Bill scoffing in the background. 'Voodoo rubbish,' he was shouting. 'Bloody women with their horoscopes and tea leaves and mumbo jumbo.' Jenny did not say that she'd seen a dangerous road in her granddaughter's cup. She knew when to keep her mouth shut.

'The girl can read cups for herself.' Bill could hardly believe this cup business. 'She could make a cup of tea, drink it, look at the stuff at the bottom and think, goodness me, I'm behaving like a prat.'

'You can't read your own cup,' Irene scoffed. 'Surely after all these years you know that.'

'He knows nothing,' his mother said down the phone. 'Someone like Cora, the way of her, she'd only ever see sunny roads and winning posts. It's an optimist she is.'

So knowing nothing about her family's worry and the grandmother's secret gleanings from the bottom of her cup, Cora returned to university. She was longing to get back to her new life and her new friends. Her family came down to the ferry to see her off. They stood in a straggled row in the car park watching the boat and the girl on board it sail away. Cora leaned over the rails waving and waving. She had her chemistry books in her bag, was still wrestling with the nature of matter, the nature of things. But irreversible chemical changes were happening in her.

Chapter Fourteen

In April Cora phoned home to say she wasn't coming home for Easter. She wanted to be with her friends. 'And,' she said, 'there's nothing up there for me. Oh,' she added casually in a detached disinterested manner, 'by the way . . .'

Irene gripped the receiver and held her breath. Something dire was coming. Through her parenting years Irene had learned to beware the words 'oh by the way.' Oh by the way, Mum, someone's thrown a lump of coal down the lavatory and water's pouring over the sides. Oh by the way, I've failed all my exams. Oh by the way, I've crashed the car.

' . . . I'm moving out of hall. I'll be sharing a flat with a friend,' Cora said.

Irene stood in her long green candlewick dressing gown, clutching the phone. 'Oh no, you don't my girl. Oh no, you don't,' she shouted.

She stormed into the kitchen where Bill was mildly drinking tea and reading the paper. 'That young madam thinks she can do what she likes. But she can't. Oh no, she can't.'

To Bill's surprise they were within the hour rattling down the road to catch the nine o'clock ferry. 'You're surprised,' Irene thundered. 'Just wait till you see the look on her face.'

But it was she who was shocked. The changes in Cora, eyebrow-raising at Christmas, were now, four months later, dramatic. Her hair was purple and green, shaven at the sides and worn in a long vibrant tumble down the middle. Her ears were multi-pierced rows of chain-and-charm-laden hoops. She wore black lipstick and her eyebrows were plucked almost out of existence. She openly smoked, blowing rebellious blasts of smoke past Irene. Her right eye was ornately made up. She seemed to be scowling out from the depths of a five-pointed star. There was a black spider drawn on her left cheek.

'Is that a tattoo?' Irene pointed, horrified.

'It washes off,' Cora heaved the words out. The trial it was speaking to people over twenty-five. 'Actually,' she added, 'I was thinking of changing my name to Spyder.'

Irene felt her knees tremble, though she didn't know if it was shock or rage.

Cora took them to the pub round the corner and introduced them to her turbulently clothed friends, who all looked at them briefly and nodded.

'My parents,' Cora said. Wasn't it awful and embarrassing to have two middle-aged people in tow? she said to her friends with a slight movement of her eyebrows. And her friends shot her sympathetic glances.

Bill bought drinks. Cora, to Irene's horror, asked for a pint of Guinness but hardly touched it. After a while she went to the bar and bought herself a Coke.

'It's a pity they don't have sneering at the Olympics. We'd have a roomful of champions here,' Irene said to Bill when Cora left their table. 'And our daughter is turning into the queen of the lip curl. Where did she learn that?'

They sat slowly drinking, communicating occasionally across their silence with sudden questions and bits of information. 'How's Gran's flu?' 'We had the hall painted.' 'Can you walk in them boots? Are they not heavy?'

'They're very comfortable. They last.'

Cora's friends across the bar rose to leave. They waved laconically. ''Bye, Cora. 'Bye, Cora's parents,' someone said. Irene seethed. She felt old. She felt frumpy. An outcast in a lurid world of wild music and rebel clothes. All around her were people in leather jackets and T-shirts. She was an old fool in her best navy coat. She was sitting in a strange bar drinking a glass of wine at two in the afternoon when she'd rather be having a cup of tea and a sandwich. These people, she thought, would know nothing about a nice cup of tea. They'd all be drinking or taking drugs or listening to funny loud music. In the end, though, she had nothing to say to Cora about her moving out of hall. She and Bill both realised that their daughter would just do what she wanted to do. More than that, she would really want to do what they didn't want her to do.

'Did you hear them?' Irene said on the way back to the car. She was hoarse with indignation. ' " 'Bye, Cora's parents." Parents. They called us parents.' And though she never swore, now she lapsed and delivered what she considered a mouthful. There was no other way to say what she felt. 'Bloody children. You bloody give birth to them, then one bloody day they bloody turn bloody round and bloody call you their parents. The cheek of it. I may be a mother but I'm nobody's parent. I refuse to be a parent.' She grabbed the car door handle and rattled it furiously, waiting for Bill to come to open it for her.

Bill shrugged. He too felt old and foolish and past it and envious. He thought that they didn't have youth when he was young. He had a sports jacket and a Gene Vincent record. Somehow it wasn't the same. 'They'll all grow out of it,' he said. 'They'll end up accountants and they'll look back not in anger, but sheepishly.'

Irene had looked at her daughter long and hard. She'd changed. The girl who had left home dreaming of becoming a chemist had grown up, gone away. Irene could tell, didn't know how she could tell. But she could tell. It was the swelling of her daughter's breasts. The curve of her stomach. The consumption of fizzy drinks. The lowering of her eyes. The shame. Irene saw it all. The physical changes in Cora, the clothes, the hair – were easily reversed. But the other change was chemical and at four months was becoming irreversible.

'That child's pregnant,' Irene said to Bill when they got back to the car. She sat heavily in the passenger seat, put her handbag on her knee. She was not going to get comfortable for the long drive home. She refused to get comfortable. Her daughter was behaving like a wanton fool, and – dare she even let the word flit through her head? – a whore. She could not possibly allow herself to get comfortable. She rounded on her husband. 'It's all your fault.'

'Me?' Bill pointed to himself. 'Me? Don't be disgusting. I won't be accused of that. You're not blaming me there. God. She's down here and I'm miles away. I haven't even seen the child—'

'No.' She was exasperated enough to hit him. 'No. You with all that running nonsense. It started then. We lost her then. It turned her head.'

Dear Cora, *she wrote when she got home.*

I know all about you. You can't hide such a thing from your mother, you know. A woman knows. I don't even want to imagine all the nonsense you are getting up to. But it was plain to me, if not your father, that you are pregnant. I only hope you know who is the father of your child. But I'm so disappointed in you. It didn't take you long to go off the rails, did it? Obviously we will support you. But I have to tell you this – you have broken your father's heart.

'You have broken your father's heart.' Cora read and reread that phrase. All day she turned it over and over in her mind. 'You have broken your father's heart.' Did he cry? She shed tears for her father's tears.

Dear Mum, *she wrote back.*

Of course I know who is the father of my child. He is Claude, a Frenchman I met at a party. I love him very much and I know he loves me. I am proud to be having his baby. This is the best thing that has ever happened to me. Having a baby is more important than any education. I am bringing a new life into the world. Nothing can surpass this . . .

Her handwriting swept and curved deeper and deeper the more she expressed her passion. Before she signed off she added: 'I'm sorry I've broken Dad's heart. Tell him that I love him.'

All her life she remembered that letter, and no matter how hard she tried to forgive herself for writing it, she never could overcome the cringe inside it brought. There is no fool like an old fool, what bollocks, she thought. There is no fool as dire as a young and headstrong fool. They are the biggest fools of all.

'But,' she would cry in the night, years later, when remembering and cringing kept her from sleeping, 'but, what the fuck are you meant to say when your mother says, "A woman knows"? How dare she?' And she would pummel her pillow before banging her head on it, furiously trying to sleep.

Years and years later, after a night lying awake staring into the dark plagued by memories and cursing herself for the fool she'd been when she was young, she sat at her kitchen table sharing wine, cigarettes, regrets and New York cheddar crisps with Ellen.

'I think,' Cora said, 'that I live a lie.'

'You? Rubbish.'

'No. Really. My mother used to say, "A woman knows". Know what I mean?'

Ellen nodded. 'I know the saying. I just don't ever say it. Because I don't know what it is I'm meant to know in my capacity as a woman.'

'I said it myself just the other day,' Cora confessed. ' " A woman knows," I said to my class. Knowingly, I said it, arrogant even. But what does a woman know? How to bake a sponge? How big is a ball of string? The meaning of life?'

Ellen shrugged.

'No good will come of it. I'll be found out. I know nothing,' Cora said.

'I don't think that's true.'

'I know nothing about the knowing thing that women are meant to have. I look about at women in the street and I wonder if they know what it is we are meant to know. If it's only me that is ignorant about the secret business of being a woman. I had children too young. I left home too young. I rushed at everything and I didn't stop to learn. And now, even though I do a job and I have brought up two sons, I still think I know nothing. There's so much I'm ashamed of. Do you think that's what women know? That in the end we'll shame our parents?'

After her father learned about the baby he sent money every week. It came on Thursdays in a brown envelope, always with a small note: 'Everyone's well here and thinking about you. Take care, Cora, and don't you go thinking we've forgotten you.'

She never found out if her mother knew about this money. 'You broke your father's heart.' She knew of course that she hadn't. But she knew how broken-hearted he'd have been if he ever found out about the things she did. It wasn't Bill's heart she broke with her fatherless babies and her wildness. It was her own.

Chapter Fifteen

Cora met Claude at a party. She was standing leaning on a wall, drinking Guinness, smoking dope, rolling her head from side to side in time to a cracked and overplayed copy of *Pretzel Logic*. Her mind was numb. But she was watching him, and thinking she would get to know him. The way she did. When he eventually came over to speak to her she realised how befuddled by chemicals she was. She'd quite lost control of her lower lip.

Conversation was limited. He said, 'Hello,' and she said, 'Uh-huh.' He said, 'Can I get you another drink?' and she said, 'Uh-huh.' But she thought, isn't it a bitch? Just when you need them most your brain and your tongue abandon you. However, with a debilitated lower lip and malfunctioning brain such a thing was far too complex to say. But her uh-huhs must have been more alluring than she imagined. He took her back to his place and showed her everything he knew about sex. Which was a great deal more than she knew.

His flat in the Grassmarket, three floors up, was the filthiest place Cora had ever seen. It smelled damp and she did not know if the floorboards were up to the strain of her walking across them. She tiptoed when she made her way to his bed. She drunkenly thought that way there might be less of her.

There was a cooker, a grubby rug, a table, a chair, a frying pan and a small pot. And, of course, the bed. It was unmade, sheetless, that tangle of blankets he'd left when he rose in the morning. Or, as Cora would discover, in the early afternoon.

As soon as they got in the door he kissed her. They had been kissing and groping a bit all the way home. Now they were alone, in private, and free to really kiss. And grope. Though when Claude did it, it wasn't like groping. He knew how to make a woman squirm. It was what he was best at. He ran his hands up her thighs, and removed her underwear as if that was what underwear was for. Removing. He set Cora moaning, 'Oh please. Oh please. Touch me there.' She was just eighteen. When he entered her, and they were still just by the door, he did not move, did not shove or thrust. She was against the wall, legs curled round his waist. He pressed against her. He smelled of garlic.

'I could stay like this for ever,' he boasted. 'We could die like this.'

'You couldn't. You couldn't,' Cora said. Or panted. 'Bet you couldn't.'

'I could.' Then facing the truth, 'No, you're right. I couldn't.'

In the morning she lay, arms spread, his head between her thighs. This was lovely. This could replace running. She started to count the milk bottles lined up beneath the window, beside the cooker. They were unwashed, stained, milk streaked and they only slightly glistened in the sunlight, smelled sour. There were hundreds and hundreds of them. A little army of them. 'One, two, three, oh. Four, five, oooh.' Her counting got to seven before she was distracted.

She moved in with him. She bought sheets and started a Get Rid Of The Milk Bottles campaign. She rarely went to lectures. She'd made a significant discovery about herself that was devastatingly to waylay her progress in life. She was horny as anything.

When as a teacher she considered the scattering of wriggling infant, tiny beings in constant motion, in her class, she thought: Shame, most of them are going to get waylaid, too. And she thought: Damned hormones. They've had such a diabolical effect on my life and I don't even know what one looks like. God, I really, really needed sex. I couldn't understand why people studied or worked when they could be shagging. It was more than throbbing hormones. I was a teenage hormone.

And though she was not prone to recriminations she knew it was a pity that she had discovered sex for real, so important and so grown up, when she was eighteen. She could not sit still for thinking about it. She took up serious shagging when she was supposed to be making lifetime career decisions. She supposed lots of other people were similarly caught out. No wonder folk got to forty and started to scream and cry. They'd got distracted a couple of decades earlier and were feeling the chill of naff decisions, heated doings.

But she'd been more than distracted. Something had got into her. A thing. A wildness. She couldn't, now, properly define it, but remembering sometimes made her reel. Not with shame. No, it was relief she felt. Thank heavens she hadn't got caught. Her mischief came screaming back to her when she hadn't got a proper grip on her thoughts. She'd be wiping the kitchen unit, peeling a potato, hoovering the carpet and the boredom of it would numb her mind. It was then the raw naughtiness of her brief life with Claude would come back to her.

There they were, furiously fucking up some alley, high on the rush of shoplifting. It was too exciting, thieving, too exciting by far to wait to get home before they started their celebrations. Adrenalin belted through them, the spoils of the day spread at their feet – well, Claude's feet. Cora's were always well and truly off the ground.

'Oh my God,' she would moan. 'A fool, me.'

Then rounding on her boys, 'I don't want either of you growing up to be like me.'

They would dismiss this with a sigh. Considering the life she led – the noise, the constant blat of music that she had to have with her in the car, in the kitchen, in her bedroom, the irritating musical sizzle that eeked from her earphones when she set off running; her mess, the tissues, nail varnish, lipsticks, scatterings of female stuff and God knows what under the bed, her relationships – men who never reappeared, thrown out at one or two in the morning because she could not bear to let go and actually sleep, dip into unconsciousness, with somebody – considering everything they knew about her, neither of them had any intention of growing up to be like her. Though they loved her. Oh yes they did that. That was what made her mess tolerable.

'I mean,' Cora continued, 'what's the point of me making all those mistakes if you're going to make them too? The very least you could do is make some new mistakes. That'd be interesting for me.'

Cora knew her mistakes. They visited her often. She had crammed all her youth into two years. Blister and hurtle, Cora. She threw herself at everything. She thought she was still suffering from some lingering adolescence she hadn't got out of her system – the music and the mess. She didn't think having two children before she was twenty a mistake – a vast and absurd inconvenience, yes. But they weren't a mistake. There was the shoplifting, big mistake that. And then there was the breaking of her father's heart. Oh, she did not want to think about that.

'You have broken your father's heart,' her mother wrote. Cora caught hold of those words and locked them within her. When she was torturing herself about her wrongdoings she brought them out to increase her torturings. Her biggest mistake, though, was not challenging it. She should have blistered and hurtled to the nearest phone and demanded of her mother, 'What the hell do you mean by that?'

Chapter Sixteen

'What's the worst thing you've ever done?' Ellen asked once. They were drinking where they usually drank – Cora's kitchen, having one of those best and worst confessional conversations. Best sex ever. Worst dinner party. Most embarrassing date. Silliest outfit. Worst buy.

'Oh,' said Cora. 'Hard to say.' Was it all the stuff she stole? Or lying about what she saw in tea cups? Or was it forcing a lifestyle she did not cherish on her children? There was so much.

'What's the worst thing you've ever done?' Cora asked Ellen.

'Dunno. I slept with two men at the same time once. But that's not so terrible really. They were my love slaves. I quite enjoyed it. But it's sweaty. If you fall asleep you have to be careful not to be the one in the middle. You wake in a terrible lather. Damp, hungover and ashamed of yourself.'

'Oh that,' said Cora. 'Yes, we all know that.'

Ellen met her lovers at a comic convention in London. They were fans. She didn't know she had any and was quite delighted with them. They were younger than her, but very presentable. Well, presentable enough for someone who'd decided it was time to avenge her husband's philandering. They didn't wear back-to-front baseball caps, that was enough for Ellen. They'd gone for a drink in the hotel bar and one thing led to another, and another. She couldn't choose between them so they'd all ended up in her bed. That seemed fair.

Stanley had looked at her coolly when they appeared all three in the morning, rumpled and bleary. 'Behave yourself,' he told her.

'I know. Sleeping three in a bed is tricky,' said Cora. She'd had two boys in her bed for years. They slept like a heap of puppies, Cora and Sam and Col. She hadn't needed to chase them away.

They each decided when they were too grown up for such cuddles and each went his own way to his own bed. Let them go, Cora thought. And having a bed to herself was lovely. She did not wake with a damp biscuit sticking to her thigh, or a brutally hard little car wedged at the small of her back. Nor did she wake at three in the morning hanging uncovered and shivering over the side of the bed whilst two little people in Peter Rabbit pyjamas spread themselves in the warm, snoring sweetly.

But there was a time in Cora's life when she had not felt complete unless some little body was curled comfortably against her, little lips pursed, little fists clenched – such serious sleepers, children. And then when they'd left her bed they still came back to it every morning, icy little feet on her naked thighs, to relate to her their adventures whilst sleeping. The dreams they had.

It was Claude's elixir of life that got them started on their shopping sprees.

'This is the secret of perfect health, good skin and a sturdy heart,' he said, scraping crushed garlic into some extra virgin olive oil. 'Take this every day and nothing will go wrong with you.' He thumped his chest demonstrating the healthy sturdy thing beating within. And coughed. Cora adored him. He was pale-skinned, thin and fragile, like a poet, she thought. And she was robust. She could run up the three flights to their flat, whilst he came slowly behind. He was sensitive. He had beautiful dark eyes and was prone to night sweats. His life was pained and he was misunderstood. She was coarse and too healthy by far. She felt crude beside him.

He could withstand the Scottish weather, but the food drove him to distraction. The only time Cora saw him lose his temper was during their first week together when she cooked for him. She lovingly prepared her speciality.

'What's this?' he said, looking in horror at the plate before him.

'It's sausages and eggs and beans. A fry up.'

'This isn't food. It's pig shit.'

Cora was hurt. How could he insult her cooking like this? How could he speak to her like this?

'I will not eat this,' he waved at it in disgust. 'Take it away.'

'No. This is good nutrition. I won't see it wasted. I hate waste.'

'You don't hate waste as much as I hate pig shit.' Peeg sheet.

He opened the window and hurled the food, plate and all, out into the night. She heard the faint whistle as it took to the air, then seconds later the smash as it landed on the pavement below – cries of protest from passing pedestrians who'd just had a narrow escape from flying food.

'What was that?'

'Good grief! It's a plate of sausage and egg. God's sake. Where did that come from?'

Cora and Claude, three floors above, did not dare look out and declare themselves. In the morning it was still there, lying on the pavement, one smashed plate thick with congealed fat. Some night creature, human or four-legged, had eaten the rest.

It was, then, the need for the elixir of life and the lack of money to buy it that started them shoplifting. It was so simple. Claude in the delicatessen simply slipped a bottle of olive oil up his sleeve as Cora bought a single croissant. They left. Burst jubilantly on to the street.

'Did it. Got it. Aha.' Neither of them had ever felt such wicked glee. They walked, stifling their delight, carefully from the shop. Don't run. Running's a sign of guilt. Walk. Walk quicker. And quicker. Faces glowing. No smiling. No running. Control. Quicker then. Till they were tanking up the street. Till they had to run. Racing away, then. Laughing. They'd been naughty and got away with it. It started there. It started then.

Within weeks they were both hooked on the rush it brought them. Their little grubby room filled with nonsensical goodies. What had started as an act of survival – neither of them had the money to eat properly, and certainly couldn't afford to eat the sort of food Claude wanted – became a thrill.

Every morning they lay in bed together promising each other not to do it today. That's what they called it, doing it. They couldn't bring themselves to say 'stealing' or 'shoplifting'.

'We won't go to the shops today,' he'd say.

'No,' she'd agree. 'Better not. Someone will spot us. They're bound to notice us. We can't keep doing it.' Nor did they voice the words, 'get caught'. Neither could bear the thought of what might happen to them if they did.

They'd rise around noon, and, after several cups of coffee to wake them and set their blood flowing, they'd breakfast on the remains of last night's dinner, the previous day's spoils. Bits of garlicky chicken picked from the carcass, straight-from-the-pot spoonfuls of Claude's daube, dark chocolate biscuits, wine, brandy. They'd dress in their acquired outfits, splash on acquired colognes, and, vowing they weren't going to take any more risks, they'd set out for their day's adventures.

Always they'd hit the department stores in the centre of town, heading first for the food hall. 'We have to eat,' she'd say. 'We'll only take what's necessary.'

'What we need. What we have to.'

'We have to eat.'

But there were such natty things to have, tasty jars of grainy white wine mustard, jams and jellies, pralines, quails' eggs, cheeses. They'd walk together slowly, staring, quietly discussing, scarcely breathing. Just beneath this control, their hearts were beating wildly. Hammering. Cora had the knack of looking about, watching whilst not appearing to be watching. The casual, yawning gaze rather than the furtive guiltily wild look about. 'Take it. Take it now.' Claude would hand over a couple of things at the checkout. Cora, carrying the loot, would wait for him. They'd walk through the rest of the store, fingering this, ogling that, shoving whatever into their pockets. Didn't matter what, scarves, earrings, a tie or two, and out the door. Along the street into the next store.

Sometimes they'd split up. Claude would wander, she would wait by the door. Her heart would pound when she saw him through the crowd, heading for her. Then she'd wander and he'd wait, till their exuberance got the better of them. It was a high that hit each of them simultaneously. They would gather speed. Out the door, walking. Along the street. Don't run. Don't draw attention. Pushing through the afternoon crowds. Faster, faster. Till running became inevitable. Cora in front, blister and hurtle, he some way behind, panting. But both faces lit with the glee, triumph. 'We did it. Did it.' If they could have raised their arms and taken a bow they would have. 'Yes. Yes. Yes. Yes. Easy.'

Running top speed was the only way to express the wildness of it. Head back, Cora went. Claude, pale and eventually breathless, followed. Off Princes Street into Rose Street and into the dark of its little lanes, back doors of pubs and restaurants. The smell of food and booze. Cora off the ground against the wall and he on her, fucking. They'd pull at each other's clothing, kissing, licking, touching, desperate to consummate the rush. 'Oh please, please, now. Do it.' Drained and shaky with exhaustion they'd stagger wanly home, pockets and bag filled, sometimes – often – with rubbish. They'd get home, pour out their prizes and always, always be surprised with what they had.

'We'll have some brandy. I need some brandy,' Claude said.

But Cora shook her head. 'No. I don't want that.' She was consumed by new needs that she didn't understand. She felt that her body was bossing her about. She wanted brandy. It didn't. She wanted coffee. It didn't. 'I need something fizzy. And none of your Perrier. I want something sweet and fizzy.'

Cora got ill. She lay in bed mornings, moaning and throwing up. Her breasts hurt. She was bloated and couldn't run. Going to the shops with Claude to *do it* no longer interested her. In fact she found all that excitement nauseating. 'I can't, Claude. I just can't. Look at my legs. I'm all swollen and horrible. I hate myself.'

Claude stroked her leg. 'It's just as well, really. We'd get caught. What do they do to shoplifters?' There, he'd said it. They were shoplifters. They'd get caught. The spell was broken.

'I don't know,' Cora said. 'Prison? Probation? My mother and father would make me go back home.' She turned and faced the wall. 'I don't want that.'

She was, of course, pregnant. Nine weeks, the doctor said. He offered her an abortion which she refused. She thought it was her punishment for behaving so badly. Or maybe it was a bit of reality come to save her from the horrors her wildness would bring. However, except for when her children had nothing to eat, she never stole again.

'Do you have a worst dread?' Ellen asked her once. 'I have. A sound. After Daniel and all his stuff, you know? I dread the sound of the mail box in the morning, and sometimes the sound of someone knocking on the door gives me a chill.'

Cora shrugged. The sound she dreaded was simple. When she went to Princes Street shopping she always worried that someone had spotted her on her stealing rampages and would recognise her. To this day she worried about it. The sound she dreaded was a simple belligerent cry, 'Oi you!'

Chapter Seventeen

It was Ellen who first interested Cora in the movement of starlings. 'Look at them,' Ellen said. 'They are not what they seem. You'd think them dowdy. But they're little dandy birds, tricked out in all colours. They glisten. And you'd think them cheeky, pushy. But they're worse than that, they're little mobsters. They're only happy in a gang. Watch them. When they take to the sky and fly, they all fly together. There isn't a sergeant major yelling, "Yo, starlings, right wheel, left turn." How do they know which way to go? Why is there never one, just one, banging into the others, causing mayhem, going left when everyone else is wheeling right? For there sure as hell always is with humans.'

'That's you,' Cora said. 'Always turning the wrong way.'

When the day faded Cora would stand in the park watching starlings cluster in the trees. As darkness turned the leaves and branches to silhouette, the starlings would chatter. Their wheezy chirrupings went unnoticed. People passed but they did not comment. The raspings of starlings were, like the rattle of cars and the whoosh of lorries skimming by too close, so common they went unheeded. Come full evening blackness, the starlings would silence. Nobody knew they were there. But if you clapped your hands, or blew a whistle or yelled and waved your arms, flapping and complaining hugely they would rise, squalling from their evening branches, and take to the air. They would start their panic flight as individuals but would, within seconds, flock. Every one would be part of the whole flight. As one they would pass in their thousands over the tops of trees. As one they would wheel one way, then the other, and when the shock and danger were gone, as one they would come in to land. How did they do that? Cora always watched them, trying to identify one that was the leader of the flight. A chief

117

starling that yelled, 'This way, lads.' Or, 'Right turn at the last tree and wheel sharp left at the steeple across the road, lads.' But no. Each one knew the ways of the whole. The movement of starlings was not for individuals. There were no rebels.

If Cora hadn't been so young she might have known that Claude was ill. He must have been ill when they met, and slowly, without her noticing any change, got more and more sick. But she had no experience of the nature of illness, how it smelled, the colour of it. Thinking back she knew she noticed that there was a difference in Claude, she just didn't make much of it. She was too taken up with the dramatic changes in her own body. The lump within was getting larger and lumpier. She could feel its bits, elbows, feet and knees – or so she imagined. Nights she could feel it wriggle and dance, little feet pattered inside, and sometimes she could see the little thing banging in there, blips on her tummy. 'Goodness look at that.' She had settled into being pregnant. She had not grasped the reality of it – that it would end with an actual baby.

After three nauseous months, Cora bloomed. Pregnancy suited her. Her skin was clear and lovely, hair shiny. She was filled with a new vibrant energy. She scrubbed the little flat, painted the walls – three a pale buff colour, one dark red. She pinned up purloined posters and record sleeves. She washed the window and cleaned the cooker with Brillo Pads. Her energy was boundless.

Claude lay in bed watching the nest-making, saying nothing. The whole business irritated him hugely. When he wasn't yelling at her to stop, he sullenly smoked Gauloises and drank brandy, neither of which he could afford. His ulcerous temper and malice surprised him. When he swore at Cora, he meant it. He wanted to hurt her for existing so healthily when he felt so constantly tired. His back and chest ached so much sometimes he could not stand up.

'Stop it, you stupid shit woman,' he cursed her.

'Stop what?' She had only been sitting by the bed listening to the radio.

'Stop being there. Stop it. Get out. Get away from me. Just stop existing. You're so . . . so . . . smug, so content. I hate it. You. I hate you.'

He hit her. She put her hand to her face, surprised and wounded, unwelcome tears spilling down her cheeks. He was vile. Why was he doing this? He hated himself and hit her again.

He was beginning to suspect there was something wrong with him. When they ran Cora sweated copiously, youthfully. Fresh, it smelled fabulously human. His sweat was slow and thick, smelled shrill. He could not stand the foul rancid taste in his mouth every morning. He was so thin, he hated Cora to see him naked. 'Don't look at me,' he spat. Often he was overcome with a sweeping exhaustion; face pale, he'd heave air into his lungs trying to overcome it. He thought this exhaustion was caused by the strain of his finals. The pains that, without warning, suddenly shot through his stomach were excruciating, but it was just nerves causing them, surely. He noticed all this, but said nothing. It made his heart stop. Waves of fear surged though him. Cancer, he had cancer. He knew it. Maybe it would all go away. Maybe there was nothing wrong really. His shit was black.

One night he woke up screaming. He curled into his pain, held it and shouted for help. Something from within was cutting him in two. Cora dressed and ran down into the street to the phone. She could not persuade her doctor to come to him.

'It'll be a spot of indigestion,' he patronised. 'Give him some Andrews Liver Salts. He'll be fine in the morning. You students and your curries.'

Cora went home and stood at the end of the bed, chewing her fingers as Claude howled. This wasn't like any indigestion she knew. Still dressed she got in beside him. Quiet now, lost in his pain, he clung to her. At six when a slow light crept into their room she rose, went out into the street, found a taxi and took him to hospital.

Cora always thought of the days that followed as a time of corridors. Confused and anxious she rushed along endless municipal miles, following signs, breathing in the nervy medical reek that pervades all hospitals. On that first morning she stood with Claude. He was stretchered and waiting for something to happen.

'What's going on?' he said. She could hardly hear him.

'We're waiting for the doctor. They're going to admit you to the ward.' She held his hand.

'What's wrong with me?'

'I don't know.' The words sang out. Scared little Highland voice amidst the rattle and thrum of medical doings. She was wearing a lurid green T-shirt, coffee-stained and crumpled. Her jeans were skin tight, worn through and calculatedly ripped down one leg. They didn't fasten over her pregnancy. Her multi-pierced left ear hung with rings, small chains that rattled moons and stars. Her boots were scraped and grubby. Her choice of hair colour this week was defiant strands of black and purple. She wore no makeup. When the doctor arrived he did not spare her his look of disapproving loathing before having the nurse usher her from the cubicle. She sat outside whilst Claude was examined and admitted. She watched as he was wheeled off into a lift. Other people were taking over the life of the one she loved.

A nurse told her, 'Your . . . ?'

'Boyfriend,' said Cora.

' . . . is being admitted to the ward. He has a duodenal ulcer that has burst. We'll be operating later this morning. It must have been bleeding for some time.' She looked accusingly at Cora.

She shrugged. 'I didn't know. Can I see him?'

'After he's been admitted to the ward we'll be preparing him for the theatre. Why don't you go home? Phone later this afternoon.' She wasn't unkind. She just had a lot to do. And she didn't reckon someone who looked like Cora. Not many people did.

Cora didn't go home. There was nothing there. She sat stranded amidst the rush and whisper of people who had things to do, and who always, always ignored her. All day she sat. At four she went to find out how he was. Corridors. Stares. They would not let her on the ward. Claude was recovering. She could see him tomorrow at visiting time. She walked home slowly, making her journey last. She watched her feet move against the pavement, dreading that moment when there would be nothing left to do but go into that empty room. Then there would be no escape from the thought that was running, unwelcome, through her head. *Claude is going to die.*

She went back next day. Walked fearfully down the ward

searching each face for that one she knew, his face. He was not there.

'He's down in ICU,' the sister told her. Cora looked at her vacantly. 'Intensive care,' the sister smiled.

Cora knew then something was wrong. Suddenly someone was being kind. Something was definitely wrong. She had never known such worry. It hurt. It pained her face and neck. She did not trust her legs to make it through the corridors any more. She was shown into a little waiting room and offered tea. They were being awfully kind. She hated it. I can't deal with sympathy, she whined to herself. A male nurse came to talk to her.

Cora's memory of that time was of sounds, colours – mostly green and red – and expressions. The expressions on the faces that moved through that small part of her life stayed with her for the rest of her life. She had been delivered into the hands of people who had made a lifetime's calling dealing with the seriously sick. The bewilderment and fear of relatives and friends were routine, part of their day-to-day dealings. She felt safe. She sat on a red plastic seat. The nurse was wearing green. He sat by her, turned towards her as he spoke gently, looked her in the eye, smiled. Claude's condition was more serious than they first thought. The ulcer had exploded inside him. Would she like to see him? He was attached to a monitor and there were tubes attached to him draining the poison. She must not be alarmed.

Cora was finding this sudden kindness increasingly hard. If it continued she was going to give in to it and cry.

She was helped, childlike, into a sterile gown – one arm, good girl, now other arm. Looking back, she thought he even fastened it for her. He led her into the unit. Six beds, widely spaced, red blankets, a nurse at the foot of each one. A guardian angel, Cora thought. A television softly beamed bland afternoon shows to a bed in the corner. There were defibrillator paddles, red, centre of the ward.

For an insane moment Cora was tempted to take them up and clamp them against her own heart. 'Clear. One. Two . . .' It was all so familiar from visions in soap operas and trips through movies. Cora had been here a hundred times before. A huge sign on the wall, white on green, 'DO NOT CROSS YOUR LEGS.' She thought vaguely that was exactly what she should have done six or seven months ago. But it was calm here, serene. People had left their lives and were battling within themselves with the business of staying alive. The sun streamed in. She thought she would like to sit here, quietly warm, for hours and hours if only they would let her. It was the first time in her life that Cora felt round her, and breathed, humanity.

She sat neatly by Claude's bed, hands folded in her lap, listening to the clack clack of the ventilator attached to a patient across the room and the insistent bleep of Claude's monitor. Claude lay still. A gunge-like bile seeped along a tube that snaked down from under his light blanket to a bottle on the floor. He was not sleeping. He just turned to her, gazed a cold moment, then turned away. She didn't think, she listened to her own body. Nerves, and the occasional kick and squirm of infant within.

Once, the monitor stopped. A loud alarming constant squeal shook the room. This was it. Cora knew this moment. Her own body throbbed fear and dread. It always happened in films. The nurse moved efficiently from the end of the bed, raised her fist, thumped, not Claude's arrested heart, but the monitor. The comforting bleep started again.

'That one's always doing that,' said the nurse. Then seeing Cora's frantic look, 'Don't worry. He's going to be fine. This is only a precaution. We're only keeping an eye. He'll be back in the ward tomorrow.'

And so he was. Almost to Cora's regret he was removed from the comforting tranquillity of intensive care to the frenetic bustle of the ward. He lay, thin and pale, seemingly lost, in the high little bed. He looked furious when she came to him. There was a flask of water and a glass on his locker.

'I have to drink this piss,' he said. She had never seen him so tired or angry. Before she could reply his anger continued, 'They have sliced me open. There's a great fucking zipper down my front.'

'I always wanted a scar. Like Zorro,' Cora stupidly said. She thought she was being cheering.

He stared at her cruelly. 'I'm a mess. It's all your fault. You did it. You with your let's do it today. Let's shop. All that strain and tension did it. Look at me, you bitch. Look at me.' He pulled up his gown. The cut, deep and straight, stretched from his groin up to his chest. He was stitched up, great black stitches, deep red surgical welts where the healing thread tightened and dug in.

Cora was shocked. 'I'll bring you Evian,' she said. These were the only words exchanged till it was time for her to go. She made to kiss him, but he waved her away.

Every day, then, for a week, she walked the long way from the Grassmarket to the Royal Infirmary. Every day she moved, raddled with anxiety and fear, along the corridors to the ward. Every day she sat by his bed, scarcely ever speaking. He still wore the open-backed institutional hospital bed frock. He had nothing else. Every day he was bullied from bed and forced to spend some hours sitting up. Every day he protested in French. It did not take any imagination at all to know that what he was saying was vile. He could not bear what had happened to him.

After six days of harrowing visits – blistering resentment, silent rages – Cora walked up the ward. In a few days Claude would be allowed home. Fresh sheets on their bed, roses in a milk bottle. She had spent the last of her money on a bottle of Evian and a purple African violet. She scanned faces looking for her favourite face, that set of features that was beloved. It was not there.

'Where's Claude?' she asked a passing nurse.

A shrug, a shake of the head.

'Isn't he here?' Cora indicated the bed, empty, stripped, scrubbed and regimentally tidy.

'Ask Sister,' said the nurse.

Cora looked wildly round. 'Where's Claude?' she said again. There must be some mistake. He must be here. She just couldn't see him. The nurse walked off. Cora ran after her. 'Where's Claude?' She was aware of how absurd she looked. A vivid little person blistering and hurtling down the ward. A raging splat of colour in an orderly world. She was beginning to shout. 'Where is he? Where is he?'

She saw the sister rattling down the ward, anxious to get to her, shut her up. Her arms were spread before her, pleading for quiet.

'Please, please. We can't disturb the patients.'

Everyone was staring. But then everyone stared at Cora anyway. She ran past all the beds, little gaudy speeding figure, spiked hair, hugely pregnant on skinny legs yelling, 'Where is he? Where is he? What have you done with him?'

This was her worst moment. This was her dread. He'd died, hadn't he?

The sister and a passing nurse caught hold of her and took her to the office. Cora was sobbing hysterically, mascara melting down her face.

'Fetch some tea,' the sister ordered, then, turning to Cora, switched her voice to concern. 'He's gone. Didn't he tell you?'

Cora shook her head. 'Gone where?'

'Back to France. His parents took him last night. You didn't know?'

'No.' Cora was quiet. This was a mistake. Claude was there. He was waiting for her. He hadn't left her. He wouldn't do that. Would he? 'I don't believe you,' she said finally.

'No, I expect you'd like to think it isn't true. But I'm afraid he's gone.'

'Is there a note?'

The sister shook her head.

'Nothing?'

'Nothing.'

They looked at each other. Cora was embarrassed. This woman knew she'd been abandoned, knew the failure she was. It was something Cora would prefer to be a secret.

'Is he the father of your baby?'

'Yes,' Cora nodded.

'It wouldn't have been easy. He would have needed a lot of looking after. You might not have managed.'

'I would have.' Cora was indignant.

'Yes. You probably would.' The sister recognised a valiant soul when she met one. 'I'm so sorry.'

Cora looked at her defiantly. There were tears in her eyes. Her throat was blocked and lumpen. 'Don't you effing be sorry for me. I don't want your sympathy. I can't stand all this fucking kindness.'

The sister smiled. There was, it seemed to Cora, not a thing she did not know about the business of being human. 'Yes. Kindness is a bitch, isn't it?' She handed Cora a box of medical tissues. 'Here. I'll leave you a minute to get yourself together. Then someone'll bring you some tea.'

Cora, trying to contain, or at least understand, her loss, put her head in her hands. The nurse reached out, touched her shoulder and that was all it took. That tiny bit of human contact broke Cora's resolve. She could hide her hurt no longer. She let go and wept.

The sister walked from the room. Shut the door. When she returned a few minutes later, Cora was gone.

For the rest of the day Cora walked. She walked through old Edinburgh, cobbled streets, ancient grey and fume-blackened buildings. Maroon buses grumbled past her. She moved with the bustle of the day. Stared down tiny darkened lanes, saw sudden bright signs, brilliant against the drab of the rest of the street, braying about galleries, pubs and shops she'd never noticed before. Haunted by her sadness, she read menus pinned outside restaurants: salmon with something or other wrapped in filo pastry, pan fried thingy in redcurrant coulis. 'I'll never have stuff like that,' she moaned. 'Life isn't that good to me.'

She looked at the glossily fed people on the pavement outside who, stuffed with bonhomie, were busy being interesting, making a fine public show of being fabulously happy, linking arms, putting gorgeous haircut against gorgeous haircut. They would briefly stop their display to watch gaudy Cora glumly pass, 'The state of that.' She decided that when her time came to join the greedy people on pavements outside restaurants hooting fruitily about holidays and glorious puddings whilst watching the less fortunate go by in their less fortunate outfits she would not laugh. 'I'll have been there,' she would say. 'Nothing to laugh at.' All the time the shock of what had happened lay within her. It was a twist in her stomach. A lump in her throat. It was an ache waiting to course through her if only she'd let it. But she kept it at bay, walking.

She walked through the Grassmarket past her flat. 'I'm never going in there again.' Past unshaven old men, long-term drinkers, who greeted her and other passers-by from the depth of their derelict lives with a cough, a lump of phlegm, and a 'Yumph.' They sat, multi-overcoated heaps on benches, against a backdrop of plush boutiques, pizza joints and antique shops. Only a few yards down the road and now she'd abandoned the notion of ever joining the glossy, greedy people. That was not for her. No, it would not be long before she joined the forsaken, drinking Eldorado wine, looking for fag ends in the gutter. She'd be a bag lady. She'd wear luminous socks and carry her life around in a selection of battered Tesco's carriers.

She walked up West Bow. She walked past the comic shop, a visual blast of wham and splat windows where men in masks and capes flew to save the poor and lowly. But not her. Past the joke shop – fat red false noses, fart powder and whoopee cushions, silly times. But she couldn't join in. And the coffee shop – air laden with the thick waft of a dark and tempting brew that she couldn't afford.

Down the Mound now, dragging her hand against the railings. She went into Princes Street Gardens and trailed with tourists, watching squirrels. She sat on a bench, mesmerised by the fountain, eating an ice cream that gave her heartburn. Children played at the swings beyond, little Pollyannas. She walked across the railway bridge, stood in mild shock, feeling through her the rattle of a train thundering beneath her. Panting now, she climbed the hill, went through the gate at the top of the gardens on to the Esplanade, then through the Castle. She stood staring across the top of the city – glittering roofs, spires and chimneys – to the river beyond, that expanse of pewtery blue water, shining. She loved it. But today she watched the view and knew the first real fear of her life. It had never once crossed her mind that Claude would leave her. Even while he was ill she stayed in their room alone at nights knowing he'd soon be back. Love, for some people, is the fear of losing the loved one. Love, for Cora, was the knowledge that she and Claude would never part.

'What am I going to do?' she barely whispered. All day she'd held her fear in. She'd walked the city, bent, huddled against her misery, clutching her stomach, refusing to acknowledge the dread growing within her. Now she stood up, breathed deeply and said out loud, 'I am well and truly up shit creek.'

She still could not face going back to their room. It was so full of him, his things. Out here there were people she could follow around, listen to their touristy small talk. She could pretend to be with somebody. Back home she'd have to face the start of her life alone.

Instead, when she was too tired to walk, she leaned in the doorway across the road and stared up at her window. As night came she crouched low. 'I am not going back there. I am never going back there.' In a doorway nearby a tramp coughed. People passed and momentarily stopped their laughter and chat to look at her.

'I will never go back to that room,' she vowed. 'Never. Never. Never.'

To ease the pain of this night, she did what she had done as a child to ease other pains, other dire moments; a nightmarish trip to the dentist to get her back teeth extracted, making space for her wisdom teeth; a long wait for the doctor to come when she broke her arm; a slow walk home with a dreadful report card. She took refuge in her beautiful moments past. The time she'd seen a lone swan come flying from behind a clump of trees. White it was against the forest green, wings whooshing and whistling. The perfect air on the top of a mountain, standing in that clean chill with the heathered grass wind-mown and lush like Wilton beneath her feet. That line on her father's face where, as a child, she wanted to curl up and lie for the rest of her life. Her life with Claude.

They had reached a time in their sex life when they could do it and chat. He would reach for her, lick her tits. Kiss her, tongue moving in her mouth. He'd put his hand between her legs. Watching her. And she would stroke him. Take him in her mouth sometimes. He liked her to move her tongue over his chest, his nipples. Then he'd enter her. Moving together they'd talk. It was their special trick. They'd worked at it. Oh, nothing mundane. He wouldn't say that they were out of washing powder and toothpaste. She wouldn't tell him the bulb in the light above the bed was gone. Nothing like that. This was when their conversation became fabulous.

'I saw a blue stone on the beach once,' he might say.

'I love blue. Sometimes if you climb a mountain the air is blue.

You feel you are walking through blue.'

'It was perfect. Round and perfect. I didn't pick it up. I don't want anything perfect. And I have seen a purple heron on a hill and a golden bird with soft yellow fronds flying lazily through larch trees.'

She might say, 'Oh.' Then a longer, 'Oooh.' He would watch her face.

'The loveliest thing I have seen was swans, seven white swans, only they weren't on a lake they were on grass,' she said, struggling to speak, working at controlling her body. She would finish this. 'Swimming on a deep green moist sea of grass, they were. It was twilight, and the trees were darkening in front of a promising sky. There was a slip of a moon.' She always remembered that moment. Then oh. They would move off into their private worlds. Glad to be with each other, aching for pleasure.

By four in the morning Cora could hardly move. Groaning, she rose from her despair. Cold knotted her bones. Her eyes were gummed shut and she felt her feet were glued to the floor of the world. She was chilled, shaking with chill. 'This is not good for me,' she told herself. 'And this is not good for the lump either.' She went slowly home. Slowly, for stiffness made moving problematic. She shuffled. Shuffled home.

Inside the flat she took off her boots and, still clothed, shaking like an old wino from cold and hunger, she crawled into bed. Not for Cora, then, the comfort and closeness of starlings. She was alone.

Chapter Eighteen

When Ellen and Cora were at Cora's they drank at the kitchen table. When they were at Ellen's they sat on the sofa, legs curled. Their conversations, though, always went the same way – long visits to their separate pasts, justifications, explanations and pontifications. On the sofa one night, a bottle of chianti wedged in the cushions between them, and the bottle they'd just finished lying on the floor, Ellen said, 'What happens to you when you marry? You go through this absurd ceremony. Do you, Ellen Frances, take this Daniel to be your lawful wedded husband and promise whatever it was I promised. I wasn't paying attention. Blah blah blah. And a few days later you find yourself in the supermarket queue buying Vim. There was no mention of Vim in that ceremony. I never bought it when I was single.'

'You must have been really filthy,' Cora said.

Ellen considered this. 'Do you know, I think I was. I think I was born filthy. I don't think you develop. I think you are born what you are.'

'Maybe it's to do with conception. Maybe you take on the mood of the moment you were conceived. Happy people will have been conceived in orgasm. Miserable people not. And those crazed, unsatisfied, frustrated folk – well, say no more. We've all been there.'

'So what's all that got to do with me being filthy?'

Cora pulled a face. 'Knowing your mother, she was probably worried about the sheet getting rumpled and stained. Now I come to think about it, Sam was conceived in absurd passion, and with Col I was looking for a little comfort. And look, Sam's all hot-headed and difficult to deal with and Col is the easiest human being alive. He's a joy.' Warming to her theme, she was convincing herself that there was some substance in her theory.

'What about you, then? How do you explain yourself, Cora O'Brien?'

'I was conceived in a warm marital bed by two loving parents. I have no excuse for myself. Unless of course my mother was faking it. There's that. Maybe that explains everything.'

When Cora had been in labour for four hours she phoned home. There was, she realised, nothing else to do.

'Mum,' she wailed down the line, 'I think the baby's coming.'

There was a brief terse silence before her mother gave in to her maternal concerns and heaped Cora with questions.

'Where are you? Are you at the hospital? How far apart are the pains? If you're not at the hospital, did you get in touch with your doctor? Where's that young man of yours?'

'I'm not at the hospital. I haven't phoned the doctor. And my young man has gone back to France.'

'What do you mean, gone back to France?'

'Just that. He's gone.'

'Are you on your own?' Her mother sounded horrified.

'Yes.'

'What have you been doing?'

'Reading paperbacks. Eating baked potatoes and going to the clinic. That's about it.'

'We're on our way.'

Of course Cora could not hold on. By the time Irene and Bill packed the car, got someone to look after the rest of the family and drove to Edinburgh, they were grandparents.

There is nothing like a baby, a grandchild, to heal family feuds. If Irene left home still bristling disapproval at her errant daughter's behaviour it took only one glimpse of the infant for her to forgive Cora her naughtiness, her hairstyle, her makeup, her big boots, her pierced ears – everything.

'Oh, what are you going to call him?' she crooned.

'Sam,' said Cora. 'Sam William O'Brien.'

'That's lovely,' Irene wept, great tears falling from her eyes. A grandchild was lovely. Cora was lovely. Life was lovely. Irene was hugely happy and was planning to go out and spend as much as possible on baby things. Baby things were lovely.

'What have you been doing all alone?' Bill asked Cora. 'That's a terrible thing to be – alone. When you're having a baby and all.'

Cora shrugged. Alone, she'd discovered, was not as bad as she'd thought it would be. Besides, she hadn't really been on her own. She'd formed quite a relationship with the child within, chatting to it, reading to it, planning with it, discussing songs on the radio. 'Oh, that's my fave of the moment.' In fact, after a while she'd become hooked on alone. But alone was not to last long.

Claude wrote to her. He wept on to the paper that he did not want to leave her, and he did not want to stay any longer. 'I would not get well staying in that room. I need space. I need time. Food, wine. I need air.'

'Huh!' Cora was incensed. 'Air indeed. We might not be so hot on the food and wine but we've got air. We have got air. Air we have aplenty,' she told the room. A week alone and she was already talking to herself. It was a habit that would stay for the rest of her life.

She'd find herself the subject of strangers' stares and smirks in the supermarket when looking through the veg. Picking up carrots and onions, carefully squeezing them and tossing back the unacceptable. 'We're not having you. And you're too soft. You'll do. And you. But *you're* not coming home with me.' If the starer got too critical Cora would turn. 'Speaking to the carrots and to myself,' she'd say briskly. 'Well, mostly to myself. I like speaking to myself. I know I'm not going to give me an argument.'

'How are you?' Claude asked in his letter. 'Are you well?'

'Ha,' Cora cried out loud. 'No, I'm not well. I'm effing up the spout with your baby. I've got constant indigestion and I'm spending my days sitting by the window retaining water. That's all I do these days – retain water. I'm all puffy and squishy,' she howled.

'Take care,' he wrote. 'Please take care of yourself.'

'You don't mean take care of me,' Cora said. 'You mean take care of it. The baby you are working hard at not mentioning. You haven't told your folks, have you? They don't know about me, and they don't know about it. Damn you.'

She threw down the letter. But that was not enough; he deserved rougher treatment than that. She stamped on it. Still not enough. She jumped on it. Then she picked it up and tore in two. Then two again. And two again till tearing it became too difficult. Feeling a little tired she threw it in the bin and sank on to the bed.

He sent money which she held now. He must have got it from his parents. She considered throwing it away too, but didn't. There was too much of it to toss aside temperamentally. She was furious, but she wasn't daft. She needed all she could get. He had, he told her, posted to the landlord money to pay the rent for the next six months. If she needed anything, anything at all, just write, just ask. She never did. After Sam was born she never even told him he had a son. She suspected he was relieved she never got in touch.

She washed the junk from her face, let her hair grow and joined the library. She ate sensibly, drank milk and read. Every night she sat by her open window watching summertime people passing below, listening to songs on her radio, a book in her lap.

One day, walking home with this week's armful from the library shelves, she was overcome with an urgent need to stop feeling scared and alone. 'I have to do this,' she told herself. 'I have to get a grip on myself. I will cross the road and the fear and loneliness will be over,' she said. 'I will be fine.' She crossed the road. Stood and took stock of herself and her nerves. No. She was still scared, still a wreck. 'Cross back. The moment my feet hit the other side, I will be fine. I will be fine.' She crossed again. It came from nowhere, a feeling of calm. My goodness, she thought, I'm almost happy. Only almost, of course. But if this is as good as it gets, it'll do. It'll have to do. She walked on. 'I matter,' she said. And knowing the truth of her condition, 'I have to matter.'

After Sam was born Cora's mother was convinced she would come home. 'She'll have to,' she said to Bill when they went to visit her on her last day in hospital. 'She can't go back to that room. It's not right. It's not hygienic.'

Bill shook his head. 'You better not be telling her that.' He knew Cora would not come home. 'You don't understand, do you?' he said. 'She feels she's let us down. And she thinks she's let herself down. She'll not be coming back till she's redeemed herself.'

'Redeemed herself!' Irene had never heard such rot. 'She'll not have a lot of time for that sort of thing. She's a child to rear. She better put redeeming herself out of her head.'

But Bill knew the truth of it. 'All I'm saying,' he said, 'is she's ashamed to go back. She left with high hopes and she's not likely to return with bloody pierced ears and a bloody baby till she's got her dignity. So if you want to see your grandson you better get used to long journeys in the car and not sit tutting and sighing for miles and miles with that damned bag on your knee.'

Irene allowed herself one last tut and sigh and turned on Bill. 'Damn you and your "blister and hurtle, Cora". You started it. Now here you are with your redemption and dignity.' She feebly hit his shoulder. 'I hate it when you're right. She'll need a fridge.'

'What,' said Bill, sensing that his flash of insight was going to cost him money, 'has that got to do with anything? And why does everything end with me paying out?'

'Dignity and redemption are all very well but she's got a young baby, she can't go running out for food whenever. She'll need a fridge. And I'll bet the silly bugger hasn't even got herself down on the housing list.'

Cora came home to a little room transformed. There was a cot in the corner, an armchair and a fridge full of food.

'Oh,' Irene withered defensively, 'I know it's not to your taste. It's all pinks and blues and babyish. And that chair's not your sort of chair. But you'll be glad of a proper sit down soon enough. And it folds down into a single bed so there'll be somewhere for you to sleep when your father and me come to stay.'

'I know. I know,' Cora said, vaguely dismissing all this. She had her baby home and she was anxious to get on with being a mother, whatever that entailed. She wasn't sure.

Oh no, Irene thought. You don't know anything.

Cora was to discover in the next few weeks the difference between knowing and *knowing*.

'It's like,' she told Ellen, 'knowing that if you shove your finger in the electric socket you'll get a shock, and actually doing it. Then the *knowing* starts. You are flung across the room, land on your bum, hair on end, heart shuddering and stomping. And you think:

Right enough that's what happens. That's when the *knowing* starts.'

She spent the first six weeks of Sam's life at full hurtle. Milky, stained, bleeding and knackered, she zombied from feed to feed, carrying bundles of laundry. It hurt to sit. And it hurt to stand. She lived on bacon sandwiches and the only thing she did for herself was make the bed the instant she got out of it. She knew she'd be too wrecked to do it when it was time to crawl back in. Every four hours it seemed her breasts filled up, itched and ached. Sweet, nutty milk dribbled down her front. Hot and sticky, she could not wait for him to take his fill, empty her out. It was her pleasure, so, so nice, that little mouth on her nipple, the small noises he made, tiny perfect hand clenching on her as he fed. But she cried a lot. She did not know it was possible to feel this tired. When the baby cried, and oh how he cried, she cried. They howled together. When he cried the sound of it, the pitch, cut right through to the depth of her. She had to stop the noise, she had to. When feeding, comforting, changing the nappy did not stop it the only relief she could find was to cry along. She stood clutching him to her, patting him, rocking him, wailing too.

'What a pair of major dweebs we are. Scream along with Cora and Sam,' she snivelled.

Once a day at first, then once a week, the health visitor called. She worried about such a young girl alone with a baby, so she fussed and looked discreetly around for signs of Cora not managing. But Cora wasn't going to let her weariness show to anybody official. Every time she called, Cora could not wait for her to go away.

There was nobody but the baby in her life. Sometimes she longed for someone else to talk to, someone else to pick him up, to feed him so that she could sleep, just sleep. She felt she was moving, wall-eyed with despair, through a bad dream. 'Please let it end.' She was slave to a tiny, incontinent, hairless, toothless master. Then one day in mid-nightmare, the baby smiled. The little bald and gummy face lit up when she came looming into view. She felt like a star.

'Good job you did that,' she said to him. 'Things were getting a bit one-sided between us. Know what I mean? I was beginning to feel I was doing all the running.' The baby smiled again. Her heart turned over. She didn't know it could do that. They stood, mother

and baby, beaming at each other, rock 'n' roll tinnily blaring from
the little tranny on the sink, babygros dripping, traffic rumbling in
the street outside.

'We can do this, kid,' she said.

By the time Sam was six months old she'd sung him her entire
range of Neil Young and Van Morrison. She explained to the little
face in her arms that people like her who could not properly sing a
note could do Neil Young for, truth be told, he couldn't properly
sing either. In the pubs of her days of abandonment her old friends
were sneering still.

It mattered not one whit what she read him. When she was stuck
it was the leader column in an old newspaper that she'd brought
home wrapped round a pound of carrots. A sweet soft whisper
lilting through the evening. He seemed to like Robert Frost – 'And
miles to go before I sleep, And miles to go before I sleep' – but
Kerouac was the one. *Big Sur* was never intended as a lullaby but
set him sleeping every time, didn't let them down. The sea was the
sea wherever it was – California or the Inner Hebrides. Cora read
and remembered picnics at Calgary Bay years ago. White sand hot
between her toes, clear green water, salt on her lips, and Irene
sitting on a tartan rug waiting with the family's huge blue and white
towel for her children to come shivering and wet to her. She'd wrap
them up, rub them dry, then dish out ginger biscuits and American
cream soda. In her little room Cora read and drifted back to softer
days when sand coated her skinny legs and the sea cooled and
slipped over her. She moved her tongue over her lips and could
have sworn she tasted salt. The movement, the surf, Cora's endless
rolling whisper and little thumb moved into little mouth, eyes
rolled back and there it was – the most precious moment of the day.
The baby slept, leaving her free to do whatever she wanted, which
was mostly sleep, too.

By the time Sam was nine months old they had games they
played, hiding and making faces and zooming the aeroplane full of
boiled egg in through the air to the mouth. 'Here it comes. Here it
comes.' Zigzagging the laden spoon across the sky, little mouth
open wide. Going out for walks Cora would charge the pushchair
along the pavement top speed, baby laughing. Blister and hurtle,

Cora, blister and hurtle. If shoppers and tourists got in her way she'd yell, 'Peep, peep. Toot, toot. Stand aside please, incontinent person coming through.' She'd shove the child forward. Coming home they would, when traffic allowed, always walk on the cobbles. The rough roads suited them. Battered through them, 'Ah. Aaaaah . . .' they sang. Jagged and rough like the road, their song would rattle out of their throats.

Once a month Irene and Bill came to visit. And at last, after nine visits, Irene admitted that her daughter was managing. To her surprise, their grandson was beaming and healthy.

'You seem to be managing,' she accused.

'Oh yes,' said Cora. 'We're doing fine.' She did not mention the nightmare time before the smile when she'd been tempted to place a soothing pillow over the howls just for a second, just for some peace. Just for a small guilt-free, silent moment.

'And,' Irene said eventually – as if this was a continuation of some previous conversation. It wasn't. It was the worry that had been rattling round her head since she'd discovered her daughter was pregnant – 'what are you going to do now? What about money? How are you going to manage?'

'I get social security. I get my rent paid. Family allowance. You send me money.' Every week they sent her money. 'But, I was thinking,' Cora said, 'Sam could go to a nursery and I could go back to college. Otherwise I'll have to get a job.'

'What doing?'

'What can I do? Wait tables? Wash dishes? I'll have to take what I can get.'

Cora sulked. For nine intense months she'd been cocooned in this little room with her child, hiding herself away from her wrecked ambitions, refusing to face up to the looming fact that she had the rest of her life to get through. Now here was Irene confronting her, the world was out there and it was time to get back to it. She had responsibilities now. She tutted and huffed.

Irene responded with a piece of disapproving breathing and told Cora she should get out for the night. They would baby-sit. She was so adamant about it, so eager to be left in charge of her first grandson, Cora didn't like to spoil her fun. A baby needed a grandmother, she figured. She couldn't bring herself, then, to tell her mother that she'd lost touch with her friends. She had nobody to go anywhere with. For the first time in months she dressed up, did her hair, painted her face, and set out. She couldn't say she had no money and nowhere to go. For an hour she walked up and down outside then, feeling the cold, went to the pub across the road to spend tomorrow's lunch money on a pint of Guinness.

She thought she would make it last. She would sit in the corner unnoticed, sipping slowly till ten, then she could go home. She worried about the baby. Longed to check that her mother was doing everything right, going through his little routine. Was he crying? Would she read to him? And what about his bath? Could her mother cope? She fretted. And fretting made her drink.

It was not part of her plan to get picked up. But it was nice to be noticed as a woman again. She'd quite forgotten she was one. She thought he said his name was Michael. He slipped into her life so easily, sitting opposite her, starting that flirtatious small talk that's so exciting because, well, you never know where it's going to get you. Was she alone? Was she a student? Well yes, she said, sort of. Not exactly any more. But she was going to get back to it, definitely that, yes. She did not tell him about Sam. Later, remembering, she was ashamed of herself. Did she want another drink? Oh no, she shook her head. I'm fine. She indicated her glass, noticing for the first time that it was empty.

'I'll get you another anyway,' he said. And that went down so easily, so quickly, he got her yet another. She felt the tension ease from her shoulders, and knew she was smiling too much. It was that pleasant drunkenness when she knew she'd had too much to drink and was too drunk to care. She realised though that it had been a while since she'd touched alcohol. She wasn't cool any more. It rushed to her head.

He lived in Jeffrey Street, and took her back to his place. It smelled of curry. There was a view of the railway from the back window. The only drink he had was cherry brandy and they were both drunk enough to think themselves sober enough to drink it.

It was so nice, so nice to be touched again. 'Put your hands on my back,' she said. 'Touch me.' They made love in an inebriated calm.

It was wonderful. So wonderful to feel someone next to her, on her, in her. She put her head on his chest. Kissed his neck, slid on top of him and made love again. 'It's the comfort,' she said, whispering in the dark. 'I just want some comfort. Someone to take my mind off it all.' He was happy to oblige. 'Sometimes,' she told him, 'it gets so lonely. It's nice to have someone who talks back. He likes Dylan, but my favourite is Van Morrison. Do you like Van? Say goodbye to Madam George,' she sang. 'I like your skin,' she stroked him. 'I love it. Look at me, pale and unhealthy. You're fabulous,' she laughed. She was very, very drunk. He hadn't a clue what she was talking about. 'How was it for you?' she asked.

'Wonderful,' he smiled. He was so polite. Such a gent, she thought.

'And how was it for me?' she asked.

'From the sounds of it wonderful too,' he told her. After they made love a third time they slipped into an alcoholic void.

Oh, the shame when she woke. She brought herself to life with her own snoring. Naked, she sprawled across the bed, and for a moment she did not know where she was, or who it was snoring next to her. There was a blissful blank a few seconds before she remembered. 'Oh no,' she said. 'Oh, please no.' Her head hurt, her mouth was dry and horrible. 'Oh God,' she whispered, for speaking any louder would be too painful. She looked about the room for her clothes. Then went to find the lavatory.

She was sick and lay on the floor, curled and clutching her knees, thinking the thing to do would be to stay like that here on the floor for the rest of her life. This unsanitary place smelling of pee is all I deserve as a resting place. Why do men miss? She lay gazing at the Harpic and the loo brush, and hanging just above her a greying comfortless towel. Someone somewhere was playing Steely Dan, 'Rikki Don't Lose That Number'. She wept a little. 'I have done a dreadful thing,' she said. 'I'm not fit. I'm not fit . . .' to be a mother, she thought.

Four o'clock in the morning she ran through the streets though she wasn't dressed for speed. Her heels stormed the silence. There was panic in her throat, her heart pounded. Oh God, oh God, oh God. What if something's happened? What if the baby's ill? What if they're waiting up for me? She ran, handbag banging on her leg, and conjured dread scenarios in her head. Her mother had dropped the baby and they were all in hospital but they couldn't find her. Now she'd turn up at this time and find the police waiting. Her mother and father had waited up for her and would be sitting bolt upright, looking grim. They'd declare her an unfit mother and look at her and know from that one glance the mischief she'd been up to. Oh God.

Normally she enjoyed being up early. She liked the feel of having the city to herself and a moment's easy breathing when the air is clear, unleaded before everything wakes and the bustle and rush starts up again. Not this morning though. This morning her throat was tight and lumpen; several times she had to stop and lean on a doorpost, gasping and panic-stricken. She reached her doorway, ran up the stairs, then stopped outside her door. Silence. She straightened her clothes and worked at her breathing, hauling great draughts of air into her lungs. Calm down, she told herself. Then she went in.

There was only people sleeping. There was a curtain pulled round her bed, behind it Irene and Bill snored. In his cot the baby lay, fists clenched, head to one side, a small sweat damping his head. Cora let her fingers trail across his brow. Then she slipped from her clothes and crawled into the bed her mother had made up in the fold-down chair.

At seven she heard her mother move about the room. She lay watching her.

'I can't lie,' Irene said. Irene, it seemed to Cora, had the knack of knowing what other people were thinking or doing seemingly without casting even the smallest glance in their direction. How did she do that? Without turning her head Irene knew Cora was awake. 'I know I should, but I can't lie. Soon as my eyes are open I have to get up. Did you have a good time?'

'Yes,' said Cora. 'Wonderful.'

'What time did you get back?'

'... Um,' said Cora. 'Don't really know.'

Irene turned to look at her daughter. 'Goodness, you look awful. Are you all right?'

'I'm fine. I've got a bit of a headache. I think I've got flu coming on.' Cora coughed a bit and sniffed. Irene sighed. She knew a hangover when she saw one. Why did her children always pretend to her? She tutted and turned to switch off the kettle. Was there, perhaps, something naïve about her that her children always put on this absurd display of innocence? 'This'll sort you out.' She gave Cora a cup of tea and a long piercing look. Cora winced.

'I hope you haven't been up to what I think you've been up to,' Irene accused.

'What do you mean by that?' Cora was defensive but, sipping her tea, avoided eye contact.

'You know fine what I mean,' Irene said.

Cora shrugged. 'No I don't.' She hid her face behind her cup, drinking. She wondered if, when her son grew up, she'd be as perceptive as Irene. Would she accuse with fierce glances and tight-lipped silences? Oh no, not her. She'd be the perfect understanding mother. She was sure of that.

Remembering – and how could she forget? – she said to Ellen, 'One day you wake with the hangover that is a hangover too far and you realise your time has come. The reckoning is no longer nigh. The reckoning is here.'

The reckoning was there for Cora six weeks later when she threw up first thing in the morning, when her breasts felt tingly and she had that old familiar longing for a sweet and fizzy drink.

'Oh Christ,' she said to Sam, 'I'm fucked.'

'Fucked,' said Sam, clear and loud, ten and a bit months old. It was his first word. And considering the times ahead, very appropriate.

Cora picked him up, held him aloft. 'Oh cool,' she crooned. 'I love it. You're so clever. What a clever boy.' Then, realising the word he'd mastered, decided this was when the swearing had to stop. 'Pity, I like a good curse. There are some things you just have to swear about. Like being pregnant. Oh God,' clutching the child to her, 'what am I going to do?'

She ignored it. For three months she vaguely hoped it would go away. But when plainly it was here to stay she went to the doctor and had her condition confirmed. By then it was too late to do anything about it. She did not, however, confess her folly to her mother and father. More than she worried about her pregnancy, she worried about them, what they would say. She had let them down again. She was about to break their hearts again. Every time she phoned home she meant to mention it, but couldn't.

'How are you?' Irene would breezily ask down the phone. 'And more important, how's my boy?'

'Fine,' Cora would say. 'We're both fine.' She told them that Sam had started to talk, but didn't mention what he'd said.

'Any word on the nursery? Have you tried to get Sam in anywhere? Have you gone to see about getting back into college?'

'Um . . . not exactly. Soon. I'll do it soon.'

When she was five months into her pregnancy the terror set in. The what-ifs started. What if social workers found out about her and took her babies away? The room could not contain three people. How was she going to live? What was to become of her?

'Only one thing for it,' she said to Sam. 'Face up to it. It's a bitch but there you are.' She went to the council offices to see about getting rehoused and found to her astonishment that she was already high on the list. Her mother had put her name down months ago.

'With another one on the way you'll be a priority,' she was told. 'It won't be great but better than one room.'

'Anything,' said Cora. 'Anything.'

Two weeks later she got word that she'd been allocated a three-room flat in Leith. 'Near the water,' she said to Sam. 'We'll love it.'

They got the bus, riding upstairs for the view, and went to explore. She found her new address in Giles Street. One floor up and along a lengthy balcony. There was a motorbike under construction outside her door, bits of oily things lying scattered. She was aware of curtains moving in flats nearby. Children stopped playing to stare blatantly.

'Look, Sam, pals. You'll have friends here.' She was working hard at convincing herself.

That night she phoned home to tell her mother and father she was moving. Bill insisted they come to help.

'No. No.' Standing in the phone box Cora shook her head, waved her hands. 'No, really. I don't need help. It's too far to come. I'll be fine.'

'We'll be there,' Bill said.

A week later Irene took one look at Cora, turned and walked out the room.

'How could you?' she yelled when, seconds later, she returned. She had too much anger battering through her veins to cope with stairs or the street. She wanted to throw something. She wanted to hit someone. Cora. 'How could you?'

Cora shrugged. 'It was easy,' she said. 'The tricky bit starts in a few months. And it goes on for the rest of my life.'

'Good glib remark,' said Irene. 'Don't get smart with me. I know when this happened. That night. That night we baby-sat. You were doing this . . .' She waved her hand at Cora's pregnancy. 'What kind of slut are you, anyway?'

'The best kind,' said Cora simply. 'I enjoy it.'

Her mother hit her. The baby started to howl. Bawl. Bill picked him up and walked him up and down. Cora glumly rubbed her stinging cheek.

'There's no need to smack the girl,' Bill said. 'What's done's done.'

'What's done's done. Just like you. Just like a man. You have no idea. Two children, no father. There is nothing to be philosophical about. She'll need a cooker.' She turned on Cora again. 'I don't suppose you've even given that a thought.'

'Actually I have. But I didn't give it much of a thought.' She was frightened of moving from her room. For months she had shared it with her son, and in it they had built up a small world of their own. She felt safe here, bricked in, tucked away from her worries which she knew were out there beyond her four walls waiting for her, refusing to go away. Nights now were starting to crowd in on her. What am I going to do? No money and in that place. Me, a pushchair and two bleating infants needing their noses wiped. That's what will become of me. Miles and miles with shopping and tired moaning babies. Miles and miles.

'I will not trudge,' she said.

'Well,' said Irene, 'it will take all that passion of yours to stop yourself. Trudging with babes, we've all done it. When you've two little ones and miles to go before you shop, trudging comes naturally.'

142

And miles to go before I shop, And miles to go before I shop. Cora's brain was running on empty. It was the first time she had heard her mother speak as if passion were normal, a part of her. It was the first time she realised her mother had passion too. It was the first time they'd spoken as women.

'I'm scared,' she said.

'Yes,' her mother heaved, agreeing. 'I'd be scared if I were you.'

It was a grubby day, struggle and woe. They took Cora's few possessions from her room. Sweating and swearing, bitterly blaming each other as they wedged round corners and bashed fingers, they got everything into the hired van. Cora listened to her father and mother battering down three flights, arguing all the way.

'It's you can't carry furniture.'

'No, it's you.'

'You can be married to someone for umpteen years,' Irene scathed, 'but it isn't till you carry an armchair down three flights of stairs with them that you discover the truth about them.'

Cora wandered about her room touching things for the last time. Saying goodbye. Goodbye to everything, her little life with her son and the times she'd had with Claude. He wouldn't come back, she knew that now. She'd spent weeks, months, thinking that any moment he would burst in carrying goodies. When she went out she always wondered if when she got back he'd be there lounging on the bed, waiting for her. She looked at the spot under the window where the army of milk bottles had stood. He'd be leaving other messes in other flats now, nothing to do with her. She'd never see him again.

At the other end, bleary with effort and scarcely speaking, they carried her bed, Sam's cot and her armchair up past the skeletal motorbike and in the main door, painted yellow, wire mesh in the glass, a heavy-duty spring that creaked hugely whenever it opened.

There was a comfortless institutionalised hallway with a begrudging and bleakly clean smell and a constant wind that swirled up skirts, flapped jackets. It was a low-rise grey stone block with bright doors and windows, unsubtle slabs of colour – blue, orange, yellow – a municipal notion of cheerful. Someone somewhere had conjured a life that worked well on a drawing board, on a cardboard model. It was the living of it that was the bitch.

Cora's flat was first floor left. Every room was painted orange. The tiles in the kitchen were grey marl filthy. She wandered through her three rooms saying, 'This is fine. I can do this.' Over and over she said it, ignoring Irene's scrutiny

'Where are you going to plant the hollyhocks?' Irene asked, staring out the window at the building across the road.

'Oh,' said Cora. 'Down at the bottom where it gets the sun. I'll have a herb garden just beyond the croquet lawn and beech hedges. I'll wander the flowerbeds snipping lupins and delphiniums, laying them gently side by side in my trug basket. In summer I'll snip a little fresh mint to put on my new potatoes. And I'll have honeysuckle at the door so I can get the scent in summer. It'll waft in. Waft. Waft. I'll breathe it in as I sit on the back step shelling peas and singing lullabies.' She indicated the flow of scented breeze with a soft wave.

'Oh well. If you can still dream . . .' Irene's voice trailed off.

Next day, driving home, she said, 'I think Cora might be all right.'

And Bill, enthusiastic as ever, said, 'Of course she'll be all right. She won all those races, didn't she? She's got fire. She would have won the final only she pushed too soon.'

'It seems to be developing into a lifetime's bad habit,' Irene scathed. Then, softly, after a small silence: 'She'll be fine. As long as she doesn't look at other women.'

'Why would she be doing that?'

'Women look at each other. They watch. They judge. If Cora looks at other women she'll see herself as they see her, and it'll break her heart.'

Cora, meantime, was setting about her kitchen floor with a bucket of hot water, some Flash and a deal of optimism. Sam watched.

'Look!' she shouted. 'It isn't grey marl at all. It's black-and-white tiles. I can live with this.' And she scrubbed with even more fervour.

Halfway across the floor her enthusiasm waned. She fell forward, laid her face on her arms, bum in the air. 'This is hell, Sam.

Sodding floor. I know, I know. Don't swear, you'll only pick it up.'
She sighed deeply, took up her brush, did a single swift two-handed
scrub and collapsed once more. She fell into a human heap, then
rolled on to her back, stared up. Sam, seizing the moment, as
children will, climbed on top of her. He was clutching a bright
yellow plastic squeaky hammer that among all his toys had become
beloved.

'I can't say I think much of your taste in toys, Sam. I prefer the
red bricks. Is this a statement of your maleness, this hammer?' She
took it, squeaked it violently. Gently batted his forehead. 'You can
see the sky from here, Sam.' Then a confession, a swift relating of a
few truths before he was old enough to understand what she was
saying to him.

'I have led a scrawny life, Sam. My successes are all unmention-
able moments of pleasure. I don't even know the name of the man
who is father to squidge number two. Know what I mean, Sam?
Shameful. I have let my folks down. Oh, I have climbed a few
mountains, and won a couple of races. Other people are doing
worthwhile, happening, career-motivating things and I am lying
here on the floor on my back looking out at baby clothes flapping
on the line. I have ruined my chances.'

The child took his hammer, and sucked it. He put his little arms
round her neck. She kissed the warm top of his blonding head, held
him to her. 'Still,' she said, 'we've a new cooker arriving in the
morning. The tiles are black and white. You can see the sky from the
kitchen floor. The social security will get us a sofa. Is this as good as
it gets? What do you think? Someone up there likes us? Ha ha. Some
boozer angel perhaps has put in a slurred word for me. God, Sam,
how are we going to cope?' She would have cried but pregnant,
hormones and all, she seemed to have left tears behind. Pity, crying
helped. 'How do you do that again?'

Four months later Col was born. Three days before Cora went
into labour Bill and Irene came to stay. Bill took Cora to hospital,
stayed with her, then chickened out just before the birth, backing
out of the delivery room waving his arms saying, 'No. No. I don't
think so.' And, 'Please don't ask me to stay. I couldn't. I just
couldn't.'

When he took his second grandson into his arms all he said was, 'He's gorgeous, Cora. You make a beautiful baby, so you do.' Next day Irene took the child to her and gazed down with unreserved love. 'Hello you,' she said. She turned to her daughter. 'Well, Cora, never a dull moment, eh?'

'What do you think?' said Cora. 'As we are conceived so we continue? Sam's all passion.'

'Blister and hurtle?' suggested Ellen.

Cora ignored her. 'And Col is a constant comfort, smiley and sweet-natured.'

'And they both love their mum,' said Ellen.

'The sex and drugs and rock 'n' roll I gave up for them, they better,' Cora blistered. 'They bloody better.'

Chapter Nineteen

'What's the most important thing in your life?' Ellen asked.

'Moisturiser,' said Cora.

'Apart from that.'

'There is nothing else. I have my children. And the pleasure of being me and just me – not mother, not daughter – just Cora, now that I have forsaken sex. And I had to give up swearing in front of the children, smoking on account of the children. So there is vodka, and there is moisturiser. It has come to that.'

'Swearing's good,' said Ellen. 'I seem to swear more now that I'm getting older.'

'Yes, you're getting angry. You get angry young men who are furious about all the things they'll never have. And angry middle-aged women furious when they realise all the things they might have had.'

'We will not trudge,' said Cora. 'We will buy some cornflakes and some potatoes and milk and bread.' We will walk there and back and we will not look at people, she thought. I do not want to see myself in their faces. She noted the fear of it in her diary.

She'd started writing down her feelings in a small notebook. She thought that since giving birth, which was the biggest thing that had happened to her, her feelings had become smaller and smaller, and were now on the same scale as the book. She thought about laundry and feeds. She was aware that she was demanding absurd standards of herself. 'Each day,' she wrote, 'I try to give my children love, fresh air, clean clothes, some education, chocolate, play, a bath, stories . . . So who do I think I am? God? Is this what they call coping?'

She thought it silly, but living as she did with only two small children to talk to and neighbours who did not indulge in the sort of brutal self-scourging she did, it was really a conversation with herself.

A year in her new home and Cora knew every lamppost between her house and the shops. She knew a million shades of grey. Blue-grey, green-grey but always grey. Walking with children, eyes constantly at child level she was keenly aware of the concrete bases of lampposts. 'And God created man,' she sighed. 'And man created lamppost bases. And you do not guide yourself through the maze by the stars. Forget them. Guide yourself home to safety by the graffiti. Left by the big red "Fuck off", left again at the third sprayed blue "Shag" and on to the end of the road.'

The grass was grey. Not the grass in the little postage stamp patches of garden between pavement and house, that were either vibrantly, greenly neglected or defiantly tamed and nurtured. It was the municipal grass that scrubbily grew along the outside edge of the pavements and in the small parks that never made it to lushness. Underdog grass, Cora thought. Trampled and peed on, denied the right to be green.

Every day she walked down to the river. She found it wasn't as far as she'd imagined to the shops, which were an eclectic mix of delicatessen and corner newsagent. There were new restaurants, striped canopies alongside old pubs. She liked it here. She belonged. Every day she sat on a bench staring out at the water. There were new buildings heaving into the skyline. It wasn't like home. At home the water was bluer, cleaner. There were fishing boats and all sorts of sailing boats. There were mountains. She ached to see them again. 'But I will not go back. I will not go back till I can face them again.' Sometimes she'd sit till the cold cut through her – she almost enjoyed the chill. Only her children's protesting howls – they were cold and they were hungry – made her get up and go back to her flat.

Cora had a brown carpet on her floor, a sofa of sorts in her living room, a cooker in her kitchen. And she had the thin and terrifying Mrs Lawrence across the hallway looking out for her. Mrs Lawrence arrived at Cora's door two days after she moved in.

'Just called to introduce myself,' she said, ducking her head from side to side so that she could see past Cora, openly nosy. 'I'm Betty from across the way there. You're all settled, then?'

'As much as I can be,' said Cora. Betty had already noted her new neighbour's condition, her child and the obvious lack of a man in her life.

'On your own, then?'

Cora shook her head, looked her new neighbour in the eye. 'I've got Sam.'

'Great age,' said Betty. 'I love them that age. Pity they have to grow.' Then smiling, 'Come and have some tea.'

Wasn't it odd, Cora thought. One minute you were charging about stores getting hot and horny shoplifting, or fucking some bloke for all your worth with Steely Dan playing somewhere off stage. And the next here you were sitting taking comfort in some shiny yellow kitchen, breathing in the fumes of Mr Sheen and Jif, sipping milky tea, talking children. How did that happen? And what was it about having children that you found such a moment soothing when it should send you screaming for the horizon, waving your arms and bawling, 'Let me outta here'? Why, this was almost pleasant. Only almost, though. Keep a grip on that almost, girl, Cora warned herself.

Betty drained her cup, rose to take it to the sink and rinse it out. But Cora reached for it, and gazed deeply in.

'You're safe,' she said. 'There's an umbrella here. You've been in some sort of danger. Exposed. Some worry perhaps. But you're safe now.'

Betty cried out, 'Amazing. How did you know? I've just had the all-clear. Just this morning. That's why I came, really.' Lowering her voice, about to confide a truth, she said, 'I needed to talk.' She brought a letter from her apron. 'They thought it was cancer. But it's not. A benign lump. I've been worried. There was nobody to tell. Oh, I could tell my husband, Will. But he's a man.' A man – what did he know about lumps?

Betty clasped her hands and considered Cora anew. 'You read cups,' she said delighted. What a find. What a fabulous friend. There was awe in her voice.

Cora nodded. 'My grandmother taught me.'

'Amazing,' said her neighbour. Cora smiled. She was made. She had a baby-sitter for life.

Word spread. Cora became, in a small street-to-street way, famous. Every morning brought a new invitation to tea. Every morning she was handed cup after hopeful cup. Tell me how it is, Cora. Tell me what I want to hear, Cora. Sometimes women would knock on her door at eight or nine at night and hand her cups with strange tea leaf patterns brought gingerly through the dark.

'What does this mean?' she'd be asked. 'What's going to happen to me?'

Cora would take the cup, turn it to the light, look into it and give her verdict. 'Tea leaves do not predict the future,' she would always say. 'They only tell you what is. It helps you realise to the full the time you are living through. That's all.'

Afterwards she would throw herself on her battered sofa, loudly declaring her despair. Sam, and later Col, would watch quietly. They were used to their mother's outbursts.

'What do they want? What can I say? Oh, I know what to tell them. Everything's fine, that's what. Everything's fine. God's in His heaven and your mummy still loves you.'

Still, being a soothsayer she was forgiven her sins. Nobody mentioned her children's lack of a father or her strange clothes. In fact, strange clothes were now expected of her. Nobody minded what they considered to be smelly and oily French cooking. And nobody minded her strange daily wanderings, crisply telling her children not to trudge.

'We're off to explore the neighbourhood. No trudging.'

And on the way home, Sam and Col would plead, 'Please, please let's trudge. Trudging's best.'

'OK. Just this once, you can trudge for three lampposts, then walk three, then trudge three.'

She was forgiven the weird things she brought home, goodies liberated from skips carried triumphantly home in the pushchair whilst behind her back her children defiantly trudged. Stamp, stamp, stamp of little feet. Gleeful looks, there is no pleasure finer than not doing what you're told. Well, Cora knew all about that.

'Look, an old oval mirror. A picture frame. A bentwood chair needing stripped.'

'Christ, Cora. My granny threw stuff like that out.' The rubbish Cora brought home puzzled Betty. It mysteriously stopped being rubbish and would appear transformed and desirable in Cora's kitchen, living room, or bathroom. In lieu of daily tea cup readings Betty lent Will to help paint over the orange walls. Cora rescued roots and cast-off bits of plant from dustbins and skips, a more legitimate plunder than her earlier thievings. She planted them in pots out on the balcony outside her door. At first they were dug up and tossed on to cars parked in the street below. But Cora just planted more. Things grew for Cora. In time her tiny potted garden became part of the backdrop and it was for most of the time left alone.

Every day she walked to the play park or the shops and every day she and the boys played games. The bears, Sam's invention, lived behind the wall with 'Shag' sprayed blue and they wore checked trousers and red caps, and they were watching them. There were thirty-three manhole covers between the house and the play park. Stamp on each one and count. Look for a four-leafed clover in amongst the weeds, we need all the luck we can get. Catch a drifting seed and you could get a wish. Watch all the wishes you didn't catch floating away into the autumn air. Wasted wishes.

'What do you wish for, Sam?'

'I wish for a motorbike and an orange lolly.'

Whirl on the roundabout and watch the sky whirl. There was a life. You just had to find it. But never say: is this it? Is this all there is? Through it all Cora listened to the radio. Songs of the day, chart toppers, filled her kitchen. She could tell the time of day by the direction she had to turn her radio to catch the best reception.

Once on her way back to her flat she noticed that a church round the corner had been turned into an enterprise scheme. There was a list of projects on a board outside. One was Starless Enterprises.

'What's that?' she asked a fat scruffy bloke coming out of the building. 'Starless Enterprises, what on earth's that?'

The bloke looked at her and her two children. 'Comic strips,' he said. 'Some for syndication, some one-off ideas for adverts.'

'Why call it that? What a depressing name?' She was incensed.

Stanley Macpherson smiled and indicated the sky. 'City nights. You can't see the stars any more – starless.'

'And enterprises?' Cora asked crisply, noticing the bloke's jeans, straining at the crotch and rumpled. He had a beer stain on his sweat shirt and one of his baseball boots didn't have a lace. What a mess, she thought. He's worse than me.

He shrugged. 'Yes, enterprises. Starless, yes. But I'm not going to let it get me down – enterprises. Starless Enterprises.'

'Right,' said Cora. 'I see. That sort of figures.'

So Cora got to know Stanley. They weren't friends, didn't say hello. They acknowledged each other with a nod. Not nodding acquaintances. Just mutual nodders.

When Sam was two and Col one, Cora took a job wiping tables and serving in a local pub. Patsy Cline and Hank Williams twanged sorrowfully on the juke box, 'Yore cheatin' heart . . .' and men flirted. But Cora was having none of it. She had done with men. Still, the chat was occasionally cheering.

'Ah, Cora, a woman like you won't be used to a place as grand as this.' A customer looking round glumly at the drab vinyl seating and stained red carpet.

'Oh, bugger off. Thing to say. Hope there's more going on between your legs than there is between your ears. That'll mean you're not totally useless.'

'Ah. You've a mean streak in you.'

'I need it. A mean streak keeps a woman alive.'

Cora started to go to night school three times a week. She read tea leaves to pay for baby-sitting. Baby-sitters would arrive with cups wrapped in plastic bags, keen for an update on their lives. Was something good in the offing? Cora always took time to look meaningfully at the patterns in the leaves. She twisted and turned the cup, considered the possibilities. She always gave out good news. She figured nobody would want to stay alone in someone else's house, looking after someone else's children deliberating grim prospects and a murky future.

She did English Literature and French. Afternoons, after the park and before work, she studied. At work she kept a book under the bar and sat chewing gum and reading. She wriggled as she read, rattling through her consciousness the constant twang of Tammy Wynette or Johnny Cash. Customers bought her drinks and asked about her books.

'What're you readin' there, Cora?'

'Pride and Prejudice.'

'Any good?'

'I like it.'

'Any good bits?'

'Not in the way you're thinking.'

'Why are you reading it, then?'

'There's more to life than cars, sex, shopping and cheap thrills.'

'What?'

Cora chewed and solemnly stared ahead. 'Love. Honesty. Dignity. Stuff like that.'

'You have them, then. I'll have the sex, shopping, cars and cheap thrills. Wouldn't you rather have them. Really now?'

'Yes. But I'm working on it. See, that's honesty.' She beamed enthusiastically.

'I'm getting there.' She fetched drinks, emptied ashtrays and carried on chewing, wriggling and reading.

Still when scrubbing her kitchen floor, and she very occasionally did, she would lie back and stare at the sky. And sigh, 'What in the name of hell am I doing?' One day she stopped and sat up. 'This floor,' she said, thumping the black-and-white tiles with hatred, 'will be here long after I'm gone. I'll be dead but this floor will go on and on.' A horrible bout of truth hit her. Her hands came slowly up to her cheeks. 'God, who does that sound like? I have skipped a generation. I haven't turned into my mother. I've grown up to be my grandmother.'

She wanted to start screaming, but relieved the tension her revelation set up in her by running through the rooms stripping off her clothes. She ended up in the bathroom where she filled the bath and climbed in. Her sons joined her. They sat side by side at one end watching in amazement as Cora furiously scrubbed at herself saying, 'That's it. That's it. That's definitely it,' over and over. She caused a small tidal wave by suddenly standing up and stepping out. She wrapped herself in a towel and strode the flat once more. 'When you find yourself turning into your granny it's time to do something.' She slumped on the sofa. 'What do I want?' Then slowly: 'I want to teach. I could do that. What do you think of that, Col?'

Col smiled and handed her a towel. 'Dry me.'

'What do you think of that, Sam?'

'It's crap.'

'Don't say crap.'

'You say crap.'

'Yes, but I'm a grown-up.'

'Why do grown-ups get to say rude words and children not?'

'Dunno, Sam. I think we need it more.'

'Well, that's not fair. And all the other children round here get to eat fishfingers and beans when we get olive oil and horrible French stuff. And also when I go to nursery when you're not there I trudge.'

'Ah,' said Cora. 'Well, trudge away. I'm sure you do it magnificently.' It was dawning on her that her children weren't children really. They were people. And the two people she'd landed with both seemed to be a lot smarter than she was.

She phoned Irene and Bill. 'I'm going to be a teacher,' she said. 'I've decided I'd be good at it.'

Irene was tempted to say she hoped this would last, remember when she wanted to be a chemist, but she held her tongue.

Bill was enthused. 'That's great. You can do it. Just go for it.' Blister and hurtle, Cora.

She passed her exams in night school, applied for and got a place in teacher training college. Betty picked up the children from school and fed them secret fishfingers and oven chips. Evenings, Cora studied. It took her mind off her great longing and it helped her to keep at bay those shameful memories that floated back to her when her brain was idle.

Whilst her children watched television she worked, earphones on, jaws working out the rhythms that thrummed through her head on Wrigley's Spearmint Gum. Keep going, Cora. Don't think, Cora. Thinking's a killer, Cora. Thinking will be the end of you. But sometimes the memories battered through the noise and gum.

They'd walk the length of Princes Street. Where shall we shop today? They could both feel the heat, a sizzling glee that started in the groin and rose up through them. They had to do it. Had to. Into Marks and Spencer and start small. Don't get greedy. A pair of tights, one swift, fluid movement. Chat to each other, quietly, like proper shoppers, and inside the blood is hurtling through the veins. Then a shirt. Grinning and getting hot. The thrill of it, looking about, checking that nobody was watching them. Through the food department, a quiche, some cheese, a pot of apricot jam, a funny-looking raisiny cake that neither of them would eat. But this wasn't about wanting or needing. It was the rush. The rush. Back through the store, just look at the door, chat and laugh. A scarf, a pair of socks, a single shoe, ah ha. Be still my hammering heart. Slowly walk to the door. Relax. Relax. Can't breathe. Hit the street. Walk, chat. Laugh. Then move faster, through the crowd. Laughing louder. Thrilling. Oh yes. Oh yes. Oh yes. She was always miles ahead, miles ahead. Running and yelping glee. Up Frederick Street, into Rose Street. Find an empty alley round the back of some pub. Bottle banks and bins. They'd kiss. Too thrilled to speak. That wild fanatical kissing that has nothing to do with love, it's the only way to blast the last of the rush away. Hands on each other, pushing aside clothes. She'd feel him. Oh yes. Oh yes. He'd be far from her on his own high, moaning. He would always have some extra thing she hadn't seen him take, up his sleeve. Olive oil, wine. Claude was a far, far better thief than she was.

When she'd stopped going with him he went out alone. He'd approach wealthy shoppers outside Marks and Spencer, offering to plunder the food department for them for twenty pounds. 'Fifty pounds of food for twenty,' he'd smile. There was always someone who took him on. He squandered his takings on cognac, wine and Gauloises which he'd toss flamboyantly in front of Cora when he got home.

'Where did you get the money for all that?' She'd point at the booty accusingly.

'Somebody has to keep us going. And it's not going to be you, is it?'

Oh God, what might have become of them. Done for shoplifting, done for indecent exposure, lewd behaviour in public, and her pregnant at the time though she did not know it. Sam might have been born in prison. She imagined the phone call home. 'Hello, Mum. I've been arrested for shoplifting and shagging a bloke in public.' They would never have forgiven her. Their kindness would never have stretched that far.

'Oh no,' she would call, yelling loudly above the roar in her earphones into the quiet of the room. 'Oh God, no. I did that.' Her sons would exchange a look across the room, eyes lifted. Their mother, God help her, was always doing that – shouting out, squealing and squirming. Cora would take her head in her hands and shake it from side to side trying to shift the shame from her head. Sometimes she would bang her head on the table. 'Oh no. Oh no. Please no.' There was nobody in the world could give Cora a talking to that was worse than the regular beating up she gave herself.

She bought a tracksuit and started running again to see if a spot of vigorous exercise would help.

'You're not off running again, are you?' Betty looked horrified. Running was no fit thing for a woman to do.

'Yes,' said Cora. 'It helps.'

'What does it help with?'

'If I effing knew that, I wouldn't have to do it.'

But really she knew her two main problems. There was her shame, and her great longing. She needed sex. She wanted a man in her bed. She sighed and sighed and when she could no longer keep the longing away she remembered Claude. Her nights with him. The things they did. He could take her to extremes and when she was moving with joy he would stop.

'Don't,' he'd say. 'Don't you dare come without me. I want to be with you. In you. I want to feel your pleasure.' For that time they had together he filled all of her. She thought of nothing other than pleasing him. There would, she knew, never be anything like it again.

'Thank heavens for that,' she'd say. 'I couldn't stand the pace.'

'Think, Cora,' he would say. 'Think about all the world. Everyone coming at once.'

'They couldn't. People are doing all sorts of things.'

'Imagine the roar.'

'What are people doing now, right now when we're in bed doing this, you inside me?' Gasping and trying to hold on, they'd list the doings of the world.

'A child in Brazil is stealing a watch from the arm of a driver parked at the traffic lights.'

'A woman in Minneapolis is hanging out her washing.'

'Pigeons in Trafalgar Square are flapping and shoving aside as a bag lady in orange luminous socks walks through them.'

'A man in Australia wears torrid shorts as he rides a wave.'

'There are blizzards of butterflies in Burma.'

'In the paddy fields of China people are making dirty jokes as they plant rice.'

'A woman in Pakistan is singing her baby to sleep.'

On and on they went. 'Oh God,' Cora would cry when it all came flooding back, 'what a precious pair of pretentious wankers we were.' Hollering from the isolation and the din in her earphoned head, she was unaware of how loud she shouted. Her boys would exchange the pitying look. Mother was torturing herself again.

There were, of course, very occasional one-night stands. Men Cora brought home, shushing and holding her finger to her lips as they tiptoed past the children's bedroom. They got coffee, sex and a small snooze. They were her indiscretions. But they never got to stay all night. If they wouldn't leave, Cora would phone Betty Lawrence across the hallway and ask if her husband, Will, would mind doing a bit of bouncing.

'Is he bothering you?' Will would say, struggling to hold his pyjamas together, and shooting Cora a disgruntled middle-of-the-night look.

'Just leaving,' the indiscretion would say, cramming himself into his clothes.

Cora couldn't bear for anyone to be there when Col and Sam came rushing through in the morning to greet her as if they hadn't seen her for years, to sing and slap hands in the air and shout at her Van Morrison tapes. 'Van the man.'

Cora's fleeting lovers always got turned out into the night. But she was more than protecting her sons from the shock of learning that their mother was only, after all, a human being with needs and lusts. Well, hell, they were finding that out every day. She found she could not bear actually to sleep with someone. Intimacy was lovely. Oh yes, she'd say. Give me that. But dipping into unconsciousness with someone she didn't know, going through the graceless business of snoring and farting and dreaming with a stranger seemed, well, somehow sort of rude. And she'd no intention of ever doing it. Eventually she had to put a stop to her indiscretions. Betty's uninhibited show of disapproval became too much to bear.

'What's got into you, bringing these men home? You never know where they've been.' She made them sound like some dubious sweet she'd found in the gutter and was about to pop into her mouth. 'It's got to stop.' Betty was adamant. 'You can't go waking folk up in the middle of the night . . .'

Cora raised her hands, stopping her flow. 'I know. I know,' she said. It was bad enough taking the scoldings she gave herself without receiving another from her neighbour. 'You don't have to tell me. It'll never happen again.'

When Betty left, Cora leaned glumly on the window, looking out. 'That's it for me, then. My youth is over. No sex, no drugs. There's only rock 'n' roll left. They'll not take that away. Oh no.'

The songs on her radio played on and on. She was listening to the music she would have danced to had she gone to clubs, jumped about to at gigs, had she gone to gigs. These were the tunes that would have marked dates, picnics, dinners, holidays, nights at bars. She was listening to the life she would have had, had she been available to live it.

Cora graduated. She started work and within a year was earning enough to move. By then, though, something had happened. She had grown up here, made friends here, felt oddly safe and accepted here. She survived here. Cora did not want to leave. She was ensconced, comfortable here. And besides, her children were growing. 'The sticky years are over,' she said. 'Thank God.'

One day Sam brought in his first single. 'Listen to this,' he said. It sounded odd to her, disjointed.

'You like that?' she asked.

"Course. It's great.'

Cora went quiet. Then: 'You young bastards. You've changed the tune.' She sighed hugely and let her arms drop by her side. 'I don't like that. It's your music. God dammit. What do you get up to listening to that? You're not doing any of the things I did, are you?'

'What did you do?'

'Mind your own business.' Then, examining his face fiercely for lies, she demanded, 'You haven't got a tattoo on your bum, have you?'

'Of course not.'

'Do you know what you've done? You've turned me into a mother.'

'But you are a mother.'

'I may be one, but I never wanted to feel like one. Actually, I was thinking of resigning from motherhood. I want to be me again. I've been waiting all my life to get to do all the things I missed, bringing you two up. I wanted to be young again. And now just when you're old enough for me to get to do it, you go and change the tune and youth doesn't seem so juicy any more.'

Sam put his arm round her, roughly squeezed her shoulders, kissed the top of her head. 'Too middle-aged to be young and turbulent. Too young and turbulent to be middle-aged. Life's a bitch.'

'You're not sneering at me, are you?' Cora asked.

'Yes. But only because I'm young and turbulent,' said Sam.

In summer swallows dipped, swooped and cried. Children, kicking a football in the street, called to each other. And in small gatherings on the balcony women stood, arms folded, gossiping and laughing. That was Cora's favourite sound. That moment on summer evenings when women standing arms folded, discussing men, children, parents, stopped being wives, mothers, daughters and relaxed. That indiscreet cackle of women talking dirty.

That summer, though, she denied herself that indiscreet cackle. She bought a car. Yellow and rusting, it was, but with the necessary tape deck and radio. She called it the fartmobile. It moved grudgingly, fartingly, from place to place. She packed the boot, put the boys in the back and with some semblance of dignity, slightly redeemed, she went home.

3

Cora and Ellen

Chapter Twenty

Ellen often dropped into Cora's after work. Cora's kitchen was sunny and cluttered, an organised mess that she hated people meddling with, tidying for her. When it was messy she knew exactly where everything was. It was her mess and she loved it. Being in Cora's kitchen was calming. Soothing, Ellen thought. She felt the stiffness and tension drain from her shoulders. She got drowsy.

Cora always made a fetish of preparing a pot of tea. Warm the pot, two spoonfuls of Earl Grey, boiling water, leave to infuse then pour.

'Tell me, Cora,' said Ellen, 'what do you want out of life? Do you ever stop to think?'

'What an adolescent question. What do I want out of life, truth or bullshit?' Cora said, giving Ellen a cup of tea. She sat across from her and started to paint her nails. One glossy chestnut, the one next to it plum.

'Truth,' said Ellen.

'I want,' sighed Cora, 'instant gratification, constant adoration and to find a bottle of quality drinkable plonk on Safeway's shelves that costs less than two pounds. Mostly I want the wine.' She waved her hand at Ellen. 'What do you think?'

'Plum,' said Ellen. 'More dramatic.'

'Yes,' agreed Cora. 'If Sarah Bernhardt painted her nails, and she probably did, this'd be the colour. Tonight's the big night. You are remembering it's my school play? You have to come.'

'Maybe,' said Ellen.

Cora pressed her palms together, a small prayer. 'Please,' she said. 'You must come. You're my best friend. It's your duty. I need somebody of my own there. Somebody rooting for me, calling my

163

name – if only silently. There's no point asking either of the boys. They'll only look frightful and sulk.'

'Oh all right. Though I hate going back to school. And you'll be all bossy. I hate it already.'

'And I hate your absurd conversations. Tell me what you want out of life, then? If we're talking profound.'

She was slowly spreading plum on to her remaining nails. Tonight she'd have beads in her hair again. She'd wear pointy-toed patent mules, her scarlet silk jacket and orange T-shirt with 'Vulgarity Thy Name Is Woman' vividly in purple across her tits. She liked to look alarming. She still got an adolescent buzz out of the unchecked expressions of surprise that fleeted across the faces of her pupils' parents when they caught their first glimpse of her. She liked people to know she was there.

'I want my very own placid dumpling,' said Ellen.

The radio across the kitchen played a selection of rock music that was familiar enough to be nostalgic. Cora was sure it was never meant to be that. From another part of the flat came the relentless thud of more agonisingly disjointed music. Now that they were nineteen and eighteen, Cora's sons were heard but rarely seen. Ellen could more than hear it, she could feel it thumping up through the floor, through her chair, through her. Though it only contained three people, Cora's was a noisy household, tackily noisy. Silence unnerved her. She did not care for the thoughts that the absence of noise allowed into her head. She looked at Ellen, alarmed. 'You want what?'

'You heard,' said Ellen, taking a ponderous sip of Earl Grey. 'I want my very own placid dumpling. You know, those women you sometimes find at supermarket checkouts. They smile and smile and look concerned for you and your Brussels sprouts and toilet rolls and think nothing of themselves.'

Cora blew softly on her nails. 'You mean you want a wife?'

'Sod that. I was a wife. I know how awful a wife can be.' She shook her head. 'Oh no, I don't want anyone like me in my life, other than me. That's enough. I want a placid dumpling. There was one in Safeway's today. She said, "We'd better get you a double bag for your wine, luvvy." And I felt wanted. I thought how nice if she took me in and stroked my hair and made me puddings or cocoa. Cocoa would do.'

Luvvy, the placid dumpling had called her. Luvvy. Ellen couldn't resist her after that. She was a sucker for affection, any kind of affection.

'Ellen, you hate cocoa.'

'I wouldn't if a placid dumpling made me some. Anyway, today I got my stuff together in the trolley and went to the kiosk to buy some cigarettes. Then on my way back to the main door there was my placid dumpling being kind to another. She was saying, "We'd better get you a double bag for your wine, luvvy," to someone else. I felt betrayed. She broke my heart.'

'Why?' Cora was exasperated. Ellen always exasperated her. 'Can't you just do your shopping like everyone else in the world and stop looking for love and acceptance everywhere you go?'

Ellen shrugged, drained her cup and stared at the formation of tea leaves left at the bottom. Cora stretched over and took it from her.

'It's still the black dog. You're still depressed.'

'I know that. I don't need tea leaves to tell me that. I'm depressed about my life. My on-off marriage. I have to do something about it. I just drifted into it. I always thought it would sort itself out. But it's not going to do that on its own, is it? What about my future? Will I ever get my act together and do something about Daniel?'

'Tea leaves only reveal your present. And you know what to do about Daniel. Throw him out. The man is unfaithful and when he's finished losing his own money, he'll start on yours. Nobody else would put up with him. I'll pick you up at six. Be ready. None of this appearing half dressed and borrowing my mascara. I have to get there early. I have some serious bossing to do,' Cora said briskly. She was warming up, getting ready for the fray.

Col came into the kitchen and started to rummage through the fridge. 'There's nothing to eat,' he complained.

'Of course there is,' Cora said. 'There's yoghurt, apples—'

'That's not proper food.' He took a banana.

Cora watched him. 'Your legs are awfully hairy,' she said. 'When did that happen?'

He shrugged. 'It's been happening all my life. Leave my legs alone.'

'One day you notice them,' Cora said, 'and their legs are all hairy and they've got stubble on their chins and their skin is suddenly clear and it's got nothing to do with Biactol. Then they kiss you goodnight or give you a cuddle and you notice they're no longer handling you like a scrum half. There's someone else out there that you're not being told about yet. Some female someone. It's all so . . . so . . .'

'Normal?' suggested Ellen.

'I'm not taking any sort of comforting sanity from you. You are the last person in the world to dispense sanity. Anyway, it just makes you feel old.'

'You would have got to this age anyway even if you hadn't had them.'

'But I wouldn't have looked it,' Cora said. Then, 'Six, OK?'

'Can't wait.' Ellen sounded morose. 'You know some parent is going to come up to you and say something utterly insensitive and daft. You'll get all upset, probably be sick afterwards and it'll all just break my heart, Cora.'

'What with your two-timing placid dumpling, that'll be twice today your heart will have been broken.'

Ellen nodded glumly.

'Only twice,' said Cora. 'This will have been a good day for you.'

Ellen nodded glumly.

At six Cora knocked on Ellen's door. True to form Ellen was still in her underwear. She led Cora through to the kitchen and continued to eat the bowl of cornflakes that was her supper.

'Look at you,' cried Cora. 'Look at how you're dressed. Look at what you're eating and look at the time.'

'It's only half-past five,' said Ellen. 'Well, it was when I looked at the clock.'

'When was that?'

'Dunno. Half an hour ago, I suppose. Before my bath.'

'You expect it to still be the time it was when you looked at the clock?'

'No,' Ellen sighed. 'Not really. It's just sort of surprising the way it keeps on moving. Relentless.'

'You're so dreamy.'

'What's wrong with that?'

'Nothing, if you're the one doing the dreaming. But really irritating to everyone else. Please get dressed.' Cora was nervous.

Ellen pulled on a pair of black jeans and a black silk shirt. Took a black jacket from the hook behind the door and followed Cora down the stairs.

'You don't have any problems deciding what to wear, then?' Cora said.

'I hate decisions. You know that. They take too long. They can cut into your dreaming time.'

A trip in the fartmobile was always thrilling. At full rattle the wind howled through the gaps between door and sill, and through the windows that would not properly shut. The car roared and shuddered. In third and fourth gear there was such a vibrating feeling of energy, speed, rushing air, it always came as a surprise to both passenger and driver to glance at the speedometer and discover they were only travelling at thirty-five miles an hour.

Cora had driven up Leith Walk to pick up Ellen. Now she was driving back down again.

'Bloody red light,' she swore, and wrestled with the gear stick. First was always sticky. And if she didn't watch it, it would slip into reverse and they'd shoot back into the Jaguar behind. 'Bloody Jag's right up my arse.' A Volkswagen pulled up alongside. Revved. The lights turned orange. The fartmobile revved. Green. They both shot forward. Cora triumphed. She beat the Volkswagen across the lights. 'Have that, you short-arsed, cheap jacket, nasty-haircutted shite,' she yelled as the rival car pulled easily ahead and shot on to the next set of lights.

'Cora!' Ellen was horrified. 'You're bossy in life and a hooligan on the road.'

'Oh bollocks. I'm just judgemental like everyone else. It doesn't do to be racist or sexist but all the advertising I soak up makes me full of other sorts of bigotry. I have my own istnesses? Istosities? Like everyone else these days I'm haircuttist, jacketist, small dickist when judging male drivers. Get in your car and throw political correctness to the wind, baby.'

The lights were against them, they couldn't surf on green and ride without stopping. So they did the traffic light dash. Draw up alongside a superior car (every car on the road was superior), swift eye contact with driver, swear and challenge. Screech of tyres and on to the next set of lights. Not exactly heat and rage in the city, just an early evening metropolitan swagger as they plunged into the depth of Leith.

Cora loved Leith. Edinburgh was style and patter, haircuts and jackets in bars. But Leith was full of folk. People spilled from pubs. Of an evening the air was boozy. You could get drunk from passive drinking. It was a place to live out a recession. And, though it was filling with bistros and bars with their names gold lettered in Palatino on their windows, low times still suited it.

Ellen normally spent trips with Cora with her hands on her head screaming, 'Stop! Brake! Pull over! Let me out! Behave yourself!' But tonight she sat rigid with nerves, chain-smoking.

'I don't know why you do this,' Ellen said as they drew up outside the school and started to reverse, exhaust at full howl, into a parking space.

The poster pinned to the railings glowingly said, 'Panto Tonite. *Jack and the Beans Talk*, a spectacle on Been Hur scale, orchestra conducted by that well-known German Heinz Bean. Starring Warren Peas. Written by Miss O'Brien and the Kids of Class Three.'

'You've been busy,' Ellen said.

The playground was already full of infants, heads and feet sticking out of red and green cardboard pods. 'The beans,' explained Cora. 'Everybody has to get a part. Casting is a masterpiece of diplomacy. Some of these kids have absolutely no self-confidence at all. Being a bean helps. If you can be a convincing bean at seven, then the rest of your life should be lived with style.'

'You think?' Ellen laughed.

'Not really. But you know us teachers – we have to wrap up everything in psychobabble nonsense.'

The air thrummed excitement. Beans sped up and down the corridor, faces aglow with glee. Jumping up and down, waving their arms, they chanted their lines. 'I'm a bean. I'm Green Bean, and this is my friend,' pointing at vacant air. 'He's a has bean.'

'These kids are as high as kites.' Ellen looked round at them. 'They'll never sleep tonight.'

'I have been busy for nights and nights and nights. Have you any idea how much paracetamol and vodka has gone into this production?'

'Yes,' Ellen said weakly. 'I have a very good idea. I contributed a deal of it.'

'Well worth it,' said Cora. 'It's surprising how many of them remember these plays.'

'It's you they remember,' Ellen told her. 'Who is Jack, anyway?'

'Melanie Johnston.'

'The one with the mother . . . ?'

'The very one,' said Cora.

Cora had once given her class the task of drawing what Mummy did all day. 'I know we usually draw what Daddy does. But mummies are busy people. Have a think about yours – what does she do all day?'

There were drawings of mummies at work behind word processors or at supermarket checkouts. There were mummies carrying home shopping, mature student mummies falling asleep at their books, angry mummies, smiley mummies, mummies wracked with PMT, mummies ironing and mummies collecting children from school and there was Melanie Johnston's mummy. She was lying on a sofa, wearing a pink dressing gown and fluffy slippers. In front of her was a huge television set and by her side a box of chocolates and a glass of wine.

'Melanie Johnston,' Cora shouted, 'this can't be what your mummy does all day.'

'Yes it is.' Melanie Johnston nodded as she spoke.

'It is, Miss.' Other children who had obviously witnessed this indolence agreed.

'I wouldn't mind but she looks great on it,' Cora protested to Ellen. 'Feminism seems to have passed her by. She feels no guilt.'

'Maybe she has reached a plain we're all striving to get to. Maybe she knows something we don't. Freedom from guilt and everything,' Ellen mused. They spent a deal of time speculating about Melanie Johnston's mum.

Walking into the school with Cora Ellen said, 'You have to point her out to me. I must see this woman.'

Cora led the way into the gym hall and indicated a seat in the front row to Ellen.

'Aw, Miss,' Ellen cried. 'I want to sit at the back.'

'At the front,' Cora ordered, waving Ellen into a chair. 'I want to keep an eye on you. No slipping out to the pub. And here's a programme. That'll be fifty pence.'

'How long does it last anyway?'

'An hour and a bit, with sandwiches, cakes and tea afterwards.'

Ellen felt herself go limp. That feeling that she'd be in this gym hall for ever. That her buttocks would go numb sitting on the hard school seat. 'Numb buttocks,' Ellen said. 'Why are municipal seats so hard? That'll be why I didn't achieve at school – I was too preoccupied with my bum. Maybe if schools had softer seats a whole different set of people would emerge as professionals and leaders of society. Maybe that's why society is such a mess, the people who have shone at school are merely the ones with insensitive backsides. Maybe—'

Cora leaned over and touched her arm, a shut up gesture. 'I have to go,' she said. 'I'll leave you to your theories. I have to switch into hyper boss.'

She disappeared behind the curtain. Ellen could hear her imperiously shrill cry. Every now and then she stuck her head out, checking Ellen hadn't slipped away, and that the hall was filling up. People were going to turn up, weren't they? They did. Of course, they did. Mothers, fathers, grans and granddads, sisters, brothers, neighbours and friends sat in expectant rows, waiting to cheer on their own little star.

At last she appeared on stage, smiled, and thanked everyone for coming tonight. 'We need all the support we can get,' she said. She was wearing a long skirt so that nobody would see the dramatic effect standing before a crowd had on her knees.

Ellen fixed her eyes on Cora's throat. It was flushed with anxiety. Her eyes shone, glassily shone. She had been working on this play for weeks and weeks. The curtain behind her billowed with little lives. There were urgent whisperings from the side of the stage, sniggers and semi-hysterical titterings. These children had been rehearsing every day since, it seemed to Cora, the beginning of time. She knew it didn't matter. Glowing parental pride, people would come and watch their own children change their socks on stage. OPCs, as Cora called other people's children, were of no interest at all. Camcorders whirred, cameras flashed. They were off.

The school spotlight wavered across the curtain, Mrs Grundy, the visiting music teacher, beefily thumped the piano, upper arms aquiver, and a cancan of beans danced on stage, kicking little legs, little faces (mostly toothless) grinning inanely, singing 'Happy Talk' from *South Pacific*.

When she was a child, Ellen recalled, school concerts were dour affairs. The choir sang 'Swing Low, Sweet Chariot' with stultifying suburban politeness, pronouncing every syllable. 'Sweeng low swe . . . ee . . . tt chaario . . .ttt'. It wasn't actually her voice but her height that got her a place in the choir. Her music teacher had a keen sense of symmetry. Ellen had fitted perfectly into the middle of the back row.

This, though, this was ebullient. The audience joined in, clapped, booed, hissed and sang. When she was little Ellen had longed to be in a school play. She had squeezed to the front when parts were being cast and stared, maniacally she now thought, at the teacher. But she was never chosen. She was considered too quiet, too distant, too dreamy to carry any starring role – any sort of role, in fact. But Ellen knew that somewhere inside her was a star trying to get out. In fact, she was quite sure the only reason she hadn't made it to Hollywood was that she was never in a school play. She hadn't been given the right sort of break. Not the sort of break the beans and Jack were getting now. They were dressed up and dancing. They were having a lovely time.

This, Ellen realised, was their first fifteen minutes. She didn't believe people only got one set. She didn't think she'd had one yet, though. It was a small glimpse Cora was giving them of what a fifteen minutes could be like. Standing backstage, prompting and bossing and organising, Cora was giving these children the chance she had had years ago when she ran in front of all those drunken cheering people – 'Come away, the wee one'. She had sensed the thrill of having a go. These children were blistering and hurtling.

At one point the excitement got too much for Jack. She tumbled from the stage. A woman rose, slowly, majestically from the mid ranks of the audience, chocolate wrappers scattering. She was tall and wearing a coat with a huge fake fur collar. She raised her hand and, pointing at the child scrambling to get back under the spotlight, roared, 'Get back up that beanstalk, you little bugger.'

Ellen stared. So that was her, Melanie's mum. Our lady of the sofa and fluffy slippers. No wonder nobody criticised her lifestyle.

By nine it was over. The volunteers who had contributed cakes, shortbread and trays of sandwiches clustered round to clear up. With an efficient snapping of yellow rubber gloves, the following of trusty mums set about wiping and cleaning. They displayed a clear upmanship over those who were sloping off home, hand in hand with infant beans. Children trying to make their moment last were refusing to take off their costumes and were walking to their cars through the evening still dressed for the show. Some of them would refuse to take their stage outfits off when they got home. They would sleep as beans tonight.

Wasn't upmanship strange? Cora thought. People will take on a bit of rivalry about anything. Cars, jeans, CDs, the neat cut of their lawns, the flatness of stomachs, food – anything. Once they had a visiting American student who expressed horror when she saw little children who lived only a street away set off for home alone. 'That wouldn't happen in the States.' The student couldn't believe her eyes. 'We got child abductors, muggers and murderers there.'

'So do we,' Cora hotly defended her country. How dare someone suggest it was, in any way at all, inferior? She was about to add that muggers and murderers over here were as good as anywhere in the world. But wondered if she was perhaps taking patriotism a tad too far.

'Can we go now?' Ellen asked.

'Oh please, let's. Oh God. What did you think of that?' Cora wanted to know. Then, 'No, don't tell me. Doing it was enough. I can't take criticism.'

'I loved it,' Ellen told her. 'Really, it was fun.'

But Cora was a wreck. She had been writing this panto for weeks. Then rehearsing it, nagging mums into making costumes and bringing along food, rounding up other teachers to help make the stage set and work the lights.

'It's over,' she said. 'It's over. Till next year it's over. Thank God . . . Oh my . . .' Her chest heaved. There were tears in her eyes. 'Quick, for Christ's sake, hold my shoes.' She swiftly freed her feet from her stilettos. 'I have to . . .' she started off down the street, ' . . . run.'

Head back, stocking-soled, she ran along the street, and disappeared round the corner. She threw herself forward and flew. She flowed, gaudy in her producer/director outfit, over the pavement. She was still fast. People saw her coming and stepped aside, turned to watch her go.

'Cora,' Ellen called. 'Cora. God damn you, Cora.' She stood holding the shoes, staring in amazement at the empty street, the space where Cora had been. Every time, every single time, Cora had a concert she did this. And every time the speed of the woman amazed Ellen. She got into the car, and started at full throttle after her. But by the time she got round the corner Cora had disappeared. She crawled kerbside, clutching the steering wheel, peering up alleys. No Cora. At last she stopped and stuck her head out through the sunroof and yelled. People stopped to stare, looked round for signs of Cora, believing Ellen to be summoning a naughty dog. Some young boys out pubbing took up the call, howling, 'Cora. Cora. Cora,' into the night as they moved from one drinking place to the next. Long after they'd gone Ellen could hear them still laughing and bawling Cora's name through the dark.

At last Ellen found her. She caught Cora in the full glare of her headlights. She was bent over, panting and gasping for breath. Her hair hung down covering her face. She gripped her sides, and wheezed, 'Oh God, I hate all that. I hate it. I hate it. I hate it.'

'Then why do you do it?' Ellen spoke quietly.

'Because I have something to say.' Her wild breathing calmed. 'I really do believe I have something to tell these children about life.'

'What?'

'This is what I have to say. Aaaaaaaaaah.'

'I don't think they heard you. They were having such a good time. Your feet are bleeding. God, you're such a fool.'

'If you truly loved me you'd bathe my bleeding feet in your teardrops and dry them with your hair,' Cora sniffed.

Ellen handed Cora her shoes. 'I'll buy you a drink.'

They went to the Oyster Bar, settled at a table. Ellen bought the first two rounds, then Cora the next two, and by then she was feeling mellow. Drinking another seemed like more than a good idea, a necessary thing to do to keep the mellowness going. She took off her jacket so that her 'Vulgarity Thy Name Is Woman' tit message was boldly on show.

'Oh God,' she said. 'All this has to stop. All this drinking.' She put her head in her hands. 'Shit, Ellen. I'm too old to be young.' She lifted her glass and half emptied it. 'Look. Look what I can do. I shouldn't drink like that. Me. I'm an old woman in the making. Droopy tits. Thighs to weep about.' She beat them ineffectually. 'I don't know.' They drank some more.

'When I worked in that pub the women all used to sing "Staynd by Yore Mayn". I used to think it'd be wonderful to have a mayn to staynd by. But now I think you only stand by your man because it saves you the awful responsibility of standing by yourself.'

Ellen nodded and said nothing. When Cora prattled it was best to let her prattle till she was all prattled out. Then she would start to sing. Then they would have an argument. Tomorrow they'd make up and be pals again. This was what was going to happen. She knew it.

'Of course,' Cora prattled, 'I don't understand men.'

'Neither do I. They are perplexing and mysterious creatures who think they can drive cars fabulously – especially backwards. Why do they go so fast in reverse?'

'See, women,' said Cora, 'women, by and large, quite like themselves but hate their bodies. Men just can't get the hang of having a body. Every month women come to terms with their body and how it behaves. Women all over the world, whoever they are, know about themselves and each other. Men don't have that. They have a bit of their body that does what it wants. It behaves badly on its own.'

Cora's face was flushed. She went to the bar, brought another round to the table and continued, 'See, if women had penises, they'd have penis encounter groups where we'd all sit round and bring them out and come to terms with ourselves. Of course we'd be bitches. "Oh, Helen," we'd say, "it doesn't matter that yours is so small." Then when she was gone, we'd say "Poor Paul, Helen's is so small. Size is everything." '

Across the room a group of young girls shrieked and laughed. They ate crisps and drank tequila. Their earrings jangled and anyone could tell just by looking at them, they were talking dirty. There goes Karen, Sharon, Alice and Katy, Ellen thought. She imagined they were out there still, running the streets, howling and calling, for ever young and free. And, of course, they were – maybe not that particular Karen, Sharon, Alice and Katy, but another lot, a new lot. They'd always be out there, Ellen thought.

'Look at you,' Cora accused. 'Drifting off. Dreaming again. You never stop.'

'I was just thinking about some people I knew years ago. I always imagine they've stayed the same whilst I've got older.'

'Ah well, that's surely the way of it,' Cora said. Her face creased with mischief. An unbounded exuberance and love of humanity filled her, booze flooded her bloodstream. The world was a lovely place full of lovely people and did anyone want to hear her doing Marlene Dietrich? Every woman over a certain age, Cora thought, could do Dietrich. She did Dietrich. Then she did Leonard Cohen. Then she deepened her voice, adding a couple of chins to her existing one and a half, and did Dietrich doing Cohen, and flatly sang, 'Oh ze zeesters of mercy.' She dipped a soulful finger into the froth of the half of Guinness that had appeared from goodness knows where, goodness knows who. Women, soul mates, fellow travellers who all longed to be deep and mysterious and loved, from here and there about the room joined in.

'Why do you do it?' Ellen asked when they staggered out. The night hit them, that whammy blat of fresh air, scorching through boozed brains and lungs. Walking was suddenly tricky. 'Why do you do it? Go drinking and, dammit, take me with you? You corrupt me.'

'I'm only abusing someone I've been trying to get fond of all my life. Me,' Cora explained.

Ellen stopped and leaned on a wall. 'I'm drunk,' she confessed. 'I'm so drunk. And you did it. You got plastered and took me along.'

'You could've said no.'

'By the time I realise that I've drunk too much I think, might as well carry on. I love you, Cora. But sometimes you're too vibrant for me. You rush at life too much for me. Blister and hurtle, Cora. But leave me at home.'

Cora was offended. 'Don't blame me if you've drunk too much. I'm fine. I'm not drunk.'

'Yes you are. You always deny it. It's so weird because you are Cora and the thing that you mostly are is honest.'

'Oh no I'm not.' Cora was hurt. She was a woman of mystery and depth. She wasn't honest. She had two sons, different fathers, and when they asked about their dads she skirted the truth. 'Oh, Sam, your father was French. We just lost touch before you were born. People do. He got ill. Don't ask.' Then feeling bad, 'Well, ask, but not now, OK?'

Ellen knocked on Cora's forehead. 'You're hiding something. Hiding. Are you in there, Cora?' She waved to Cora from the other side of the gulf, Cora's guilt.

'Oh bugger you,' cried Cora. 'What do you know. You've got it all. Stanley Macpherson sorts you out. He fixed the mess you got into with Daniel. You've done nothing for yourself, Ellen. You know nothing about life. Tucked away. Dreaming.'

'I'm not tucked away. You're the one with secrets.'

'Secrets,' Cora screamed. 'A person should be allowed their secrets.'

Start at the top of the store and work down. Scarves, lipsticks, nail varnish, chocolates, gloves, a perfume tester. Take it, take it. Above the lift, the sign to watch out for – two lights flashing. They are calling for the store detectives. Quick, quick. Time to go. Only that was when it was best. Eyes wild, crazed with the thrill, danger set the blood buzzing.

'You are bricked in, Cora. I tell you everything. I expose myself to you. And you tell me nothing,' Ellen shouted. They were yelling at each other. Drunk and yelling. It drove Ellen wild that Cora knew everything about her, and she did not know everything about Cora. She felt cheated. And they were getting older and older. Time and worry showed on Cora's face. There were valleys on it that had not been there that night when she came fabulously across the room. 'You look like you are in need of some serious corrupting,' she had said.

Oh, corrupt me, Cora, Ellen thought. Make me like you are, take me to the vile places you have secretly visited and show me how to sin marvellously like you did.

And it was true. Stanley Macpherson did look after her. Ever since she had shown him Daniel's mess he had cared for her. He sorted her accounts. But then everyone knew that Stanley, being Stanley, would have sorted Ellen out had she walked in off the street with her problems in a shoe box. Stanley had started pension plans for Ellen, Billy and Brigit. He had trust funds and savings plans for his children. The only future Stanley hadn't provided for was his own.

Stanley never left the house without a pocket full of change for the beggars he'd pass on the way to work. Stanley's living room was full of waifs. Waifs of the living room storm Ellen called them – people from his past who turned up to sit at his table, eat his food, borrow money and disappear from his life for another decade or so. He syndicated *Gangster Women* and *Engels* and all her other characters and invested her share of the profit. She was thirty-seven, comfortably off, protected and cosseted by Stanley.

'I still think you're hiding. I hate it,' she said. 'You've locked me out.'

'Not you,' her mother said when she stood in the cold bungalow. 'Not you,' on the night her daddy died and the draught rushed under the front door, freezing her feet. All her life, then, rejection had terrified her.

'And you think there isn't part of you that's locked away in your dreamings,' Cora retaliated. 'You shut yourself off. And you are so privileged. So lucky. Everybody likes you. You don't realise. You are so cool you can wear sunglasses indoors at night. At your age. I hate that.'

'Oh good one. I'm privileged and you've had it tough. I know nothing and you're worldly. You're a mother, an empowered woman . . . and . . . and I'm . . .' Ellen stopped. She was what? She was a wimp, tucked away from the world. A dweeb, geek – she had a vast selection of derogatory descriptions of herself.

'A mother,' Cora shouted. 'I'm a mother. You think that makes me something special? Guilt trippers of the world unite . . .'

A mother, me a mother, she thought. Some mother. A boss, a nag, purveyor of proteins and vitamins, clean socks and quick, gravure, easy-access philosophies.

'Who was my father?' Col asked.

'He was my love,' she replied. She lied.

'Why did he go away?' he asked.

'Sometimes people have to go away,' she said.

'Other children have fathers,' he said.

'Well, you've got me. And I've got you. We don't need a father.'

Oh good one, Cora, she chastised herself. You really tackled the issues there. That'll see him through life's ups and downs. He can cling to that. You've done the lad proud. Watch him face the world.

Sometimes she would stand in the hall outside her children's room listening to them sleep. And she was filled with shame. She had brought these boys into the world and what could she give them? She had little money. She had worked through their early childhood. She felt she had missed out on part of their infancy, and they had not had the mother they deserved. And their mother's sins had denied them both a father.

'I have failed. I have failed,' alone in the dark she accused herself.

And here she was, nearly forty, wearing an absurd T-shirt and bawling at her best friend in the street. Why stop at shouting? Why didn't they let go and fight? Why didn't they just start battering each other with their handbags? Passing cars were already slowing so that passengers and driver could stare and enjoy the show.

'I'm too old for all this,' she sighed. 'Where's the car?' She was jealous of her friend and hated herself for it. Furthermore, her head hurt. She was sure she was going to have an embarrassing bruise where Ellen had knocked on her forehead. 'I think you have injured me.'

'Have I? Oh sorry,' said Ellen. 'And I can't remember where I left your car. Can't drive anyway. Get a taxi.'

'I'm so pissed. And I have to get up in the morning and go to work. Unlike some,' Cora said pointedly.

'Sorry,' said Ellen. 'Sorry I don't have to turn up at exactly nine o'clock and I can lie in bed when you can't. Sorry I'm such a wanker.'

'So you should be.' They shared a taxi and parted in the glum reckoning of throbbing and painful sobriety. Sore hearts and tears, parched mouths and a headache coming searing in.

Chapter Twenty-one

Daniel didn't leave with one wild flamboyant sweeping farewell. He drifted out of Ellen's life. Then back in again. And out again. In again. Out again. Their parting took a lot longer than their getting together. They became expert at arguing with each other, and could slip with ease from bickering to quarrelling to full-scale screaming and throwing things. And then make love. They could yell foul things at one another. Stop. Go to bed. Make love. Fight lying down. Stop. Make love again. Get up in the morning, and still be fighting. It was draining.

The disintegration of the relationship started with Friendly Mary's lovebite and never recovered. Daniel often came home with an armful of fruit and veg. With shrinking heart she remembered on the night of the lovebite Daniel came home with a huge bag of apples. Once she got up after sleeping with Daniel and ate a particularly juicy pear.

'Where do you get all the fruit you come home with?'

He shrugged. 'Here and there.'

'Don't lie to me,' she cried, throwing an apple at his head. It hit – a beautiful strike just above his left ear.

'Jesus.' He rubbed the damaged spot. He was astonished. He was surprised that someone as utterly non-confrontational as Ellen should suddenly start throwing things. Then there was the devastating accuracy of her aim. Thank heavens she did not know about Louise, his old tutor – not only were the pickings from her flat more up-market, they were also heavier. A bottle of claret from her wine rack fitted into the deep pocket of his raincoat, a couple of frozen veal cutlets from her freezer that they'd eaten the other night – with apple sauce – things like that could, when thrown over a six-foot distance, cause some serious damage. He felt aggrieved.

Ellen had no idea the trouble he went to.

'Bugger you,' he snarled. It never once crossed his mind that what he was doing was wrong. It was just the way he was. Evenings on his way home he'd stick his head round the door of the fruit shop. A big smile and a wave and Mary would fill a bag with this and that. 'Oh take it. They'll not be worth putting out tomorrow,' she'd say, dismissing his protests.

Daniel would say, 'Ta,' and smile again at her. It was part of his life, his job. If he didn't smile and wave and take, he'd have to buy food. His money was far too precious for that. He needed it for horses, music and booze. But mostly for the horses.

Ellen did not understand how much he needed to gamble. It was winning that did it. Just winning once was enough to make up for losing twenty times. If he got really low, he knew just one little win would bring him back up again. He just had to have that moment when his horse was flying at full canter past the winning post. 'Yes,' he'd shout to himself, an inward and silent roar of triumph, fists clenched. 'Yes. Me. Me. I picked that horse. I did that. Have that.' In his head he'd line up his mother and father, old teachers, tutors, lovers, people who doubted or mocked him, and, these days, Ellen. 'Have that, all of you. I knew that horse would win. Me.' He'd take his winnings, and, if he didn't put them on another horse, he'd lavishly squander them. Saving money, being sensible, would break the lucky flow. You had to laugh in the face of the lucky gods.

The thing he hated most about sharing his flat with Ellen was that she found out about his lucky routine. She had no sympathy with it at all.

'You've washed my red socks,' he screamed. 'I need them today. They worked for me last week. Got up nine thirty. Grey striped boxers,' he waved his lucky book in front of her, 'white shirt, Levi's, red socks. Look, *red socks* . . .' rapping the page with his finger, pointing, 'played The Smiths. Coffee. Walked down left side of street. Ten pounds on Heartbeat. Won. See that? Won.'

She looked dumbfounded at his precise, absurd notes, his small neat writing, listing every event in his diabolical life. Said nothing.

'Now you've ruined it. I can't repeat last week's lucky routine. You've broken the divine flow.'

Realising she might read his own carefully documented evidence against himself he snapped the book shut and shoved it into his back pocket. His lucky jottings included no mercy details of who he slept with, positions and what he'd filled his pockets with as he made post-coital tea or coffee. Ellen would not appreciate knowing that his other lovers provided her meals. Especially when they caused her so much trouble. She did not have his iron digestive system. The other night she'd lain in bed, complaining and belching – and there was nothing worse than a woman belching – put him right off.

'What was that we had tonight?'

'Chicken,' he said. Casually he thought.

'I know it was chicken. But how did it get red like that, and so sweet?'

'Oh, it's an old recipe of mine.'

'What was it?'

He'd stolen a bottle of white burgundy from Louise along with some frozen chicken thighs, a carton of yoghurt and a can of Coca-Cola. He'd planned to drink the Coke as he cooked the chicken in the wine. But somehow as he chopped onions and mushrooms (a gift from Friendly Mary) he'd poured and drunk a glass of wine, then another and before he knew it there wasn't any left to put in his casserole. Congratulating himself on his inventiveness, he cooked the chicken in the Coke instead. The result he thought surprisingly interesting. A culinary discovery, he decided. The chicken went fascinatingly red, and tasted sweet.

'It's Thai,' he told Ellen.

'Oh clever,' she enthused. He could tell she wasn't keen on eating it, but was, as ever, too polite to say so. It wasn't quite vile. In fact, he thought, a little garlic and ginger and it could be palatable.

He blamed this sudden throwing of fruit on old Mrs Boyle downstairs. Her and her damned mushroom quests that were now a regular Saturday afternoon outing were turning Ellen's head. But he was wrong. It was Ellen's dreams that were driving her to distraction.

She dreamed she was in a boat and the sea was heaving, a huge swell. The vast, heavy wall of water washed over the land, over small single palm tree cartoon islands, sent them rocking and sinking. The boat was still but everything around was going under. She dreamed she was walking through a city that had a vast canyon in the middle of it, a sudden plunging gap that stretched the full length of the ancient, worn paving slabs. To cross the gulch and get to her friends Ellen had to use a narrow, shaky rope bridge. People were bustling across easily back and forth, but it scared her. She couldn't bring herself to cross it. She dreamed she was driving to a park and suddenly realised she did not know the way. She stopped the car and ran into a huge building where she confessed to the man at the counter that she did not have a driving licence. They took her out right away in a car covered with gaudy signs, one neon lit on top, and a PA that boomed, 'Keep back. Learner.'

'What do they all mean, Stanley?' she asked at lunch one day.

'Overwhelming odds, feeling of inadequacy,' Stanley said. 'You've some sort of crisis you're not facing up to. Something you feel you can't cope with. That sort of thing.'

'Ah. My dreams are a bit obvious, aren't they? Not intricate and Freudian – well, if Freud wrote for the *Beano*, I suppose,' said Ellen.

'Only you would offer an apology for your dreams,' Stanley said. 'It's that bloke of yours, isn't it?'

'No,' she lied.

'Thought so,' said Stanley. He sniffed, took her bacon and brie sandwich and chewing it, told her. 'Brigit has left me.'

'No. Why?'

'I eat too much. I'm never home. I get agitated and fret if I take a day off. I annoy her. Not as much as I annoy me, I can tell you.'

'What are you going to do?'

'Eat too much. Stay at work too late and get agitated and fret if I take a day off. I don't have to change now, do I?' Staring glumly ahead, they shook their heads in unison.

'I really think Daniel cares for you in his way,' he said.

'Oh yes. I think that. But I can't stand him being with other women. I mean,' she lowered her voice, 'among other things, the unfaithfulness and the holding and kissing someone who isn't me. Well, frankly, I don't want to share him. You know . . .'

Stanley finished her sandwich and considered going to the bar for something else to eat. 'No, what?'

'His thing. His thing.' Ellen never mastered talking frankly about intimate parts of anybody's body – her own included. Stanley looked blank. How irritating. 'His thing,' louder now. 'I think about where he's putting it. What he's doing with it. What these other women are doing with it. And I don't want it near me.'

'It'd be a little more than near,' said Stanley seriously, wondering what it was about him that women always confided in him. Whatever it was, if he knew, he would fix it. He didn't want to know this.

'I think I'll have a pork pie,' he said.

Ellen burst out crying. It hurt so much. She thought Daniel was hers, her prize. He was so beautiful. Nights she waited – straining to hear his footfall on the stairs, his key in the lock – for him to come home to her. He always arrived bursting in, his marvellous life pouring from him. He'd carelessly toss his jacket over the back of the sofa and sit down, hands clasped behind his head. He'd tell her his day. She thought his life mystical and wild. He met this geezer who . . . knew a bloke who . . . he had a drink with, and . . . there was this deal brewing, and if . . . he put thirty quid on Joker's Wild and had won this . . . look. He'd hold up a wad of notes or he'd bring out something – a silk scarf, a pair of earrings – to give to her. He was so fabulous, and look at her. What did she do? She came and she went. She left for work at half-past eight. She came home again at six. She knew nothing of geezers and blokes and deals. She sat at her desk writing comic strips, correcting proofs, having the odd script conference – whatever. She ate lunch and in the afternoon she did it all over again. I'm so boring, she thought. So ordinary. I live a little life. Give me my Nescafé, give me a Twix and watch me go.

Every Saturday afternoon Emily Boyle would link arms with Ellen and they would set off on a mushroom quest. They rarely returned with mushrooms, they rarely returned sober. They weren't drunk, of course, just drunkish, deliciously touching the gigglish edges of silliness. Enraged, Daniel would hear them coming along the street, laughing, and there was always the telltale clank of bottles in their Oddbins bag. Emily would invite Ellen in and cook for her. It was the only decent meal she ate all week.

'I'm not teaching you to cook,' she said. 'I'm teaching you the meaning of food. It brings sanity and wellbeing. Never make decisions or love on an empty stomach. In other words, if you are ever in the position of having a man propose to you again, insist, absolutely insist, on having a bacon sandwich before you reply.'

They sat in Pierre Victoire's eating dish of the day, drinking wine. They'd order more wine, drink it and smoke. They'd be there all afternoon. Cora too.

'Oh,' said Emily Boyle. 'People accuse Rachmaninov of being romantic. Yet the Rhapsody on a theme of Paganini was quite terse, completely devoid of any overblown nonsense. And,' taking one of Ellen's cigarettes, 'the ending begins with consecutive fifths. That's hardly nineteenth century, is it?'

Cora and Ellen shook their heads.

'Did you sleep with him?' Cora asked.

'Sleep with Rachmaninov? Me? For heaven's sake, one didn't sleep with a man like that. He was so dour. Tall and glum. And devoted to his family. Oh no, I had other lovers.' She had a special way of saying Rachmaninov and piano. She rested her voice on the As. Prolonged them, as if she loved saying them and didn't want to let go – Raaachmaaaninov. Piaaano. Ellen loved it. Alone, in the bath she often imitated the old lady. 'Rachmaaaninov. Aaaaabominable. Aaan aaabsolutely aaadorable aaarse.' She thought Mrs Boyle's a golden voice.

'No, I just played a duet with him, that's all,' Emily said.

'I know you did that. You told me.'

'And I will tell you again. You can depend on it.'

'Ah,' said Cora. 'I just wondered.'

'I'll have a vodka martini.' Emily flapped her hand at the waiter. 'Will either of you join me?'

Cora and Ellen shook their heads in unison. But they were dazzled by Emily's drinking bravura.

'Oh I know,' Emily said, abashed at her consumption, but only slightly. 'I shouldn't. But at my age what can possibly happen to me? My liver is as old as I am. Things I've already put it through, another few years of abuse is hardly going to matter. Thank God I never have to look at the thing. Oh, I give myself the odd ticking off, tell myself to stop. But it's so lovely being naughty. The spirit has always been willing, and so has the flesh. So I'm at one with myself.'

She was holding court, expounding her theories about life. Half a bottle of barolo and a couple of vodka martinis and her life story and philosophies were anybody's.

'You people, you young people are all the same. Every generation of young people, all the same. You think you invented sex. I don't know. My goodness we used to have a lovely time. All the better because we weren't as lewd as you lot. You're so explicit.'

Ellen drank. Cora switched to Evian, espresso and inhaling the smoke from Ellen's cigarette.

'During the war there was such urgency – the shagging that went on. Let me tell you. We thought we were going to die. Or we thought the ones we loved were going to die. Of course we made the best of what time we had. Ah . . .' she was remembering, 'it all stopped in the fifties. People bought bungalows and sat inside neatly with their hands clasped in their laps – front doors shut. It was trauma did it. They were stressed, traumatised. No doubt about it. Philip Larkin says sexual intercourse was invented in 1963. But that's nonsense. People just came to themselves. They just noticed there were jolly tunes playing on the radio and they thought, time to get shagging again. And that's what they did. Time to get shagging again.'

Her golden voice hung gloriously on to the A. Shaaagging. She took an expert swig of her drink. 'That's the sexual revolution according to Emily Boyle.' She finished one vodka martini, ordered another and said, 'He never made faces as he played.'

'Sorry. Who?'

'Rachmaninov. He kept his face still. I never saw that in anyone else. Everyone else showed the emotions that were running through them with the music.'

Ellen said, 'Ah. Fancy that. I never knew.'

'Practice. Practice. Practice. That's what does it. That's how I spent my nights for years and years. Four, five hours a day. One day

I looked up and my life was hurtling past me. You people with your sex and drugs and rock 'n' roll are so lucky. I wish I'd had that.'

'So do I,' said Ellen. 'It kind of passed me by.'

'I was too busy with children. It all went on without me. Sex, oh yes, did that, smoked a little dope but it was mostly rock 'n' roll for me, other people's sins,' Cora sighed. 'Not that I didn't enjoy what sinning I managed. Sinning was fine. Loved it. But look what happened: two children, no father. And look at the environment I gave them.'

Emily gazed at her, ancient eyes. She reached her veiny old hand across the table and patted Cora's. 'Look at my hand,' she said. 'I have watched my life passing on the back of my hand. There it was, getting older and older in front of my eyes, whilst I stayed the same.' Then, 'You give yourself such a hard time. You don't see it, do you? *You* were your children's environment. Your body at first. Then your thoughts, your presence.'

'I wasn't there that much. I was working,' Cora said.

'Oh, stop chastising yourself. You worked for them, didn't you? Your stuff was there. Your taste. Books. Music. Give yourself a break. Children are tough. It's you middle-aged people who are fragile and broken.'

Chapter Twenty-two

Sunday lunch time, Cora put a plate of cauliflower soup before Ellen. 'There. Eat that.'

Still recovering from yesterday's hangover, Ellen stared glassily at the bowl before her. 'Women should take up physics,' she said.

'Is that some kind of incomprehensible comment on my cooking?' Cora asked. She did not take kindly to any kind of criticism.

'No. It's just soup. I mean that men are nature's physicists. Women are natural alchemists. The alchemy of our bodies and the alchemy of the mixtures we brew. Potions we put on our hair, moisturisers on our skin.' She sniffed deeply. 'Doubtless men invented the bow and arrow. Women, soup. Definitely, soup.'

'Hmmm,' said Cora.

'So I was wondering – what if,' Ellen said.

'What if?' Cora said. 'Do I have to listen to this? Your life is a mess of what-ifs and maybes.'

'What if Einstein had been a woman? Even better, what if Oppenheimer had been a woman? What if a woman had split the atom? Think about that. A man split the atom and he unleashes this abominable power. What does he do? He takes it to other men. "I have unleashed an abominable power," he says. And the other men, who are politicians and soldiers – the worst sort of people to have access to abominable power – say, "Abominable power. Does that mean we can destroy the world, then?" I ask you,' Ellen was getting quite heated now. 'I ask you, would a woman do that? "Destroy the world?" a woman would say. "You're not going to do that, I've just paid my phone bill. I've just had the curtains dry-cleaned." Oh no. If a woman had split the atom and unleashed that power she would have taken it to other women. To Helena Rubenstein or Coco Chanel and told them to see what they could do in the way of producing the ultimate moisturiser. Alchemy's creative.'

'Ellen,' Cora said, 'do you ever have any logical thought progressions? I sometimes think you are lost in some sort of dreaming. You hide in your head. Mostly from yourself. And you'll do anything rather than face up to your problems.'

'Yes,' said Ellen. 'I know. Whenever I have a problem I drift off into daydreams, vaguely hoping it'll sort itself out without me. I walked into this life I lead and sat down thinking: This'll do. I never planned it. I never plan. People look at me and think: She's OK. She's got an interesting job. But I don't know. I don't know what I want to do when I grow up. It's all right for you, you just know me. But I am me. I'm in here, and, frankly, I'm confused.'

'You need to get away. Ideally from yourself. We could go walking next Saturday. Give you a rest from Emily. She's as bad as you. Her and her mushroom quests. Have you ever bought any?'

'Once. Years ago.'

'She's leading you astray.'

'If anyone is going to lead me anywhere, astray is where I choose. I can't go anywhere on Saturday. I have to go out with her. I have to listen to her stories about Rachmaninov. I'm hooked. I have to find out if they're true.'

'Of course they're not. She is a bullshitter. I don't believe she ever met Rachmaninov. Do you?'

'Yes. I know her stories are unlikely, but I believe them because I want to. I'll go walking on Sunday if you want. I'd like to go watch geese coming in.'

'Well, we'll go on Sunday.'

They drove up to Cameron Loch. Hammering up the motorway, singing and dancing in the seat, playing at being Tina Turner.

'That's who I want to be when I grow up,' said Ellen.

'I'm going to be your Mrs Boyle. Over seventy, drinking everyone under the table and full of wonderful lies. I'm going to tell people I knew Jimi Hendrix.'

'Aren't you going to say you slept with him?'

'No, that's what's so wonderful about your old lady. She doesn't say she slept with Rachmaninov. She played the piano with him. I love it. I jammed with Jimi. I did lyrics with Jim Morrison. I sang doowop oooh in Tina Turner's backing group. I'll reinvent my life for the young and gullible people who were not around to witness my youth. Fill my glass, child, and I'll tell you a story. I'll lie and I'll lie and I'll lie and it'll be wonderful.'

They left the car in the car park overlooking the glassy expanse of icy water and set off up the tamed side of the loch along a wide track that Cora took at a brisk pace. Ellen trailed a couple of yards behind. They cut a dash in the countryside. Cora drowned in a dark green jersey, a multi-coloured selection of scarves and beads round her neck, a grey chenille hat wedged on her head, jeans tucked into striped socks, walking boots. Ellen was in black. The further from the city she got, the more of an urbanite she looked. Walking through muddy places in black jeans and black jersey, black scarf wrapped round her neck, she seemed awkward. She stuck her hands in her pockets and bent forward watching the ground as she walked. Open spaces worried her. No matter how many layers she put on she always looked cold. Her cheeks glowed chill, her lips moved slowly when she spoke. Her nose was red. She hated that.

Across the loch huge pine trees loomed into the sky. A heron stood skinnily still at the edge of the water watching them approach. When they got too near, it grudgingly took off, flying low over the water, huge wings lazily spread, a loud irritated gravelly cry.

'We really pissed him off,' said Ellen. 'He was comfortably settled there. Enjoying his daydreams. You could see him thinking: Oh bugger them. Now I'll have to fly away. Wonder if he's like us, lying in bed, putting off the moment of getting up. Does he delay the moment of flying off because he's ensconced?'

Cora shrugged.

'I love it when I wake early and realise I've another hour before I have to get up. It's my favourite pleasure,' Ellen wittered on. 'So warm and soft and I'm all relaxed. It's best if it's raining. Even better if it's pissing rain and I can hear people outside walking about in the wet and cold whilst I'm still fabulously in bed. Hee, hee, hee, I think, I'm in bed and you're not.'

'There's a nasty streak in you,' Cora said.

Ellen ignored this. 'Then if there's someone with me, someone I can wake to share my bonus hour, well, that's perfection.'

Across the water pine trees woodily creaked and moaned. Pigeons clattered unseen in amongst the deepest branches and exchanged throaty cooing. The Sioux could live here, Ellen thought. I could come see them. They'd ride along that far bank, single file. And they'd know everything – where rabbits hide, where the deer drink, the fox runs, everything.

'Who'd be in your bed rainy mornings?' Cora asked.

'Ideally all sorts of men. In reality Daniel.'

'You can't let go, can you?'

'Doesn't seem like it.'

After Ellen threw the apple at him, nursing his bruised head and ego Daniel left. He stayed away for three days. Ellen sat alone at night waiting for him to come home. Every time she heard someone on the street outside she thought it was him, and she brightened. She'd arrange herself on the sofa with a book, a cup of coffee and the television on across the room, looking, she hoped, as if she hadn't really noticed him missing. But when at last he did reappear she was out at work. When she got home, he was there, looking cool.

'Hi,' she said. Casually, she hoped.

'Hi,' he said. A better sort of casually than her. He got it right. He had no problem sounding as if he didn't care. Damn him. He was the one sitting with a coffee watching telly, looking as if he hadn't noticed her missing.

'Have you eaten?' she asked.

'Yes,' he said. Well, sod him. She malevolently hoped he had eaten the prawn salad she was planning for supper. Then she could pick a fight with him about it. But he hadn't. And now she didn't want it. She did not ask where he'd been, but knew he hadn't been alone and hadn't been with one of his mates, the interesting blokes and geezers he mixed with. They said nothing about their fight. They watched television, were polite to one another. And when they went to bed, made love. They fell easily into sex together because it was what they did best together.

Two weeks later they argued again, about Daniel's sex life again, and this time he stayed away for a couple of nights. Then he began staying away for a week, or a fortnight. In time she stopped listening for his coming home. He moved odd bits and pieces of his furniture to Friendly Mary's flat and Louise's house. Ellen replaced them with her own things. The flat started to look as if Ellen and not Daniel lived there. Neither of them addressed the overwhelming sadness they brought out in each other. This went on for years.

Once Ellen had seen him with another woman, someone blonde and thin she did not know. A soft wind, a central casting sort of wind that only added to their mutual gorgeousness, flapped their clothes and wrapped her hair round her face. Ellen could tell that they had, by unspoken agreement, decided to walk and laugh together and cast not a glance at the lesser beings who, peeping at them from the depth of their ordinariness, wondered who they were. They had the gift of celebrity. They looked famous. Daniel was carrying her shopping and, as they crossed the road, he put his arm round her shoulder to steer her safely through the traffic to the far pavement. He never did that for me, Ellen thought. Her heart was breaking. Then Daniel reappeared, letting himself into the flat late one night. She could not help but accost him.

'Who was that you were with? I saw you. You bastard. I saw you.'

Daniel shrugged. 'It was nobody,' he told her. Was that how he spoke about her? To them? His other women? 'She was nobody. A woman I once knew. Someone I married'?

'You shit,' she said. 'You shit. You are so nice to these other women. You put your arm round them. You carry their shopping. You look at them and smile. You were never that nice to me, Daniel. Never. Why couldn't you be nice like that to me?'

He picked up the jacket he'd thrown off, put it on and walked out the door. As he went she heard him say, 'Because you matter.' That hurt more than anything. She raced after him down the hall and caught him by the sleeve just before he left. 'What the hell do you mean by that? "You matter." How can I matter when you treat me so badly?'

'I never pretended for you,' he said flatly. 'I never let you believe I was the ideal bloke other women always think I am. Want me to be.' He shrugged, looked at her sadly.

'Oh thank you for that,' she shrilled. 'Just what I needed, someone who was totally honest about his affairs. Thank you for that.'

He shrugged again. 'I'm sorry,' he said.

It was not what she wanted to hear, an apology for refusing to be perfect for her when he worked so hard at being perfect for everyone else. This was some kind of privilege? She should thank him?

'Bastard,' she said. 'Bastard. I love you.' It was the only time she ever said it to him. As far as she could remember he never once said it to her; she didn't ask it of him. He slipped out the door, shut it against her tirade and stood, head down, listening to her.

'Bastard. Bastard. Bastard,' was all she said over and over. He did not know what he was hearing. The demented howl of a worm turning. But she did not run after him, or call him back. She returned to the living room, curled on the sofa and wept instead.

After that he stopped coming by so often. When he did he no longer let himself in, but rang the bell and waited for her to open the door. A small thing, but it meant a lot. It said, I no longer live here. I am a visitor. And yet she couldn't resist him. If he was there in her living room, she had to have him. No matter what ideals she set herself – I will send him packing, I won't give in – when he was there, when he was for the having, she would have him. Afterwards she always felt that she'd let herself down.

Daniel kept coming back. He came back when she was at work. And on Saturday afternoons when he knew she'd be on mushroom quests with Mrs Boyle. Yesterday as he was leaving he'd met her on the stairs and she'd let him know she was going walking with Cora. Right now, then, though she did not know it, he was standing in her bedroom breathing in the scent of her, slowly going through her things. He did it all the time, visited her when she was not there to receive him. He'd let himself in and wander through the rooms, touching her things, keeping himself informed about the details of her life. He'd scrutinise her cheque stubs, look at her supermarket receipts, read her mail, eavesdrop on the messages on her answering machine, thumb through her books, criticise her records. He noted she'd developed a taste for opera, something he knew nothing about. He blamed Mrs Boyle for that. He'd rake through her kitchen cupboards, stare into her fridge. He'd look at her dishes in the sink, and in the bathroom open her scent, sniff it deeply, splash a little on. He'd read her notebooks, check on her plots and characters and the fast-flowing speeches she planned for them. He'd lie on her bed and touch the tumble of clothes she always left draped on the chair. He listened to her silence.

He always thought Ellen had wonderful silences. She was, by and large, content with what went on in her head; plots, dreams, memories. Her silences, then, were deeper than his – more profound, mature, grammatical, more glossily silent. His silence was always the same – a wild syncopated clamour, bits of songs, racing facts, things people said to him years ago, that went battering round and round, a mind out of control, no matter how he tried to make it stop.

When he left, he always took something. He knew better than to take food. She bought so little she'd notice. There was so much else she would not miss. He could take an earring and she'd think she'd lost it in the street somewhere. A CD and she'd think she'd lent it to someone and had forgotten who. A cup, a glass, and she'd think, I'm sure I had more of these. A lipstick and she'd think she'd mislaid it. Once he took the soap she washed with and knew she'd only be momentarily puzzled by its disappearance. 'Funny,' she'd say, looking vaguely around. Thinking of her, he smiled as he wrapped it in toilet paper before slipping it into his pocket. Today he found her favourite silver ring lying on the dresser in her bedroom and couldn't resist it.

He would put it in a box he kept in the room across from Short Price Frankie's, the bookie, where he now lived. It was a small bed-sit but it suited him. He had his records and his stereo and a bed to lie on. Not that he used it much. There were other beds. He would sleep with Louise and take her mangoes and prickly pears that Mary gave him. He would sleep with Mary and take her white wine and Belgian chocolate that he stole from Louise. Mary wore a necklace he'd taken from Louise's jewel box and growing on Louise's kitchen window sill was a white begonia that once had been growing on Mary's. Daniel slept with them, made them tea or coffee and made up cheering horoscopes he pretended to read from their magazines. One day he knew he'd be found out. Meantime, what the hell, they all enjoyed it. Still, he thought about Ellen. He could not leave her alone. In her way she drove him crazy – if anybody, anything could drive him crazy. He could not get through to her. He could not penetrate the wall she'd put up years and years ago. He'd talk to her then notice she wasn't listening. She'd be staring off into the distance, a slight smile moving on her mouth. She'd be dreaming. She'd be off somewhere with someone else, visiting some moment from her past and creating in her whimsy a moment better than the one she was having with him. He hated that.

Cora and Ellen walked along the dam at the top of the loch, a wide grassy path. Swans came whooping across the water, dipping their necks, watching them. Their calling cut through the afternoon chill, spread eerily to them. Ellen was beginning to long for the city. She did not like to spend too long walking on untarmacked surfaces. She was uneasy with horizons. There was something about built-up places, city smells, music playing in streets, international wafts from restaurants, the drift of booze from pubs, heavily leaded fumes, that made her feel safe. They walked down the far side of the loch, moving slowly through long grasses, thick bushes. Shoving branches of trees to one side as they went. It was getting dark, a textured velvet black in amongst the pines.

'Are you sure you know where we're going?' Ellen asked.

'There is one path that leads round the loch,' Cora said. And pointing back, 'That is where you've been.' Pointing forward, 'That is where you're going.'

Chaffinches cheesed in thickets and occasional rabbits thudded out of view.

'There're scuttly things here,' Ellen protested. 'I don't like that.'

'Oh shut up. I always forget what a pest you are when we walk. I always forget that I vow never to take you again.' Then she heard the first geese. Her stomach fluttered, as it did when walking at a favourite estuary on north Mull she'd seen five o'clock eagles take to the sky. Every evening for years she'd cycled to her spot to watch them. Two of them rose straight up calling, declaring their presence.

Vast magnificent beasts they were, occupying a huge piece of sky.

The first geese flew in a small skein high above them.

'They've overshot,' said Ellen, 'they'll never get down.'

'Of course they will,' said Cora, pushing forward to hide in amongst some trees so that she could get a closer view of them. 'They're scouts come to check the going's safe for the main party coming along behind.'

'Like the Sioux,' said Ellen.

They seemed to stop overhead. Ellen imagined one calling out, 'That's it, chaps. We're here. Everyone down.' They wheeled, almost fell out of the sky, tumbling they came. The noise they made. Jostling and hooting they formed ranks on the water, settling their wings and shoving up to make room for others. Then they'd float, heads high, dignity regained, acting as if the nonsensical fiasco of landing hadn't happened. Yammering and honking another skein came, and another, thousands of them surging up the loch just below the line where trees met sky. Floating, lookout geese called to flocking new arrivals with a wheeling urgent passion, anxious for them all to be together again. The cacophony of hoots and cackles vibrated the air. When they'd all landed they looked from a distance like one vast floating raft, only their mewling and humming gave them away. A gang they were. Constantly calling and communicating, they knew nothing of silence.

Ellen knew that the urge to fly somewhere safe for the night came to them all as one and as one they'd take to the air as if landing didn't matter. 'Now there's a trick to master,' she told herself.

'They're monogamous,' said Cora. 'When a goose dies, his partner flies alone for the rest of her life, back and forward from feeding place to resting place, morning and night. And then when spring comes, she flies all the way to Siberia alone.'

'Poor old lone goose.' Ellen was quite distraught. Cora turned to look at her. There were tears spreading across her eyes. Her nose was chilled. She'd slipped her arms out of their sleeves and shoved her hands up inside her jersey to warm them in her armpits. Two hours out of the city and the woman was a wreck, weeping openly for lost geese in a lonely sky. Widows and orphans.

'For God's sake, Ellen. They're geese. They don't ache. They are all instinct. They don't ponder what might have been.'

'You don't know that,' Ellen said. It always surprised Cora how soft Ellen was. Her gentleness was boundless. She'd lift spiders from the bath and set them down to safety on the bath mat. 'There you go.' In a crowded room hers was the lap cats chose to settle on. Strangers told her their life stories. If beggars and drunks approached her for money in the street they were never disappointed. She spoke to her plants. She had a ruined relationship with a man who had broken her heart. But she could not find it in herself to reject him, completely, utterly. It hurt her to think of him alone. So she always let him come drifting back.

'Well,' Cora sighed, 'look at it this way. Widows and orphans and all sorts of single geese join the skein. They take their place in amongst the others, and nobody minds them. They do not discriminate against those that have lost their loves.' She remembered years ago Ellen putting the boys to bed and, wondering why it was taking so long, she'd gone through to the bedroom where all three of them were in tears over an Edward Lear poem. Edward Lear, for chrissakes, this woman would weep buckets at Edward Lear.

'They never came back. No, they never came back. They never came back to me.' Ellen read and it seemed so utterly, utterly sad. The boys found it unbearable. They pleaded that Ellen never put them to bed again. 'Please don't let Ellen read us a story again. It's too sad.'

'I don't know why we're such friends,' she said now, handing Ellen a tissue. She knew Ellen would not have one of her own. 'We have absolutely nothing in common.'

'Each of us is a lone goose. We take our single place in the human skein of things,' Ellen said.

Chapter Twenty-three

'I have reached an age when I don't like anybody to see my naked face. It's a bad habit, makeup. You get uncertain about yourself without it,' Ellen said to Cora. 'Some people have defensible space round their house, a smallish mowable area complete with hedge that is theirs. It is what they need to protect and to protect them from the world, from aggressors. I don't have a lawn. So this is my defensible face. This is what I protect and what protects me. The ever thickening layer of gunk between my face and the world.'

It was just after five. Ellen had just finished work and had popped round for a swift visit.

'You need taking out of yourself,' Cora said.

'I need taking out of myself and putting into Lauren Bacall. Somebody snazzy.'

Later that evening Emily Boyle considered Ellen and agreed with Cora. 'You need taking out of yourself,' she said.

'You're always saying that,' Ellen said. 'I'm fine the way I am. I don't want to be taken out of myself.'

'Rubbish,' said Emily. 'Everyone needs to be taken out of themselves once in a while. Me. You. Cora. We shall have a dinner party. Well, you shall.'

'I can't do that.' Ellen was horrified at the thought. 'I can't cook.'

'What's cooking got to do with it? We're going to drink and chat and eat and tell stories.'

'If it's a dinner party don't I have to supply food?' This seemed to Ellen like one of the essentials of any dinner party.

'Absolutely. If you're stuck for what to serve at a dinner party you can always do my old faithful, the edible Bloody Mary.'

Ellen had a good idea that this was not a dish to be taken lightly.

'Thing about it is,' Emily enthused, 'once you've served it

nobody is capable of eating pudding and they certainly don't remember if they've had starters, or not. It requires minimal cooking. No need to bother with salad, nobody notices it. Just some celery as a salty side dish. Oh yes.' She drifted off smiling slightly, remembering glory evenings of yesteryear.

'So what's the recipe?'

'Oh yes. Olive oil in a pan, a biggish pan, I'd say. Not huge. Large drink on the side for Cook. No ice cubes, the heat dissolves them. Melt garlic and anchovies in oil with a chopped chilli. Or two. Add onions and once they're sort of melty and transparent pop in some bacon, celery and grated carrots. Not too many carrots. But lots of garlic. After all, everybody's going to be eating it so everybody's going to be smelly, aren't they? And, by the way, it's good for vegetarians. Everyone knows they love bacon really. Add some tomato pulp to this mixture. Oregano, if you like. Let it simmer. Top up Cook's drink. Season your brew. Salt, pepper – lots of pepper – a pinch of sugar. Let it simmer some. Now pour in lots and lots of vodka. Lots and lots. Do not stint on the vodka. Some Tabasco and a good dash of Worcester sauce. A squish of lemon. You could even pop in a dash of sherry. And more vodka. Serve as a sauce for pasta.'

'What sort of pasta?'

'Do you honestly think anybody is going to notice or care? Plain spaghetti, linguini, penne, what difference does it make? And a side dish of celery with salt. Or you could make a salad with lettuce hearts and celery in a sour cream dressing. But that's a bit complicated for you.'

'What sort of wine do you think?'

'When I had it in Paris in the thirties it was served with vodka. But wine, yes why not?'

'Red? White?'

'Absolutely.'

'Do you put Parmesan on it?'

'Child, this is a recipe guaranteed to disguise the fact that you can't cook. Parmesan yes, Parmesan no. Trust me they won't know the difference.'

So she cooked it, and invited Ronald and George to share it with

Emily and Cora. On a whim as she was leaving the office on the Friday, she asked Stanley if he'd like to come along.

'I don't do dinner parties,' he grumped.

'Neither do I.'

'Will there be food?'

'Of a sort. I'm not good at food.'

He looked at her suspiciously. 'What are we having?'

'The edible Bloody Mary.'

There was a long, long silence. 'I don't do much since Brigit. She's pregnant again, by the way.'

'Is she ever anything else?'

He shrugged. Ellen knew he'd end up supporting this child like he did all Brigit's offspring though he'd only fathered two. She missed him since he separated from Brigit. She'd been a regular visitor to their house, a rambling, messy place filled with children, their noise and their tawdry plastic clutter and filled with Stanley and his books. Visions of Stanley at home were of a man, child in one arm, shovelling oven chips and fishfingers on to Peter Rabbit plates, eating as he went. But now he lived alone, she didn't drop by to see him any more. It wasn't the same.

'You'll never be a millionaire if you keep carrying on like this,' she softly ticked him off.

'It isn't me carrying on, is it? I don't know, life keeps intervening with my plans. I'll bring some food. Your menu sounds dubious.'

It was a drunken evening. The edible Bloody Mary steamed on plates, drizzled with olive oil, glistening with olives, Parmesaned and parsleyed. It was extraordinarily good. The room was candlelit. Conversations staccatoed. People started to say something, wandered off mid-sentence, mid-thought and ended up saying something else.

'I don't mind what we talk about,' Emily was adamant, 'as long as we don't talk about death. When you get to my age all the people you know talk about death. Who has gone, is going, will go next. It's very depressing.'

Candles flickered and the wine bottles dwindled.

'Have you always been faithful to George?' Ellen said to Ronald when George was out of the room.

'What in Christ's name was in that sauce?' Stanley wanted to know. 'It had a real depth of flavour. And I feel . . .'

'Of course I have,' smiled Ronald, though somehow Ellen didn't quite believe him. 'Darling, I'm far too insecure to be anything else but faithful. I don't take risks.' He smiled wickedly.

'Have you ever thought about getting a new pair of trousers?' Emily eyed Stanley's crotch.

'You are treading in dangerous territory when you cast aspersions on a chap's trousers,' Stanley said. 'A chap and his trousers are, well, close. I'm a stout trouser sort of a chap.' Stanley was drunk.

Emily beamed to Ellen. 'See. I told you the edible Bloody Mary worked. Stanley is being gorgeously affable. I love him. I have a trouser theory, too.'

'What could that be?' asked Stanley.

'That people always go too far. You can tell that by the state of women's heels and men's trousers. Look at them in the seventies. Vast flapping things. People went round with yards and yards of material waving round their ankles. Then they went all tight. You can tell the state of the world by the width of men's trousers and the height of women's heels. I tell you.'

Cora put a familiar hand on the intimately straining threads of Stanley's jeans. He always wore jeans, but had, for the evening, abandoned the stained and dubious sweat shirt for a denim shirt and spotted tie. 'These aren't as stout as you think, Stanley,' she told him. Her face glowed. Umpteen glasses of wine and more vodka than she knew about made her more forward than she planned to be. 'I think you give your trousers qualities they do not possess.'

He looked at her with unreserved longing. He adored her. Always had. He'd first spotted her marching along the shore, crisply ordering her sons not to trudge, and had desperately wanted to introduce himself and say if she would love him for ever he wouldn't trudge either. Then one day she'd been standing outside the building when he finished work. 'What does that mean – Starless Enterprises?' she'd officiously asked. He told her, then she'd gone on her way before he could declare himself. When she'd turned up at the office visiting Ellen he couldn't believe his luck.

'You know her?' he asked. In a loose disinterested fashion, he hoped.

'Yes,' said Ellen. 'Cora O'Brien. A chum. Do you want me to introduce you?'

'No. No,' he shook his head. 'Life is complex enough.'

'You don't have to have a relationship. You could just buy her a drink. Have a chat.'

'I can't afford a drink. I can't afford a chat.'

'Cora isn't like that,' Ellen hotly defended her friend. 'Cora is wonderful.'

Stanley didn't dispute it.

They opened more wine and cooed over his runny Camembert and provolone.

'Cora,' George said, 'I declare you have a chip on your shoulder.'

'Jealous,' said Cora, 'because you're too old to have one. Your shoulder's past it in the chip stakes.'

'How did you guess?' George smiled. It was a joke they had. They did not greet each other with a 'how are you?' or a 'hello'. It was always, 'You've got a chip on your shoulder, Cora.' George was always amused by the replies. She never let him down.

'You've got a chip on your shoulder, Cora.'

'Of course I have. Where would a low-class girl like me be without one.'

'You've got a chip on your shoulder, Cora.'

'It suits me. It is me. I am that chip.'

'You've got a chip on your shoulder, Cora.'

'And you haven't with your murky past, George? I'll show you mine if you show me yours.'

'Cora, my sweet, I don't think that would be a treat for either of us.'

'Have you always been faithful to Ronald?' Ellen to George when Ronald was out of the room.

'Oh for heaven's sake, how old-fashioned you are,' George sighed. 'Of course not. Darling, who is? If not in fact, then in daydream, in longing. I, of course, am far too insecure to be faithful. I have to know I still have what it takes. My ego, my libido depends on it. My insecurity, you could say, does the relationship proud.'

'Oh that old thing,' Emily derided him.

George beamed at her. 'You no doubt have heard it all before.'

'Absolutely,' said Emily. Aaaabsolutely. Then, when Ronald returned to the table, 'Our Ellen has been digging into the intimacies of your relationship.'

'Good heavens,' said Ronald. 'I hope the child has a strong stomach and a stout heart. It doesn't make pretty telling.'

They all smiled. Ellen often watched Ronald and George walking home from the pub, summer evenings, close, so close. Their quiet, constant almost rhythmic bickering cutting through the soft air. She envied them. I'll never have that – a chum, lover, companion, she thought.

'She wants to know if you have been faithful to George and if he's been faithful to you.'

'And now she knows,' said George.

'See,' said Emily. 'Their neuroses match perfectly. It makes them friends. They know all about each other. Unlike you and Daniel.'

'What about me and Daniel?' Ellen refilled her glass and other glasses nearby.

'Your neuroses match disastrously,' Emily told her.

'What do you mean by that?' Ellen wanted to know.

'Well,' Emily cut herself a wedge of Camembert and heaped some grapes on to her plate, 'Daniel simply hasn't learned to give.'

'You can say that again,' Ellen nodded, a kind of hypernod, a nod of someone who has had far too much undeclared vodka and declared wine.

'You on the other hand,' Emily looked at her sternly, 'have never learned to take.'

Cora pointed a loving finger at her friend. 'She's certainly got the measure of you,' she said.

'I'll make coffee,' Ellen said. Rising unsteadily from the table. She was concentrating on the long drunken walk from table to kitchen and the heroic effort needed to make it. She returned in time with her cafetiere and only five matching cups.

'Funny,' she said. 'I used to have six of these. I don't remember breaking one.'

Stanley and Cora shared a taxi home. He got out, paid, and walked her to her door. He leaned on the front door. In those golden days of yore before satellite dishes and mountain bikes, when her children were young and sleeping, Cora used to lean here to listen to and breathe in other people's lives. The Robinsons upstairs were making chips, the Lawrences were arguing. A low moan somewhere – someone was making love. And she would shut her eyes, trying not to envy them – them all – arguers, chipmakers and lovers. None of them was alone.

'I have a theory about bad housing and anoraks,' said Stanley.

'Oh, this housing isn't that bad. There is an odd comfort in the closeness of other people.'

'If it wasn't for sex,' said Stanley, 'there would be no housing schemes and no anoraks.'

'You'll have to explain that,' Cora said.

'You grow up. You get horny. You screw somebody. She gets pregnant. You need some place to live, you've got no money, you move into a housing scheme – two rooms and a kitchen four floors up, no furniture except a bed, a sofa and a telly. What else is there to do but screw? You have more children. They use up all your energy and sense, so the only thing you can bring yourself to do in the evening is watch crap on the telly. Then you're so bored when you get to bed you screw some more. You have more kids. They use up all your money. No energy, no sense, no money, the only thing you can afford to wear is an anorak. And you're stupid enough to think you look good in it. If there was no sex there'd be no tower blocks, no housing schemes, no shit on the telly and no anoraks. We do it to ourselves.'

'Stanley!' Cora chided. 'You old cynic. Life isn't that bad.' She was laughing, but still she felt a flicker in her stomach. It was registering some sort of truth. No energy, no sense, no money. She recognised herself in some of this outpouring.

'No. I know it isn't that bad,' he said.

She reached up on tiptoe. 'I have to go. It's late.' She kissed him. It was just a small peck on the cheek but she surprised them both. 'Sorry,' she said. Then, absurdly, tried to rub it off, wiping the kissed spot with her fingers. 'I don't know what came over me. It's a reaction. Just something I do. Please don't think I mean it.' Then realising how awful that sounded, 'Well, don't think I didn't mean it. I mean . . .' She was being silly now. 'Oh good night,' she said. And left him leaning there, smiling vaguely, with his nonsensical theories and his damp cheek.

Two in the morning and all that was left was debris. A wine-stained tablecloth covered with crumbs. There were dishes piled in the sink, and dishes on the unit and dishes on the table. Candle wax drippings, overflowing ashtrays, remains of soggy salad, grape stalks, grubby glasses, burned pots and a pristine lump of Roquefort left, drunkenly neglected, in the fridge. Oh, someone's had a dinner party, Ellen thought, glumly looking round. I'll deal with it in the morning.

She was feeling a little leftoverish and liverish herself. Her mouth was raw with smoking, her head ached and just beneath the deepening ache of her hangover were the scatterings of vodkaed conversation; relationships and sex, holidays abroad, critical pronouncements about films she hadn't seen and books she hadn't read. She'd deal with it all in the morning.

She climbed naked into bed, said, 'Never again, never again. Oh, please, please, never again.' Over and over. The night she'd had, a lucid memory of drunkenness spread before her and she could see it as clearly as if her follies were lying in full view on a sheet of black silk. 'Never, never again,' she promised herself again before falling into a deep, dirty sleep.

Two hours of unconsciousness she got before she woke. There was someone in the room. Her head hurt, and she was numb, still, with fragments of dream humming in her head. It took a moment before she realised what was happening, before she could interpret into reality the rustle and movement that had woken her. She saw him, dark against the window, standing by the bed looking at her.

'Daniel?'

'You bitch,' he said. 'You bloody bitch.'

She could not think of what to say. She could not sort out her confusion.

'Daniel?'

'You've had a party and you didn't invite me. You didn't even think of me, did you?'

'We're separated, Daniel. I get to have a life.'

'You get to have a life. You. You've just taken over my life. This used to be my life. This. In this flat.'

It hurt. He imagined everyone sitting round the table drinking and laughing and never even mentioning his name. He'd lived here for years and Mrs Boyle had hardly spoken to him. Ronald and George passed him on the stairs and barely said hello. But Ellen, oh yes, his wife, with her black clothes and hair and dark glasses and shy ways, everybody wanted to know her. 'What do you do?' they'd say. 'Um. Write comic strips,' she'd answer in that deferential way of hers, and they'd ooh and aah. 'How wonderful. What fun.' And they'd invite her to tea. Or something.

'You took my life. You took my books and my music and my things and I made you. I told you things. Books, films. You knew nothing when I met you.'

She struggled to rise, propping herself up on her elbow. Her hangover took hold. Oh God, she didn't need this. She really didn't need this.

'I don't need this, Daniel. Please go away.'

'Please go away,' he mimicked her. 'Please go away. Just like that. Go away, Daniel. I'm finished with you. And away Daniel goes like a good boy. Does he bugger.'

She sighed. Their arguments were always the same, a childish peeved hurl through Daniel's anger and pain.

'I took nothing, Daniel. I picked up the tab for a year's back rent. You were lucky not to get thrown out. I paid all your bills. I got your phone reconnected. I paid your parking fines, though I still haven't seen any car.'

'I pushed it into the river.'

'God help us. And I paid your back poll tax. It was years overdue. Daniel, you'd have ended up in prison. I bailed you out.'

'Oh fuck you.' Fuck you, always fuck you when he couldn't think of anything more dire to say.

She lay down. Pulled the duvet over her head. 'Leave me alone.'

'I will not leave you alone,' he fumed, yanking the cover off her, throwing it across the room.

Naked, she squirmed, pulled a pillow over her. 'Stop this, Daniel.' It was horrible. He was horrible, out of control and unable to contain his hatred. It would be easier to deal with if he hated her and not himself. He leaned over her. Whiskied breath. He was drunker than she was. He took her wrists, held them on the pillow over her head, climbed on to the bed, on his knees over her. She hated that. Hated it. Writhed and fought. Pushed and kicked. 'Leave me, Daniel. Leave me.'

He held her, said nothing, such a vicious silence. He shoved his knee between her legs.

'Daniel, please. Please. Let me be.'

Then he fell on top of her. She felt his lips on her neck. His breath on her. He was moving on her. 'I've been watching you. You could have asked me if I wanted to come. You don't even think about me. Well – here I am.'

She felt him. He took her. Inside her. 'This is me,' he said.

There was never a time when she did not want him. But now she shouted, 'Not like this. Not like this. No.' His body always entranced her. It was not like a man's body. It was a boy she loved. A boy. Men scared her. Men were big. Men were huge and they called you cunt.

'Daniel!' she screamed. 'Don't. Leave me. Leave me be.' But her legs curled over him.

He moved and heaved into her. 'This is me. This is me. Me, here. Me.' He came. Not his usual roar of joy and release. This time he just howled, a cry of such anguish, Ellen almost forgave him. Spent, he collapsed on to her. Then rolled away. Held his knees. Shamed, he clutched his head. 'Sorry. Sorry. Sorry. I didn't mean that.'

'Oh yes you did,' she said. She lay beside him. The room was cold but she did not move to cover herself up. She would get really, really cold, blue with it, shivering. That would show him what a bastard he was. 'Oh sod this,' she said out loud, realising how foolish she was being. Daniel lay by her, quite still. Sniffing occasionally, staring ahead.

'Stop this,' she said to him. 'Either go or get into bed and sleep. I need to sleep.'

He turned to her. She had decided never to forgive him, but she still took him in her arms, stroked his hair. Kissed his head. She never could bear his pain. 'You bastard. You're such a mess. Worse than me.' She put her lips on his neck, licked it slightly. Salty, it was. He'd been sweating. 'You're all sweaty,' she told him. 'Take your things off.' She helped him out of his clothes. 'That's much better.' She surprised herself, she sounded so maternal. She didn't think she had such feelings in her. They lay entwined.

'When I was little my mother told me she didn't want me,' she told him.

'She didn't mean it,' Daniel said. 'I bet she didn't.'

It was their old game. They always bet each other pathetic absurd bets that she always lost. Listening to the radio she might say, 'I bet you a blow job to fifty pounds the next record will be U2.'

'OK,' he'd say. 'You're on.' She never won. Not once.

'You know nothing about gambling,' he told her. 'It takes you shuddering and shaking to the brink of yourself. You have to risk losing everything you have for the thrill of winning something you don't really want. It isn't the gain, though. It's the winning. I can't tell you what it's like. You have to take yourself to the edges of not just who you are, but what you have and how little you care about it. And yourself.'

'What's wrong with you?' she asked.

'I'm a shit,' he said. 'You know that.'

He hung on to her. 'We could just lie here and hold each other. Just touch. People can do that. You don't have to have sex.'

She didn't believe him. 'That has never worked for us, Daniel.'

She reached down to touch him. 'I always thought this was mine. I couldn't stand other women sharing it,' she said. She moved down him. 'It didn't need to be like that,' she said. She closed her mouth over him. Everything seemed louder, more than real. The rustle of bedclothes, the soft slap of their bodies touching. His breathing. She wanted him so much, and he was a shit, always would be. There were tears in her eyes. He pulled her back up to him, and lay on her. Stroked her, kissed her.

'I bet you,' she said, 'I bet you everything – this flat, everything I have – that after this you will never come back to me.'

He did not reply, did not take her on. He just lost himself in her. She opened her eyes. All of Daniel's Madonnas were round the walls, watching. They'd seen too much, she thought, all the nonsense that had gone on in this bedroom through the years. They with their permanently serene faces. And her with her legs in the air.

Chapter Twenty-four

Still drunk, naked and holding on to Daniel, she slept again. He was gone when she woke. The morning hurt her eyes. There was something relentless about early light, the way it bled into the room glimmering and seeping round the edges of the curtain. Stiff and shivering cold, she wrapped herself in the duvet, pulled it over her head. And hiding, remembered.

For weeks and weeks she had not visited the Sioux. They must be sitting by the campfire thinking about her. Little White-eyes has not ridden out from the bungalow to see them. She missed her old friend Mrs Robb. Maybe the Sioux would be missing her. Maybe they'd be wondering where she was.

Only, they did not live on the golf course. She was just a silly little girl that everyone laughed at because she galloped about on a pretend horse. She knew that by day. Standing up in the sunlight she could see the golf course was just a scrubby over-used expanse of grass. But at night, lying down in the dark listening to the television through the wall and trying not to think about the man in the pointy shoes and the woman in the white dress coming to kill her, she could not resist imagining them.

She could see their faces, those wise features, calm, honest eyes. She could hear the sound of their horses as they moved across the plains. School was starting tomorrow. She knew after that there would be no riding out to see them. She would be back in her gymslip and cruel schoolgirl knickers, her garters would dig into her leg and her school shoes would be heavy on her swift summer feet. She would no longer be fleet.

Summer lay outside her window. Stars in the sky. Her mother went to bed; Ellen could hear her snore. The Sioux were out there. She imagined them riding in slow single file through the golf course gates, down Wakefield Avenue to her front gate. She could hear them. A certain jingle, a clip of hooves on tarmac. Right now they'd be lining up on the pavement, standing still, pooled in lamppost light, waiting for her.

She slid out of bed, dressed and climbed out of the window. Thunder was there, of course, faithful and still as she leaped on to his back. Bareback, tonight, she gripped his mane and rode down the garden path to greet the Sioux. The chief, feathered and proud, raised his hand when he saw her come to him. Side by side, with a whole tribe coming behind, they rode down the centre of the avenue and into the golf course.

Summer had warmed the earth, the air was still and soft. She did not need her jumper. She took it off, threw it to the ground. Wanting to feel the grass on her feet, she slid them from her shoes then set off towards the hunting grounds. The night was glorious, stars above and a fat moon shining. She sang a little song as she went, a little song that was her own. 'Toot-ti-too,' breathy singing. A deer drinking at the great water lifted its head to watch her go.

The chief at her side, the tribe behind her, the night soft on her body, she was happy. Deliriously happy. She stopped. Trembling, she listened. She thought if she concentrated she would be able to hear the stars move, thump, dunt, in the sky, or the grass crushing beneath her feet. And there was a breathing. She turned. Screamed. He was standing behind her. The spy, Mr Martin, in his yellow V-neck jersey, checked trousers and a raincoat. The blood drained from her heart. She paled and shook.

'Look at this,' he said. He opened his coat. There was between his legs a huge pink thing. Heaven's sake, what was that? It was horrible. Horrible. Amazed, she took another look before she set off away from him. Running. And where was Thunder now? And where were the Sioux? Gone. All she had was her little leggies that fear turned leaden. She could hear him lumbering behind, feel his hand clutch at her shoulder, rough on her bare flesh. 'C'm 'ere,' he said. 'Don't you want to touch it?'

'Leave me. Leave me.' She opened her mouth to call for help, but nothing came. She threw herself over the grass towards the hole in Mrs Robb's fence.

He, breathing behind, called her name. 'You'll like this, Ellen. You'll enjoy this. It's what you want, isn't it? Running about alone at night.'

She couldn't find the hole in the fence. Ran up and down like an animal, searching for it.

'They've fixed the fence,' Mr Martin said, catching up with her. 'Your little bolt hole is all fenced up. Look at it. Look at what I've got for you.' He showed her again the huge pink thing. Lunged at her. She turned and ran, fled towards the golf course gate. Battering, pelting without looking back. Her face was frozen with fear and effort. Little fearful noises, yelps, came from her throat.

'What in the name of God are you doing, girl?' Her mother. Her mother standing on the sacred Sioux hunting ground in pink candlewick dressing gown and fluffy bedroom slippers. Ellen stopped, panting and trying to catch her breath, pointed back. But there was nobody there. Mr Martin must have his own bolt hole that he used when he saw Janine storming furiously towards them.

'The man,' Ellen said. 'The man was after me.'

'What man? There is no man.' Janine took her daughter by the arm and marched her home.

'The man,' Ellen cried. 'The man.'

Her mother smacked her hard and sent her to bed. 'You're more trouble than you're worth, my girl. Stupid . . . stupid . . . stupid . . .' Aching, trembling and filthy, Ellen curled up under the blankets. She was stupid and more trouble than she was worth. There really were no Sioux, and there was no gleamy black stallion.

Chapter Twenty-five

The best thing for a hangover, Cora thought, was a walk. On the Sunday after the night of the edible Bloody Mary she got up at six, filled a flask with coffee, packed her rucksack and headed for the hills. It took almost three hours from Edinburgh to reach Glen Doll and Jock's Road. A favourite walk because, whilst she liked to be alone, there were always lots of other walkers to smile and nod to in passing. Being too alone in lonesome places wasn't always advisable.

She parked the car, put on her walking boots and took the path at a lick. She liked to get some distance between herself and the rest of the world and she knew that when she started to think, as she always did when walking, her pace would slow. The more tortuous her thoughts, the slower the pace. Then when her memories came full flow she would stop, hold her head and groan, 'Oh no. Oh no. I did that.'

She chastised herself daily for the mother she'd been. Looking back it seemed to her that all she'd done was boss and nag. 'No, you can't have . . .' and, 'Just where have you been till this time of night . . .' and, 'You are not leaving this house till you've done your homework . . .' and, and, and. The trouble with having children was they turned you into a mother against your will, she thought. Nobody really mentioned when she had a baby that it would grow up. She strode and listed out loud the things she hated.

'Training shoes,' she said. 'I didn't bargain for them.' She passed through the gate of the deer fence and started up the path. Huge trees, a deep, green pine smell, and a chill in the air. Deer tracks on the soft mud at the side of the path. 'Things,' she said. 'There were all those childhood things I'd never heard of till they were demanded of me. "Oooh," they'd lie. "Everyone's got one except me." Nintendo, transformers, mountain bikes, shoes that pump up. God. Nobody mentioned any of that to me.'

The path branched off, up and up through the trees or along the wide forestry track. She took the hard way, started up the long steep slope through the trees. Breathing hard, calf muscles starting to ache.

This morning, before she left, Sam had found her kneeling on the kitchen floor, head inside the fridge, looking for food.

'What are you doing?'

'I'm kneeling here searching for food and swearing like a trooper. I'm a mother, what do you expect?'

'From you, Mother, nothing other than that.'

'Don't you mother me.'

'Sorry.'

'Don't speak to me like that.'

'Like what?'

'Patient. You're being patient with me. Don't you dare be patient with me.'

He laughed.

'There's nothing to take on my walk,' she sighed. He brought her a Mars Bar and a bottle of water from his room. 'There,' he said. 'Don't you go eating it till you arrive. I know what you're like. You can't wait, can you?'

Last year he'd left home to live with his girlfriend. When they split up he came back. But he wasn't Cora's any more. She couldn't boss or bully him. She missed him for that. It meant Col took the brunt of her bossing. She liked having someone to keep right.

Panting, she carried on up through the trees. There were fabulous views ahead, a reward for all this climbing. 'Parents' Day,' she yelled. 'I hated that. Sitting on hard seats waiting to get spoken to as if you were ten years old.' Pant, pant, stride. 'God, though, boys. Grubby little buggers.'

Out of the trees at last, and there was the whole fabulous world she'd been denied by the thick pine barrier. The river, hills – brown and only vaguely purple now that September was gone. A little wind crept over her, bringing the smell of peaks she would not reach today, peat. She was moving easily now, that fluidity she

216

loved. It came, too, when she ran mornings over the Links, a moment when movement was all. A purity in that moment that was clear and simple. She did not think. There was only her body and the world it was running through. There was only her heart beating, her lungs heaving in air and the regular thud of her feet hitting the path. She loved that moment. It cleaned her out. It kept her sane.

'They peed in old Coke tins. Ugh. Clammy hands, dangerous underpants. Ugh.'

Cora was steaming up the mountainside now, the rubbled path quaking and scattering in her wake. Great lumps of quartz jutted from the hills, a mountain hare scudded up the huge slope above her. 'Alphabetti spaghetti,' she hollered, voice bouncing off the mountains, 'goodbye to you.' She sniffed. 'Potato waffles, oven chips, Wee Willie Winkie sausages, beans – goodbye to you.' Bye to you. Bye to you. Bye to you. Her farewell echoed up the valley. Highland voice, beaming softly away from her. She sat considering the view. 'Burgers,' she said sadly, 'milk shakes, toffee yoghurt, tomato sauce flavour crisps, cherry cola, fishfingers, chunky chicken bites – goodbye to all you sticky things. I will not miss you.'

Eating her Mars Bar she started back. It was two o'clock. Two hours' walking to the car park, then three hours' driving. It would be dark when she got home, and she did not trust the lights on the car.

She listened to Rachmaninov as she drove, a new addiction. Emily Boyle played the Third Piano Concerto on the table most Saturdays after the mushroom quest, and listening now Cora realised how well the old lady played it. Why, you could almost hear it as her fingers hit the wood.

'See,' she'd say. 'Three movements and the opening theme pops up in them all. Clever, huh?'

Cora and Ellen would nod. 'Yes,' they'd say. 'Fancy that.'

Without glancing at them Mrs Boyle would smile and say, 'I suspect you two are making a fool of me. But you'll see. You'll see.'

'Maybe she did know Rachmaninov,' Cora said. The car battered down the glen, through Kirriemuir then right turn at Glamis, on to Perth, down the motorway and home. 'Not long,' she said. Music poured into the car. Cora wondered how long Mrs Boyle had been alone. And who was Mr Boyle? Soon she'd be alone. Her boys would go, and if she would not miss all the mess, and stickiness and stuff they brought, she would miss them. She would definitely miss them. The tape ended. Snapped out and the radio came on. 'Golden Oldies,' some disc jockey burbled, bending his voice round his enthusiasm. 'Blasts from the past.'

'Oh no,' said Cora. 'Not you. Not that. No more past blasts for me.' She turned the tape; Rhapsody on a theme of Paganini.

'Opus forty-three,' Cora boomed. Like Ellen she had started imitating the old lady. Would the house seem empty when the boys left? Would they come back to her? 'They never came back, no they never came back to me. Oh God, shut up.' She'd had only the Mars Bar all day and wished she'd stopped for some more chocolate. Her work with the boys was done. 'They don't need me now.' Rachmaninov's terse melody hummed out. She turned up the volume, opened her window. Put her foot down. 'I could die now,' she said, suddenly emotional, pre-menstrual, foolish. 'I could die to this tune. Die now.' Hurtling and blistering, Cora. 'I'll die to Rachmaninov.'

She hammered round a bend that the fartmobile was not up to hammering round. On two wheels, then over. Over and over. The hideous grind of aching metal, the roar of ungeared engine, before it cut out. She crashed and tumbled. Though she was in it, she could stand apart from it. She could see it. She could tell what she looked like, spinning and rolling. A car coming towards her stopped. People got out, were running towards her. Then it stopped. The car landed on its side in a ditch. She thought: Oh. This is a strange view. The cassette spat out of the machine, the radio came on: 'A blast from the past, remember this? "Bohemian Rhapsody".'

'I'm not dying to that.' Cora was appalled. 'I hate "Bohemian Rhapsody".' Hanging sideways and almost upside down, desperately reaching for the radio switch. ' "Scaramouche, Scaramouche . . ." Get stuffed. I refuse to die to that.'

She could only have hung there for a couple of minutes. Was aware of hands getting hold of her, cutting the seat belt and heaving her out of the car. She was pulled to safety through the open window. And as soon as she was free from the wreckage she got to her feet, stepped back and politely asked if someone could please switch off the bloody radio. The car was ruined, but she was fixated on stopping the music.

'You were lucky,' one of her rescuers said.

Cora considered him calmly. 'I will not die to that tune,' she told him.

She was taken to the local doctor's, declared fit, given a lift to Perth where she caught the last bus back to Edinburgh. It was after midnight when she got home.

'Where the hell have you been till this time of night?' Sam was furious with worry.

Cora was amazed. Why was he so bothered? 'I had an accident,' she said quietly. 'The car's a write-off.' She sat down to take off her shoes and rub her feet. 'I think I'll have a bath.'

'Are you all right?' She could tell he'd worked himself into a lather imagining all sorts of things. 'You might have phoned. I was going to start ringing round the hospitals.'

'I'm fine,' she said, icily calm. 'I'm absolutely fine. Nothing wrong with me. I just will not die to "Bohemian Rhapsody".'

'What do you mean, "Bohemian Rhapsody"?'

'I mean it was playing when the car went off the road and rolled. And I will not die to that tune. Rachmaninov, I'll consider. But not that.'

Shaking her head she went through to the bathroom. He stood, scarcely believing what she'd said. The scent of her ylang-ylang bath oil floated through to him, mingling with steam and her cool assurances. 'Oh no. Not that.'

He thought she'd finally gone off her head. 'She's bust her string,' he said to nobody but himself. 'Off her rocker.'

Next day Cora rose early, put on her tracksuit and running shoes and took off at a mild jog. She did not think. She felt so serene, removed from herself, as if she was standing outside herself, watching. She chose Mozart for her Walkman. Can't face rock 'n' roll, she thought. I need something perfect. Rock isn't perfect. It's a howl to match your mood. And moods are rarely perfect. She looked down at her body. 'I'm fine,' she told herself. 'No aches. No pains. No bumps or bruises. Well, look at me.'

She didn't run so much as float. The car crash was vividly with her every step she took. The colours of it – the yellow rusting bonnet, grass, road and the sweep of her mediocre lights as she rolled. Then everything spun round; cans, cups, papers showered from one side of the car to the other as she landed. Crashing past her.

'I'm fine,' she said.

The morning was crisp and raw, first frost. She had run through other mornings when the cold air rushed and burned down her throat, but this cold was a perfect cleansing chill. 'This is what I want,' she said. 'This perfection.' She got to Leith Links and did not jog. She took off, running and running over the grass, music in her ears, tears in her eyes, pouring down her cheeks. 'I'm fine.' It was the first time in her life she'd felt it. Ecstasy.

She moved through her day. She showered, dressed, went to work. She walked through corridors to her room, watered her plants, wiped the board, laid out books. She marked the register, wiped noses, tied shoelaces, marked sums and read stories. She did all her usual things, she thought, in her usual way. Only her pupils said, 'Miss O'Brien was in a funny mood today.' Friends in the staff room said, 'What's up with Cora? She's being weird.' She told them all that she'd been in a car accident and held out her arms, displaying her soundness to everyone in the room. 'Not a scratch on me. I'm so lucky.' Thinking back she recalled vaguely talking at length to rows of baffled, but polite, little faces about the joys of climbing mountains. 'It's the only place you'll find air that is totally unleaded and not recycled, that has not previously been breathed by others. Free-range air.'

Next day Melanie Johnston's fabulous mum phoned to complain to the headmaster about Miss O'Brien and the nonsense she spoke. 'My Melanie came home bright red and all but fainted. She tried to walk from school without breathing in any old air. What is the woman on about?'

Feeling positively smug about herself and her luck in the face of death she went shopping. Even the blessed have to eat, she told herself. She wandered the aisles clutching her basket, wondering what on earth it was she'd come in for.

'I nearly died,' she said out loud. People debating the merits of cornflakes over Weetabix looked round and pretended she was not there. 'But it would not matter if I did,' she continued, wandering past the toilet rolls. 'The boys wouldn't miss me,' she said. Then, considering this: 'Yes they would. I mean,' to a woman loading up with cat food, 'Col kicks off his shoes and never can find them. Every day, every single day we wander about looking for them. And I ask you, would either of them touch a vegetable if I was not there? And they don't get up in the morning without nagging. They need me. They still need me and I could have died. I didn't care. Death, I thought, take me. Take me now. This is it, now. Only "Bohemian Rhapsody" came on and I'm buggered if I'm going to die to that.'

A small crowd gathered. Cora dropped her basket. She could see her accident clearly again. The car hanging in the ditch as she calmly told her rescuers to switch off the radio. It clanked and groaned and crumpled down, and as it did the roof flattened. Had she still been in it, she would have been killed.

'I would have died,' she said. She was shaking now, visibly shaking and crying. She was completely out of control.

Stanley Macpherson always shopped on his way home. Every evening he glumly drifted past the frozen food section muttering, 'Something to eat. Something to eat. Steak pie? Frozen peas? What?'

He heard the little fracas but paid it no heed. Life was grim enough without witnessing other people's grief. If he had not remembered that he needed to wash his boxers and socks he would not have gone up the pet food and cleaning stuff aisle and he would not have seen Cora standing, ashen and weeping and passionately declaring to an astonished crowd of shoppers that she wanted to live. He pushed through them to her.

'It's all right, I know this woman.' He took her arm.

'Oh, Stanley,' wailed Cora. 'I was in an accident. The car crumpled to nothing. And ...' she spread her palms, tears streaming freely down her face. She quite forgot what she wanted to tell him. ' ... And I just realised now that I don't really want to die. I nearly died. Died, Stanley, died.'

Anxiety stretched her voice so that he could hardly make out what she was saying. He was not good at this. Emotional moments worried him. He would have liked to run away but couldn't leave her standing weeping and wailing between the cat food and washing powders like this. He put an awkward arm round her and clumsily pulled her to him. She buried her head in his shoulder. He smelled of soap and beer. His hand was on her head, fingers through her hair.

'There, there,' he said.

In her whole life, she thought it was the nicest thing anyone had ever said to her. There, there.

He took her to his car, held open the door, sat her inside.

'Thank you,' she said. 'You're kind.'

'Manners maketh the man,' he said.

'And mistakes maketh the woman,' she said. 'Is this your car, Stanley? It's quite nice.'

'Not everyone drives around in a fartmobile, Cora. Some of us think safety, you know.'

'I'd forgotten cars could be comfortable.' Then remembering her shopping. 'I came for olive oil and garlic. I can't not have them.'

'All right,' he soothed. 'Sit here. I need some food anyway.'

He returned twenty minutes later with her shopping. 'It's in the boot,' he said.

'No. I need it. I need to see it,' she fussed.

'OK.' He fetched her shopping and placed it on the floor of the car, between her feet. 'I'll take you home.'

'I don't want to go home.'

'I'll take you for a drink.'

'No. I don't want that. I don't want to sit somewhere public.'

'OK,' patiently, 'I'll take you to my flat.'

She thought about that. 'All right.'

She sat on his sofa drinking tea, shivering slightly. 'It just suddenly dawned on me, the finality of it all. It came to me in the supermarket there, I wanted to live a little longer. I could have died. And for a moment I welcomed it. This is it, I thought. This is it and I don't care.' She blubbered. Then howled. 'But I do.'

'You realised you were mortal, then. Bummer, isn't it?'

'Yes,' she nodded.

He reached over and took her cup, put it on the table.

'This flat isn't bad, Stanley. I thought it'd be all messy. But it's nice. High ceilings. I like your stuff.' She patted his sofa. She was talking quickly, her tongue and brain out of control. So he kissed her. He didn't mean to take advantage of her distress. He just thought he might shut her up. He kissed her and she let him. Such a comfort, human contact. She slipped her arms round his neck and drew herself to him. It was a gentle kiss, a may-I? kiss. Nothing passionate. A little exploratory touching of lips and tongue. But he slipped his hand across her breast and discovered that whatever was going on in her head, her nipple, at least, was willing. He'd take it from there.

He took it from there to the bedroom because fumbling about on the sofa, unbuttoning and groping, was a bit adolescent for them both. She was pleasantly relieved to find his brass bedstead was not, as she'd imagined when she realised she was inevitably on her way to it, surrounded by old beer cans, abandoned underpants and socks worn – as were socks of the men in her life so far – to the point of crispiness. It only creaked tellingly, but as there was only the pair of them in the flat it didn't matter really. All those years of silent sex, sssh, sssh, muffled pleasure, she'd almost forgotten the joys of really letting go, yelling out loud.

'I can't remember the last time I did that,' she said, surprised at herself. 'The older your children get the less privacy you have.'

'Teenagers are irritatingly omnipresent,' Stanley said, thinking glumly of Brigit's two older children. 'They hog the phone, the bathroom, the fridge and they gather in the dark outside the bedroom when you want to spend some serious knickerless time with your wife.'

'There is nothing puts you off more than a loud kitchen full of lager-raddled giants eating all your food,' Cora agreed. 'Is that what happened to your marriage? Not enough knickerless time?'

'My wife said I was never home. But I objected to the knickerless time she spent with other men. We worked up a real recipe for disaster.'

The curtains moved against the window, voices from outside

floated up, people out there embarking on their evening. Early laughter floating through the night. In a few hours, a few drinks, the laughter would be darker. She knew that. She'd done that.

'They're off pubbing. They'll drink and wish and play eye games with strangers. They're hoping to get lucky.' She judged his silence before she said, 'Like me.'

He turned and smiled to her. 'Are you hungry?' Then pushing back the duvet: 'I'll fetch you something.'

Love in the early evening, or love in the afternoon, lying in bed while the rest of the world went on with its business, was bliss. She was stretched out in a stranger's bed taking sneaky peeks at the life he led; the books he read, his pictures on the wall, shirt draped over the back of a chair, letters from credit card companies and lawyers – a divorce in the offing. His boots were lying askew where they had been kicked off, and his CDs were scattered over the floor. She leaned out of bed to examine them. Charlie Parker, Thelonious Monk, Wardell Gray, Duke Ellington, 'Oh no,' she sighed, rolling back. 'Not jazz. I hate jazz.'

There was something hugely comforting about lying in Stanley's bed. She bummed across into his bit that seemed, somehow, warmer, comfier than hers. He'd put the light on in the kitchen; a muted glow filtered up the hall into the bedroom. He clattered, whistled a bit, nothing intrusive. It was so calming to lie there with the drifting sounds of someone caring doing things for her in another room. For a few moments she let go of the tenacious grasp she'd always held on her life and allowed someone else to take responsibility for her. When Stanley came back to her, she was sleeping. He ate a bacon sandwich, drank coffee and stared out of the window before joining her.

The emptiness of his bed woke him. It was two in the morning and chilly. Cora sat in the chair across from the bed, staring at him. She had his sweat shirt pulled round her shoulders. That was all she wore. He shut his eyes, hoped she hadn't noticed him wake. He was relaxed and warm, wrapped in sleep, and was not willing to keep his eyelids raised, but he knew, he could tell, a serious conversation was coming up.

'Stanley,' Cora said. 'I hate jazz. Is that all you listen to?'

'Mostly it is.' He still was not going to open his eyes. 'I'll get you earplugs. All right?' With any luck that would be it.

'I have to go, Stanley. I know it's the middle of the night, but I have to go.'

'I didn't think you were the type to get up and go home.'

'Well, no. I never go to other men's beds. Until tonight, that is. Before that I used to make the men get up and go home. But then, that stopped.' She sighed. 'Years and years ago, when the children were little, I stopped. I didn't want them to come in and find a strange man in the house. And Betty Lawrence gave me a ticking off. And—'

'Please don't ask me to drive you. I'm tired.'

'Sam and Col will be wondering where I am.'

'I phoned them. They know you're with me.'

'Stanley, I have this thing. It's nothing to do with you, really it isn't. It's just sleeping with someone. I don't do it. I like the sex, love it. But afterwards sleeping – know what I mean? Drifting into unconsciousness whilst your body keeps on functioning without you keeping an eye on it. Snoring and farting and dreaming with someone seems somehow – I don't know – intimate.'

'Isn't that what relationships are about? Not the sex. The snoring and farting and dreaming together afterwards?'

'I don't know. It scares me.' For a while she said nothing. She sat considering the man in his bed. 'What do you think about relationships, Stanley? Do you think they work?'

'I don't know.' Then knowing he wasn't going to get away with that negativity: 'Yes. If you want them to.'

'It's just that in a relationship you become and . . . Stanley.'

He gave up. 'And? And? Now you've got me. I'll have to open my eyes. What do you mean – and?'

'People have billing in relationships. One person remains the same, the other becomes and. Daniel andEllen. Only that's sort of become Ellen andDaniel, hasn't it? Fred andGinger. Laurel andHardy. Lennon andMcCartney. You'd be Stanley. I'd be andCora. I've been Cora for years now. I don't want an and.'

'Cora, if we have a relationship, and Christ we've only just slept together, but if we do I promise you top billing. On all our

Christmas cards and in our cheque book you can have top billing. You stay Cora, I'll be andStanley, OK? Now will you fucking come snore, fart and dream with me? I need someone to hang on to in the night. Stop me drowning in my sleep.'

She couldn't move when she woke. Accident damage had set in. She was raw and stiff, bones knitted, a slow bruising was welling round her eyes and purpling down her cheek. Her neck felt as if it had been rammed down into her spine. Turning her head was impossible. To look right or left she had to turn her whole body.

'Oh God. What's happening to me?'

'You've been in a car crash. What did you think – you wouldn't hurt? The unbruisable Cora.'

'But I didn't hurt yesterday.'

Stanley shrugged. 'It took a whole day before you reacted emotionally. Here's your body having its turn.' He heaved himself into his trousers. 'I'll bring you some tea.' He brought her tea and toast on a tray and a pile of books. 'Stay in bed,' he said.

'I can't stay in bed,' she protested. 'I have to work.'

'I've phoned and said you won't be in for a few days. They weren't in the least surprised. Sleep,' he instructed, 'is what you need.' He reached across and pulled out a fraying, ancient hardback. 'I found this the other day when you were striding about the hills and defying death. Have a look through it. See if you can see what I saw.'

'Oh mystery,' she sounded sarcastic.

'No, really. You'll love it.' He pulled his sweat shirt over her bare shoulders, put the tray on her lap and kissed her.

'Stanley,' she said.

'Oh God, no. Here we go again. You can snore and fart and dream to your heart's content, I won't be here. I'll be andStanley and I'll wear headphones when I listen to jazz. What more can I do?'

'Stanley, I have to tell you something. I've done dreadful things,' she confessed. 'You brought me tea. I can't not tell you.'

He looked at her. His hands were deep in his pockets, worried about getting to work, but knew this was not a good moment to look at his watch.

'My children have different fathers,' she confessed.

'Cora, anybody can see that,' he said.

'I've done other things,' she said, fiddling with her cup, not looking at him. 'Terrible, terrible things. I can't not tell you about them.'

'Goodness,' he said.

'I went on shoplifting sprees. I loved it. I got such a high, I can't tell you. I didn't do it for the gain. I just did it for the doing of it. We'd sometimes stand outside a shop and one would send the other in to come out, say with something green from the third floor. Or something pink from the second. Didn't matter what it was. We were so naughty.'

'Oh that,' said Stanley. 'With that French bloke. Yes, naughty gets it.'

'You know about that?'

'Yes.'

'How do you know about that?'

'Daniel Quinn saw you. He told me.'

She looked astonished. 'He saw me?'

'Yes. You know what a telltale he is. He was probably up to the same thing. It's no big deal. Kids steal all the time. Christ, Cora, please don't tell me you are still recriminating about this. Please don't tell me you have been living in shame all these years. What, nineteen years?'

But she had been. She was crying. 'Not all the time. But it sneaks up on me and I feel such remorse. Then there's the boys, they deserved better.'

'Better than what?'

'Than what I gave them. You know that house. I never had any money.'

'Cora, you did fine.'

'You knew. You knew. Oh, don't tell me everybody knows.' She hid her head in her hands. 'Everyone knows, don't they?'

Sighing he lifted the tray from the bed and sat beside her. He put his big bear arm round her. 'Cora. You brisk through your life bossing and nagging. Don't trudge. Behave yourself. What's five times three. Sew your crotch, Stanley. Brush yourself down before you leave the house, Ellen. Don't eat all the biscuits, boys. I do not

227

have a chip on my shoulder, George. If we did not know you were smouldering underneath there somewhere, and that you had a mischievous past do you think we'd put up with you?'

'Oh God, Stanley,' sobbing. 'I'm so tired. So tired. I wish I was sleeping. I think it's my preferred state.'

And gently rubbing her shoulder, lips on her hair, staring at the curtain moving, worrying vaguely about getting to work, Stanley said, 'Tell you the truth, Cora, I'm beginning to prefer you that way too.'

He arrived late at the office. 'I don't know, Billy,' he said. 'Why do we bother with women when we can send out for a fat tart in nylons with a carry-out?'

Billy shook his head. 'Fucked if I know.'

'And,' Stanley waved in frustration at the empty desk across the room, 'where's Ellen? She hasn't phoned in, has she?'

Billy shook his head. 'Nope.'

'Sodding dinner party, sodding drink, sodding people. I could be happy but for these things,' Stanley said. But he picked up the phone, dialled his number, checking on Cora.

Chapter Twenty-six

It was a week before Cora was well enough to leave Stanley's. She could, of course, have gone home, but she allowed herself the luxury of having someone look after her. It was addictive. It was a week, then, before Cora got round to visiting Ellen. She battered on the door. No reply. She creakily dropped on to complaining knees and shouted through the letter box, 'Ellen. Ellen. I know you're in there. Stop being an arse and open the door.'

She heard the sound of a city door being opened. The rattle of a chain, the thick slide of a bolt, the heavy rumble of sturdy key in lock all before the doorknob turned and there was Ellen. Her childhood doors had not been like this. In the village of her youth doors were never locked. There was nothing, she fondly imagined, to lock them against.

Ellen was wearing a huge T-shirt, an ancient cardy – hardened tissues barrelling out the pockets – black knickers, rumpled grey socks. Her face was pale, washed out pale. As she stood in the sudden daylight she wiped her nose with a small stub of used tissue.

'What the hell happened to you?' Cora asked.

'I might ask the same thing,' Ellen said. 'Look at you. Who beat you up?'

'The car. It died. Unfortunately I was in it at the time.' She followed Ellen up the hall and into the bedroom. Ellen climbed back into bed.

'You are wearing the alluring outfit of a woman who sleeps alone,' Cora said.

'You should know,' said Ellen.

Ah, no longer, Cora thought. But was astute enough to know this was not the moment to mention it. She climbed carefully on to

Ellen's bed, sat beside her and said, 'So tell me.'

'Nothing,' said Ellen. 'It's nothing.'

'Doesn't look like nothing. Are you all right?'

'I'm fine.'

Cora looked at her witheringly. 'No you're not.'

'I said I'm fine. Why don't you believe me?'

'Only your lips are saying that.'

'Well, tell me which bit of my body you're reading that I can correct its language, and make it lie too.'

Cora looked round the room. Daniel's pictures, all his women – Man Ray's, George Grosz's, a Matisse – the faces who had for years looked down on Ellen's bedroom life were on the floor, looking, now, at the wall.

'They've seen too much,' Ellen said. 'I can't bear what they know about me.'

Cora said nothing. They sat side by side on the bed in the quiet silence friends develop. At last Cora took her hand. 'What happened?'

'He came here after the dinner party. He let himself in. He was so angry at me.'

'What for?'

'Having people in and not inviting him.'

'What! How did he know you were having a party? If that's what it was.'

'He watches the flat. He stands outside. And when I'm not home he comes in and hangs about.'

Cora put her hand on her stomach, controlling her sudden queasiness. 'Horrible. Horrible.'

'He forced himself on me,' Ellen said. 'At least I think he did. I don't know.'

'He raped you?'

'No. Not exactly. He forced himself on me. And then, I let him. I always let him. Is that rape?'

'Yes,' Cora was adamant. 'Surely you know?'

Ellen shrugged. 'I know. It was rape. The first time it was rape. Then we made love.'

Cora despaired. 'You're a fool, Ellen.'

'I know. But he was lying there all crumpled and rejected. I couldn't stand it. It was so sad.'

Cora threw her hands in the air. 'Pack it in, Ellen. Pack him in.' Then remembering the absurd realities of Ellen's life, 'I don't suppose you have any food in the house, do you?'

Ellen shook her head. 'I think there's an old bar of chocolate in my jacket pocket. I'll get it.'

'I'm not eating something that's been in your pocket for weeks.'

'I know. But I will.'

This was a woman, Cora well knew, who would often stand by the window staring out whilst eating cornflakes straight from the packet. Her clothes were lying in a tangled entwined heap, jeans, tights, knickers, T-shirt, jersey, where they'd landed after she'd removed them in one or two rapid unpeelings and tossed them away.

'Do you know what I remembered?' Ellen said. 'I remembered running across the golf course and being chased by the old man who lived across the road. He was flashing. I always thought he was a spy.'

'Well, you got that wrong,' Cora said.

'Yes. Then my mother came and she didn't see the bloke. She was so angry at me for running around on my own in the middle of the night she smacked me. Really hard.'

'If you'd been mine I think I might have smacked you too,' said Cora, shaking her head. She reached over and took Ellen by the hand. 'You are such a fool, sometimes.'

'I suppose. But I needed her that night. I needed a mother. I have always thought my mother didn't like me. I've always had difficulty with that. I went to terrible lengths to shock her. I really was horrible. If she disapproved of something I'd do it. Smoking, drinking, marrying Daniel. Shame on me.'

'Indeed,' said Cora. 'Is this taking stock what's made you hide away all week?'

'That, and that effing edible Bloody Mary gave me a three-day hangover.'

Cora shivered. 'It's freezing in here.'

'Central heating has softened you.'

231

'Well, certainly, I don't go to bed looking like Captain Oates.' She climbed under the duvet and, chittering, pulled it up to her chin. 'I've been sleeping with Stanley.'

'Stanley! *My* Stanley?'

'That isn't how he defines himself. But, yes, your Stanley.'

'Goodness. How did that happen?'

'He found me having a nervous breakdown in the supermarket. I thought my accident hadn't bothered me. Then suddenly as I was walking down the aisle between the pet foods and washing powders it hit me. I realised how close I had been to death or serious injury, and I started to – well – gibber. Yes, gibber gets it. He came along and rescued me. He said something lovely.'

'What?'

'Mind your own business.'

'OK, I will. But after you've told me what he said.'

'He put his arm round me and said, "There, there." There, there. Isn't that lovely? Pass it on.'

They huddled a while. At last Ellen said, 'A nervous breakdown? In the supermarket? Between the pet foods and the washing powder? God, Cora, you've no style. You could have hung on till you got to the Haagen Daz.'

They lapsed back into silence, staring ahead. Thinking.

Then Ellen said, 'Do you want a drink?'

Cora said, 'Have you any wine left?'

'Wine?' said Ellen. 'Wine? What sort of uptight middle-class drink is that? You're getting all comfy and middle-aged. You could do with some serious corrupting. I'll get you some vodka.'

Cora grinned. 'Oh, vodka. I don't drink spirits. I can't. They give me a headache. I feel wretched. I don't like not being in control.' She considered this. 'Actually, that's true. I don't like not being in control these days.'

'Not being in control.' Ellen got up and headed for the kitchen, boogieing slightly to a tune in her head as she did. 'Best feeling in the world. Really. I mean it. Really.'

'What've you got to be so happy about?'

'Dunno,' said Ellen.

Chapter Twenty-seven

'Don't you dare ask me what Stanley's like,' Cora said. 'Just don't.'

'OK,' Ellen said. She sat at Cora's table, looking vacant, saying nothing. Then: 'So, what's Stanley like?'

'Lovely,' Cora said.

'Do you think sex gets better as you get older, then?'

'Perhaps. Less urgent. Maybe. Less of a whoosh. He stops, rolls over and falls asleep. But you're sort of like a car with a dicky timer. You shudder on going ah-ah-ah on your own. 'He gave me this.' She handed Ellen the book Stanley had showed her weeks ago on their first morning together. 'See if you can find it.'

'Find what?'

'What Stanley found. And isn't he clever to have spotted it? When you were lying hungover, trying to decide if you'd been raped or not and I was dicing with death, he was poking about an old bookshop in Victoria Street spotting this.'

Ellen took the book and gently turned it over. *The Travels of Rachmaninov* by C. L. MacDonald. 'Clodagh MacDonald traces the life, travels and undiscovered music of a pianist and composer who became one of the first international performers in the age of modern communication.' Ellen opened at random and read ' . . . as early as 1907 Rachmaninov was producing work that would evoke mystery and romanticism. His *Isle of the Dead*, for example, has a quintuple rhythmic quality that matches the rich orchestration . . .'

Ellen snapped it shut. 'You've read this?'

'Well,' Cora shrugged, 'I'm more of a one to look at the pictures.'

Ellen opened the book again, and looked at the photographs. Distant times frozen for ever, people in hats looking stiff and uncomfortable in their New Age life. Rachmaninov himself was standing looming above his entourage, tall and taciturn. Nature seemed to have endowed him with more elbows than ordinary mortals. It was not the man himself, however, who caught Ellen's eye. It was the small enthusiastic woman standing behind him, wildly waving. She was exquisitely beautiful and seemed to be leaping up and down, boundlessly gleeful. Ellen pulled the book closer. 'Who is that?'

'Who do you think?'

'Is it?'

The same cheery character appeared in several other photographs, never actually playing with the man, but always looking, in the face of the great man's glumness, joyous.

'It's Emily Boyle. It is. Surely it is.' And they gave a quick burst on the air piano, a small homage to an exuberant liver of life, teller of tales and inventor of the edible Bloody Mary.

'Isn't Stanley amazing?' Cora said. 'He fixes lives, rescues me from a nervous breakdown and solves mysteries.'

Ellen was impressed.

'Chippy Norton ace detective,' she wrote, 'is shrewd and he is kindly.' She adored this character already. He was chubby, wedged into an old tweed jacket. He moved slowly through his life – by bike if possible, looking somewhat like a plum on a razor blade. And he solved his crimes by observing the trivia in his suspects' lives; their shopping, choice of television viewing, the contents of their bathroom cabinets, the books on their shelves, their laundry. He spent as much time as possible gossiping, eavesdropping, staring and eating biscuits. He was comfortable. His jeans were complaining of the strain at the crotch. The juicy and the curious might get lucky and cop a swift peek of his Calvin's.

Jack Conroy loved him. Ellen delivered it personally, stood in the midst of his clutter as he looked it over.

'He's lovable,' Jack cried. 'You don't do lovable. Neither do I. But this is different. He's so familiar, Ellen, I feel I know him.'

'Yes,' Ellen nodded. 'He has that effect on people. Do you ever vacuum, Jack?'

Jack's carpet was still thick with rubbings. 'No. Never. My wife vacuums the house, but not in here. Oh no. If she tidied in here things would get lost.'

Ellen looked round. 'I do believe you are even messier than me.'

'Really?' Jack was proud of that. Ellen's untidiness was legend. 'I take that as a compliment.' He slid off his chair, and came to her. No need for words, the look in his eye, a certain purpose in his movement said it all.

'Oh please,' she said, dismissing him. 'Not that. We've been there, done that and frankly . . .' She made a face. 'You know, frankly, the earth didn't move.' She spread her palm on her chest. She'd been feeling awfully nauseous lately. 'I don't know why they say the earth moves. If it did, you'd stop, wouldn't you? You'd think: Hold on, better stop, the earth is moving. Maybe that's why modern women prefer to go on top. If the earth moves he'll fall into the hole first. You'll have a soft landing.'

Jack looked bemused. Ellen's burst of wittering reminded him of how disastrous their attempt at sex had been. If he remembered correctly she'd spoken through it, in that shy meandering way of hers.

'Besides,' Ellen explained, 'I've been awfully queasy lately. All the time queasy. I don't know. Something I ate.'

Jack nodded. Queasiness, women. He had a feeling he knew what that was all about even if Ellen did not. He smiled to her.

'What?' she said sharply. 'What do you mean by that smile? Every time I tell somebody about my nausea they look like that. Smile. Smile, they go. And they don't say a word. I hate that.'

It was true. She'd mentioned it to Stanley.

'Sick?' he said. 'Right.' And he'd smiled.

'Queasy?' George had said. 'All the time? A sort of all over, constant sickness? Goodness.' And he had exchanged a knowing look with Ronald.

'Nauseous,' said Emily Boyle. 'Well, that's not so good. Perhaps you should stop drinking for a while.'

Cora simply said she should see a doctor.

The doctor looked at her. He did not even try to hide his surprise.

'You have sore breasts. Tingly. You feel bloated. You're being sick in the mornings. Can I ask you how old you are?'

'Um,' said Ellen. 'Thirty.'

'I have your notes, Mrs Quinn. I can see you're older than that.'

'OK. Thirty-five. Six . . . ish. I always feel ashamed of how my life has passed and I haven't got round to doing what I planned. I sort of drifted into everything, you know. Not one serious well-thought-out and planned decision. Work – I was in the right place at the right time—'

'The reason I ask,' the doctor interrupted her, 'is you seem rather old not to have considered you might be pregnant.'

Ellen looked astonished. 'Oh no. Can't be, it's ages since I had any sex.'

'How long?'

'Three months.'

'That'd do it. When was your last period?' the doctor continued.

'Gosh.' Ellen scratched her head. 'Yes, it must have been a while ago.' She measured her life by Daniel's visits. And she hadn't seen him since that night. A little churn in the stomach. That night.

'I don't know,' she whined. 'I can't remember.'

'Why don't you hop up on the bench over there and we'll take a look.'

Doctor speak. Ellen hated it. She felt doctors must do a special course in euphemism. Hop up on the bench – heave yourself on to his bench, paper towel under the bum and lie with her legs open. Take a look, he'd put on his plastic gloves and poke about her innards, whilst gazing contemplatively ahead saying, 'Relax. Relax. Let your knees drop.'

'You're three months gone, I should say, Mrs Quinn. Congratulations.' Ellen walked home in a daze.

It was over, then. Her life of late nights and drinking had to end now. After years and years of abuse she had to come to her senses. And she would spend the next five months worrying about the damage she might have done in the months of not knowing the babe was there within her.

'I suppose,' she sighed, 'I can put it down to youth. To growing up. All that time taking vodka, smoking, sitting up late listening to music, eating absurdly at absurd hours and now it's over. Oh well. It's been good. I can just put it down to an extremely long adolescence.'

She went to tell Daniel. He was holding court behind the bar and looked only slightly abashed when he saw her. She should have known when he didn't take on her bet that night, the terrible night of the Bloody Mary, that he wouldn't come round any more. He held up a glass and pointed to the vodka.

She shook her head. 'Mineral water,' she said. 'I'm off drink.'

'Goodness,' he said. 'It won't last, of course.'

'Yes, it will, Daniel. It'll last for another five or six months anyway.' She gave him her best purposeful look. 'Know what I mean, Daniel? I'm pregnant, Daniel. *We're* pregnant, Daniel.'

The colour drained from his face. She knew what he was feeling – as if his circulation had suddenly been cut short and was doing overtime in his gut, leaving his legs without support.

'And you are going to take some responsibility,' she ordered. 'None of this getting to know another woman who has a child and stealing from it to give to your child. You are going to chip in.' She'd thought about this a lot. 'If not with money, then time. Time whilst I work. Know what I mean, Daniel?' She was prodding the bar with a decisive and bossy finger. 'I won't let you get away with it.'

She thought she had, at last, come to terms with the truth about Daniel. There was some rage in him, yes. But mostly he just didn't consider the consequences of his actions. He wanted so he took. And in turn he expected others to do the same to him. When they didn't he thought them mugs, easy picking.

She could tell, though, that Daniel didn't want a baby. It would pee, he thought. It would puke. It would shit vilely into a nappy, green shit. Babies did that. He'd seen it in other people's babies' nappies. He shuddered. But worse than all of that, much much worse, it would look at him. It would look at him the way babies did, like Buddha, with their perfect faces and their terrible innocent eyes. And it would know.

It knows, he always thought when he came face to face with a baby, whingeing under its constant gaze. And he always felt shame. No, he did not want a baby.

Chapter Twenty-eight

'Cora,' Ellen said, 'what will you do when your children leave?'

'Cry,' said Cora. 'It will break my heart when they go.'

She considered this. There was, for example, the dire consumption of food in her house. There was the noise, the roar of television and CD player. There was the mess, the decaying training shoes in the middle of the bedroom floor, the damp jumble of towels in the bathroom. There was, also, the toilet roll situation. Cora had not realised the importance toilet rolls would play in her life as a parent. Their husks lay on the bathroom window sill as if nobody in the household was admitting to ever using them and therefore did not see it as up to them to throw them out. Before that, toilet roll husks were delivered to the play group and nursery in large plastic bags and were returned crudely glued to cornflake packets, roughly painted and were now, she was assured, space stations and lost planets. The constructors of space stations and lost planets were grown now, but still thought she was on constant duty as a mother. When she was in the lavatory glumly considering a cardboard heap of toilet roll husks they would bang on the door demanding, 'Where is . . . ?' and, 'Have you seen . . . ?' and, 'Is there anything for eating . . . ?' and, 'What are you doing in there?'

'Leave me alone,' Cora would cry out. 'I'm a woman. I demand to be left alone.'

Now, of course, her boys were grown and she could annoy them, bang on the bathroom door. 'What are you doing in there, Col?'

'Leave me alone.'

'I will not. I have been waiting for years to irritate you. You've got a lot of irritation coming before I'm avenged.' Yelling through the door now, 'Just wait till you leave home. I'll come round to your perfect flat and leave Smartie marks round your walls and I'll jump on your sofa and when something wonderful is on telly I'm going to whine and demand we watch old *Sesame Street* tapes. Oh yes, my boy. Just wait. Parent's revenge.' Battering on the door, both fists.

'Bugger off, Mum, will you?'

'Yes,' Cora admitted to Ellen, smiling. 'It will break my heart when they go. But sometimes I cannot wait for my heart to be broken. Though I'll cry, and it shall be wonderful, they will not be around to ask why I'm crying. Or what I'm crying about. I will have peace at last to cry and cry and cry. And when I'm finished crying for my lost children, I'll watch sad old black-and-white movies and cry some more. I've a bit of crying to catch up on. Looking forward to it.'

'You're lucky. I don't cry any more. Last time I did was when I first discovered about Daniel and his women. I think I've forgotten how.'

'Nonsense. All your tears are there. One day you'll open up and have the most fabulous howl of all time.'

Did her mother cry, Ellen wondered, now she was alone? Did she sit in her living-room gloom with fat tears rolling down her withered cheeks as darkness deepened around her? Outside in the garden a late evening blackbird would cluck a warning that night was coming. In the street a bus would rumble by. Her mother would hear the sounds of suburbanites coming home for tea. But nobody would clatter through her door, nobody would call her name. Ellen was shaken. She almost made fat tears roll down her own cheeks imagining her mother's loneliness. She phoned home.

'I'm fine, dear. How are you?'

'I'm OK,' Ellen said.

'I really can't stop,' Janine went on. 'It's my bridge night. And I've only just got rid of Rita and Betty, and Peggy's calling at seven. So I haven't long.'

Wrong again. Wasn't she always? Ellen had forgotten how many friends her mother had.

'I thought I might come over to see you tomorrow.'

'Tomorrow. That isn't your usual day. But that would be lovely.'

She was doing the washing up with her mother when she told her about the baby. She was washing, Janine wiping and putting away.

'By the way,' she said. 'I'm going to have a baby.' She looked into the soapy water.

Janine stiffened. 'When?'

'I'm four months gone.'

'Is it Daniel's?'

'Yes.'

Her mother busied herself with the plate in her hand, wiping it vigorously. 'Well,' she said at last, 'that'll learn you.'

'Learn me what?'

'Not to be silly. To start taking life seriously. To do all the things people have to do when they have babies. You'll find out.'

'Ah,' said Ellen, 'I plan to be a very good mother.' She plunged a cup into the water, let it fill with water and sink. Then she floated a plate on the surface. The cup would be lying in wait for it. She remembered that. Torpedoes on the port side, boom, whoosh.

'Don't we all,' Janine sighed. She disappeared into the pantry with a pile of plates and clattering, put them away.

'I always thought you didn't want me,' Ellen told her. She vaguely thought her mother was out of hearing range, or the clattering would drown her accusation.

'What on earth made you think that?' Janine appeared at the pantry door, astonished.

'You told me. The night Dad died you were standing at the front door and when I came to you, you said, "Not you. Not you." I've always remembered that.'

'Did I do that?' Janine took a stack of cups and started to hang them on their hooks. 'How awful,' she said mildly. She did not think it so dreadful.

'My feet got cold,' Ellen said.

'It was a cold night.' Her mother looked at her. 'You were always such a strange child. So removed. I never knew what was going on in your head. Then there was the night I found you on the golf course, half naked. What were you doing?'

'I was riding with the Sioux,' Ellen told her, grinning, squirming in embarrassment. It sounded so silly now. 'I thought they were out there waiting for me. I imagined them coming for me, riding down the avenue. The whole tribe of them. I could see it. I could really see it.'

241

Isla Dewar

Janine stopped her cup routine and looked at her daughter. 'Have you any idea how lucky you are? The rest of us just see a grubby, yellowing municipal golf course and you see hunting grounds complete with the Sioux nation. Other people see a bunch of silly girls and you see Gangster Women. Daniel, for heaven's sake, a man like that, you see an avenging philosopher. Now this Chippy Norton chap. No doubt it's some perfectly ordinary person going about his business but you see an adorable fat detective. You can imagine a Sioux tribe coming to ask you out to play in the middle of the night. You are so lucky. I am so envious.'

'You? Envious?'

'Me. I'm an ordinary oldish woman in an ordinary suburban bungalow. I know who I am. I have no illusions.' She tutted. 'Oh damn. I promised myself I wouldn't do that when you told me you were pregnant just then. Don't tut, I said to myself. Now I have. Sorry.'

'That's OK. I wouldn't have felt right if you didn't tut.'

'When you work you'll need someone to look after the baby,' Janine offered.

'Yes. Thank you,' Ellen said. 'Actually everyone's been super. Ronald and George are keen to baby-sit. And Emily is going to teach her the piano.'

'I'm having a baby,' Ellen had told Mrs Boyle.

'I know, dear. We all know. Isn't it wonderful? I shall teach her to play the piano.'

'Her?'

'Definitely. It looks like a female sort of a bump.'

'You'll teach her the good old EGBDF,' Ellen said. 'I remember that. Every Good Boy Deserves Football.'

'Football?'

'That's what my old music teacher said.'

'It's fun, dear. Fun. Favour. Frolics. Fornication? Oh, I'm sure you don't need me to fill you in on any more effs. But as you get older the effs just get better and better.'

Ellen smiled to her.

She turned to Janine. 'There's Daniel . . .' she said weakly.

'Oh goodness me, Ellen. Don't talk rot,' Janine sniped. 'Still, it's

242

good to see your absurd imagination is still functioning. You're going to need it now you have someone to support. Daniel is not getting ready access to any grandchild of mine. I mean, daughters you have to let go. But grandchildren, oh no.'

Chapter Twenty-nine

'I don't think I can do this,' Ellen said. 'I don't think I can be a mother. How did you manage, Cora?'

'I just did it. To anyone in my position I'd offer the advice: learn to love your duffel coat – you'll be wearing it for years and years and years – and keep your eyes down. Avoid the eyeflick.'

'The eyeflick?'

'That look women give each other. You know, that swift recce women give each other. The gorgeous one looks at the dowdy one and thinks, Nah-ne-nah-ne-nah-nyah, thank Christ that isn't me. I haven't let sex and doughnuts ruin my thighs and reduce me to living my life in a duffel coat. And the dowdy one looks at the gorgeous one and thinks: If only I'd taken life and sex at an easier pace I wouldn't have become the woman in the duffel coat trudging around, trailing children, taking comfort in doughnuts.'

'You're an excellent mother. I have no maternal feelings at all. In fact, I don't think I like children.'

'Other people's children, nobody likes other people's children. Your own are different,' Cora assured her. 'Becoming a mother is easy. You just do it. It's stopping that's a bitch.'

'But you're a boss. You are naturally bossy. If you hadn't anyone to shove around you'd get withdrawal symptoms.'

It was true. Recently Stanley had borne the brunt of her verbal bruisings. 'Stanley, you have never embraced the concept of leisure, have you?'

'No. I don't know what it is. Actually, it scares me. It's since I saw leisure pants in a catalogue, stay pressed leisure pants. Though these were spelled without the Y, sta-prest leisure pants. I had this vision of myself wearing them with an open-neck leisure shirt and I hated it. Terrifying. Terrifying leisure. I can't deal with it . . .' He was walking round the bedroom expounding, waving his hands about.

'Come to bed, Stanley. I just thought we should go visit my folks. You're the first decent bloke I've ever had, I thought it might do them good to see I've sorted myself out.'

'It's taken you a while.'

Cora nodded. 'You won't have to put on any sort of leisure wear, I promise.'

'So how do you do it?' Ellen said.

'Guilt'll get you through.'

'Women are good at guilt.'

'That's why they make better mothers than men. Men have no sense of stoicism,' Cora said wistfully.

They thought about this. Life without the urge to be stoic. 'Bastards,' they decided in unison.

When Ellen got home Daniel was there. He was standing in her living room with a friend, one of the people – a bloke, a geezer – with bit parts in his life. The life she had once considered fabulous, but now thought wasted, and, as he got older, sad.

'What the hell are you doing here?' she demanded. 'How dare you keep coming into my flat like this?'

'I just came for the sofa,' Daniel said, smiling. He made it sound natural. A normal sort of thing to do – uplift a person's sofa without asking.

'That's mine. You put it down.' Ellen was horrified.

'Actually,' Daniel sounded superior, 'it's mine. I bought it.'

'I love that sofa. You're not having it. You have left this flat. Get out.'

'Not till I have the sofa.'

Ellen sat on it. Thumped her body on to it, claiming what was hers. 'I bailed you out, you bastard. I paid off the rent. I—'

'I know, I know.' Daniel was beginning to turn nasty. He wanted that sofa. He had, after all, thousands of pounds, years of winnings, stuffed into the cushions. Ellen knew nothing of this.

Over the years Daniel had been through many lucky routines. And though they were not all made up of the same combinations of breakfasts, socks and boxers, two common factors ran through them all. He always had to start out with a small sum of money stolen – or as he saw it, borrowed – from the purse of whatever woman was in his life when he woke in the morning. He'd fetch her, whoever she was, a cup of coffee in bed. And when he was waiting for the kettle to boil, he'd take something from her purse. His second common factor was that he could not use his winnings, so he always put them into the cushions of the sofa that had once been his sofa, in Ellen's flat that had once been his flat. Now he was moving from his bed-sit opposite the bookie's to a larger flat. He wanted the money. He also wanted the sofa.

'I want that,' he said. 'And I will not leave without it.'

'Oh yes you bloody will.' Ellen was more adamant than he'd ever heard her before. Perhaps that's what pregnancy did for women – made them adamant. Bummer. Ellen sat harder on the cushion, pressing herself into it.

'Come on, Jake.' Daniel indicated to the bloke, geezer, he'd brought with him to take one end of the sofa as he lifted the other.

Jake was hesitant. 'I don't know about this. Whose is it?'

'Mine,' said Ellen.

'Mine,' said Daniel.

Claiming her territory, Ellen lay down. 'You are not having this,' she boiled and raged. 'You bastard. You took and you took from me and you're not getting this sofa. I love this sofa. Get out. Get out and don't ever come back.'

Daniel, remembering her accuracy, years ago, with the fruit, stepped back.

Filled with bile and venom Ellen sat up again. 'Get out.'

Jake headed for the door. 'I'll leave you to it, then, Daniel,' he said. 'See you outside.'

Daniel stood his ground. 'That sofa's mine,' he told her. 'I bought it.'

'You bastard,' she said. 'You absolute bastard. It's mine now. God, the money you took from me. I paid you for this over and over. You're not getting it. It's mine now. First time I ever came to this flat I sat on this sofa. And you seduced me on this sofa. I told you I thought one of my tits was bigger than the other. And you asked if the small one or the big one was my favourite tit. I loved that. You've made love to me on this sofa. And when you first left me I waited for you on this sofa. I've been lonely on this sofa and I've been really happy on it. I watched our favourite videos on this sofa and got drunk with Cora on this sofa. We had our honeymoon here. Drinking dubious concoctions, spraying champagne. I have lived on this sofa.'

Daniel stood quietly. His hands were deep in his pockets. He did not look at her. 'I'll leave it with you, then,' he said, and turned to go.

'In fact,' she softly told his departing back, 'I'm going to play with my baby on this sofa. Feed her. Let her lie and sleep on it whilst I work at the table there.' She was silent, contemplating her life on the sofa.

'I have plans. For the first time in my life, plans.' She affectionately patted its beloved, worn arm. A cloud of dust sighed into the air. She stared at it. 'I'm planning on getting it cleaned next week. Furthermore,' she added when he reached the front door, 'don't bother coming back. I'm having the locks changed.'

Later, when Daniel phoned her, he said that he wouldn't advise her to get the sofa cleaned without first checking inside the cushions. Puzzled, she put down the phone, crossed the room, unzipped the cushion and found a wad of notes. Ten minutes later she was still pulling out money, wads and wads of money. When she had yanked out the last of it she could hardly believe her eyes. It lay spread across the floor, a huge haul. She sat amongst it, fingering it, lifting it and putting it down again. 'Money,' she said. 'Heaps and heaps of money. See, I knew I was right about this sofa. It's lucky.'

She phoned Cora.

'What are you going to do with it?' Cora wanted to know.

'Dunno,' said Ellen. 'I just dunno. I've never seen a heap of real money before. A vast pile of cash. Daniel's winnings.'

'Is he going to get some?'

'He doesn't want it. He's decided it would break the flow of his lucky routine.'

'You can have it all.' Cora suddenly got greedy. 'You could go on a world trip. Buy a new car. A really new one that hasn't belonged to several other drivers before you. You could get amazing clothes. You could—'

'I could get one of those really, really good, expensive bottles of vodka you can get these days,' Ellen joined in.

'Vodka?' Cora roared. 'Thousands of pounds and you're going to buy a bottle of vodka!'

The force of her voice thundered down the phone. Ellen held it away from her ear. Turned it over, considering it from underneath her thick fringe. It was an old phone and sort of past it. Faded and used. Years and years, she'd been speaking to Cora down this phone. Years and years.

'I could buy a new phone,' she offered suddenly.

'Vodka and a new phone.' Cora couldn't believe it. 'Is that all you can think of? You must be really happy. I keep telling you that. You're secretly happy.'

'Happy?' Ellen whined. 'Me? Happy? How can you say I'm happy. I can't even do a backflip. I always wanted to do that.'

'A backflip,' Cora said flatly.

'Yes. I may have a job and a flat and a baby on the way, but I always wanted to be able to do a backflip. You know, you leap up, twirl round a couple of times in the air, backwards. Land. Spread your arms, shout, "Tra-ah!" and get wild applause. That. Oh no. How dare you say I'm happy? What's happy? I'm not happy. I wouldn't go that far . . .'

And Cora said, 'Bye, Ellen. Speak to you tomorrow.'